AWA...
PASSION . . .

"I will leave." She started toward the connecting door.

"Ariel."

She turned.

He picked up her shawl. "I believe you forgot this."

Chagrined, she walked back toward him and grabbed for it, but he held it just out of her reach. "You must pay a forfeit, first."

"What?"

"Another kiss."

Ariel's stomach lurched. It had been one thing to kiss him in that damp cellar last night, or later in the darkened hallway. But here, in his room, in broad daylight . . . it was much more deliberate, much more . . . exciting.

"My third lesson?" she asked.

He nodded and pulled her into his arms. "Follow my lead," he whispered before his mouth met hers.

THE
UNREPENTANT
RAKE

by
Melinda McRae

A SIGNET BOOK

SIGNET
Published by the Penguin Group
Penguin Putnam Inc., 375 Hudson Street,
New York, New York 10014, U.S.A.
Penguin Books Ltd, 27 Wrights Lane, London W8 5TZ, England
Penguin Books Australia Ltd, Ringwood, Victoria, Australia
Penguin Books Canada Ltd, 10 Alcorn Avenue,
Toronto, Ontario, Canada M4V 3B2
Penguin Books (N.Z.) Ltd, 182–190 Wairau Road, Auckland 10, New Zealand
Penguin Books Ltd, Registered Offices: Harmondsworth, Middlesex, England

First published by Signet, an imprint of Dutton NAL,
a member of Penguin Putnam Inc.

First Printing, March, 1999
10 9 8 7 6 5 4 3 2 1

Copyright © Melinda McRae, 1999

All rights reserved

 REGISTERED TRADEMARK—MARCA REGISTRADA

Printed in the United States of America

Chapter 1

Ariel Tennant glanced overhead at the sullen sky. Scattered flakes of snow drifted lazily from the leaden grey clouds—not the most favorable omen for travel. But Ariel was determined to reach Cranston by tomorrow afternoon, and she had no intention of altering her plans because of a slight dusting of snow.

The sooner she reached home, the sooner she would be free from the loving, but smothering attentions of her aunt. Aurelia Dobson meant well, but after three weeks of her doting attention, Ariel longed for the comparative freedom of her own home.

For that, she would have gladly set out in the face of the fiercest blizzard.

It soon appeared that was what she had done. Only a few miles south of Macclesfield, the snow began falling in earnest. At first it gave the landscape the appearance of having been dusted with castor sugar, but as the miles rolled by and the surrounding countryside turned solidly white, Ariel began to fear that nature intended to thwart her plans.

"Dare we go any farther?" her aunt asked when they stopped at Leek for a change of horses and a cup of hot tea.

"I spoke with the coachman. He said the snow does not bother the horses and the roads are still safe." Ariel glanced around at the tiny, cramped common room of the inn. "If the storm is truly bad, we might be stranded for days. Wouldn't you rather be at the Duck at Derby?"

Her aunt considered for a moment, and Ariel knew she had said exactly the right thing. Aunt lived for her comforts, and the

Duck, with its excellent food, clean rooms, and obsequious staff, was one of Aunt's favorites.

And Ariel had not lied—merely stretched the truth a tiny bit. John Hodges, the coachman, had said it was *possible* to continue, although he recommended remaining where they were. But as long as he did not consider the trip truly dangerous, Ariel determined to press on.

By the time they returned to the road, the countryside was blanketed with a thick layer of snow. Only spiky branches and bare tree limbs stood stark against the white. Ariel felt the first twinge of misgiving, but shrugged it aside. If worse came to worst, they would simply have to stop at the next coaching inn and not continue to Derby this day.

She felt something akin to relief when they pulled up in front of the small inn at Waterhouse. Their pace had slowed considerably over the last few miles as the horses struggled through the deepening snow. It was time to act prudently and halt for the day.

Unfortunately, other travelers had arrived before them, and the inn was jammed with those seeking to escape the storm. The innkeeper only shook his head when Ariel asked for a room.

"Not a one to be had, miss," he said. "I've got people who'll be sleeping in the taproom this night."

"A private parlor, then." It would be miserably uncomfortable sitting up all night, listening to Aunt's complaints, but they had no choice.

"There is nothing available," the innkeeper said firmly. "Nothing. I cannot even stable your horses; we're full up."

Dismay washed over her. "Is there another inn nearby?"

"Derby's but seven miles off," he said. "You could make it there, most likely."

Reluctantly, Ariel went back outside to confer with her coachman. There was little to discuss. They had come this far without mishap; surely they could make it to Derby and find soft, comfortable beds waiting for them at the Duck.

"Continue on?" Mrs. Dobson shrieked when Ariel informed her of the plan. "In this weather? It is far too dangerous. We shall remain here."

"The inn is full. All the owner can offer us is a seat in the tap-room."

"Nonsense. Tell the man who we are. He will find us a room."

"His rooms are already filled with dukes and marquesses," Ariel replied with a mischievous smile. "There is no room for a mere viscount's daughter."

Mrs. Dobson sniffed. "This would never happen at the Duck."

"True, which is why we need to travel on. Who knows—perhaps the snow will ease up in the next mile, and we will make it to Derby easily."

Her aunt regarded her doubtfully, but sighed and followed Ariel back to the carriage.

The never-ending fall of snow soon extinguished Ariel's faint hopes of a quick journey to Derby. If anything, it seemed to be snowing with more force than before.

Six miles, she told herself. It could not be farther than six miles to Derby. Less than an hour on good roads, but conditions were far from good. Still, time enough to reach Derby, and the comforts of the Duck, before nightfall.

The carriage crested a small hill and started down the other side. Suddenly, the vehicle slewed sideways, skidding across the slick surface. Ariel felt a sharp jolt, followed by a sickening crack, and the coach tilted ominously. Aunt slid across the seat, crashing into Ariel and squashing her against the side of the coach.

Mrs. Dobson screamed. "Mercy! We shall be killed."

"Nonsense." Ariel helped her aunt to sit up. "We've merely slid into a ditch."

She heard scrabbling sounds outside, and the coachman pulled open the door, peering in at them. "Be you ladies all right?"

Ariel nodded. "Are the horses unhurt?"

"They're fine. But we lost the rear wheel."

"I guessed as much. How far is it to Derby?"

"I reckon we're halfway twixt there and the last inn. I'll un-harness the horses and send the lad on ahead. He can bring back help."

Ariel sat back against the seat. There was nothing else to do.

In decent weather she might be tempted to walk to Derby. But in this snow, that was impossible.

She peered out the window at the sky. Nightfall was rapidly approaching, and it would be past dark before the groom reached Derby. Who knew how long it would take to return with a vehicle to rescue them in this snow? They could not count on meeting another carriage coming this way; sensible travelers had already stopped for the night.

As they should have. But there was no purpose served in berating herself now for a lack of judgment.

"Have we passed any houses on the road?" she asked the coachman. "Perhaps we should beg for shelter rather than wait for help from Derby."

Hodges considered. "Seems that we passed a sign at the last crossroads. I'll send the lad back to look."

He shut the door, and Ariel glanced at her aunt, who was clutching a vial of hartshorn. "The taproom at that inn in Waterhouse is starting to look more appealing."

Mrs. Dobson twisted her hands together. "It is all your fault for insisting we travel back to Cranston with such haste. We should have spent another week with your cousins."

Ariel sighed. Aunt was right, but there was nothing they could do now to turn back time. She took the carriage rug and tucked it tighter around Aunt. All they could do was sit and wait—and hope there was shelter nearby.

Simon Granville Thorson, the tenth Earl of Milford, stared out the library window at the falling snow that was rapidly obliterating the untrimmed shrubbery outside. It looked as if his houseguests would not be departing any time soon. He was not going to be left alone for a while now.

Not that he minded—much. The prattle of that bit of fluff Bates brought with him was beginning to grate on Simon's nerves, but it was easy enough to avoid her for most of the day—the women were rarely out of bed before midafternoon.

And he had to admit he relished the opportunity to feast his eyes a bit longer on the delectable morsel who'd accompanied Lynnwood. It was far past time for Simon to be rid of Claudia, but it required too much effort to seek out another mistress at this time of the year. Perhaps Lynnwood would entertain the idea of a trade.

A rap sounded on the door, then Harman, the master of Simon's domain, stepped inside.

"There is a lad outside, reports that there's been an accident out on the main road. No one is injured, but they've broken a wheel and would appreciate shelter for the night."

Simon frowned. This was his house, not a posting inn. He did not want a bunch of strangers invading his private lair.

He glanced out the window again, noticing he could barely see the far edge of the garden in the fading light. 'Twas not a fit night out for man nor beast.

With a sigh, he nodded to Harman. "I suppose I must be charitable. Have the stable lads hitch up the cart and go to the rescue."

"I will see that rooms are prepared. Do you wish them to be seated at dinner?"

"Perhaps we should see what type of people they are before I extend too much hospitality."

"Quality, no doubt, if they are traveling by private coach."

Simon grinned. "Are you suggesting that I should dress for dinner?"

The butler's expression remained impassive. "I believe that travelers in distress will be more than willing to overlook some of the social niceties in return for shelter."

"Make the arrangements." With a nod, Simon dismissed Harman.

Now, instead of being rid of his invited guests, his house was to be invaded by strangers. He reached for the brandy decanter and poured himself a fresh glass of the amber liquid. Thank God the cellar was well stocked. He just might need to make heavy use of it for the next few days.

Ariel felt limp with relief when the groom returned with the invitation to shelter at a nearby house and a cart to transport them. It was nearly dark, and cold, and Derby seemed like an impossible goal.

To her chagrin, Aunt insisted that every piece of baggage be unloaded off the coach and onto the cart to prevent them from being stolen from the abandoned carriage.

"The weather is miserable," Ariel protested. "No one is going to be out on the roads to steal anything."

"Poor weather has never deterred the hardened criminal," Aunt retorted, refusing to leave her shelter until the last trunk was loaded onto the cart.

At last, wrapped in carriage rugs to keep warm, Ariel and her aunt settled in the cart and set off toward their unknown benefactor's home.

By the time they reached the house, Ariel's teeth were chattering and her feet felt frozen through. The light that poured from the open door was a welcome sight. She climbed down from the cart and walked on cold-numbed legs toward the stairs.

Mrs. Dobson nodded approvingly as a superior-looking butler met them in the hall.

"I am Harman," he said. "Welcome to Thornhill. I trust your short journey was not too uncomfortable."

"It was most appreciated," Ariel replied.

"If you will follow me, you can warm yourselves in the small parlor." He glanced at them curiously. "There are just the two of you?"

"And my groom and coachman," Ariel said.

"We will make them welcome, as well."

"Is your master or mistress at home?" Mrs. Dobson inquired. "We should like to meet them."

The butler nodded. "His lordship thought you would prefer to refresh yourselves first."

"But I do so wish to thank him for his kind consideration. To whom should I address my appreciation?"

The butler coughed. "You are a guest of the Earl of Milford."

"The Earl of Mil—" Aunt halted in mid-sentence. "Milford?"

The man nodded.

Aunt grabbed Ariel's arm and swung her around. "We are leaving now. Immediately."

Ariel stared at her, uncomprehending. "Are you mad? It is a near blizzard outside, and we have no means of travel."

"I cannot allow you to remain in this house for another minute," Aunt said. "Better that you freeze to death in the storm."

"That seems rather foolish," Ariel said.

"Did you not hear what the man said? Milford!"

"Who is Milford?"

Aunt shuddered. "I cannot even begin to speak of the man's depravities. Your brother would never forgive me if he learned—"

"I would think that Richard would be grateful to any kind soul who took us in on such a night." Ariel caught a glimpse of the butler, who was standing at the foot of the stairs, an inscrutable look on his face. Then he slowly winked.

"That shows how little you know." Aunt grabbed her elbow. "Come, girl, we are going."

Ariel jerked her arm away. "You may do whatever you wish, but I am staying here."

"You cannot! The man's name is a byword for licentiousness! No one with any pretense of respectability dares to even speak his name."

"Surely, no one can be that bad," Ariel said. "If he is so terrible, why haven't I heard of him?"

"Names like his are not meant for the innocent ears of young ladies."

Ariel laughed. "Oh, come, do you think I don't hear Richard and his friends talking? I know far more than you think. Why, the only person who could be so horrible as you describe is the one they call the 'black-hearted ba—' oh!"

She clapped a hand over her mouth as a tall man stepped from the shadow of a doorway, a cynical smile crossing his handsome face. His dark eyes glanced between her and her aunt.

"I believe the word you want is 'bastard,'" he said, bowing low. "The Earl of Milford, at your service, ladies."

With a low moan, Mrs. Dobson crumpled to the floor.

Simon was accustomed to women having strong reactions to him—either shocked avoidance or blatant invitation. Yet he'd never had one faint at the sight of him before. Of course, he rarely had dealings with middle-aged matrons.

The young woman kneeling by her side was far more to his taste. Thick blond hair streamed over the dark wool of her cloak. He'd only caught a glimpse of her face, but he'd felt a quick flash of interest. A comely chit. And, judging from her companion's horrified reaction to him, totally respectable and not for the likes of him.

With a sigh, he sent Harman for brandy.

"I think she would be more comfortable in the drawing room," Simon said.

The girl turned to look at him, and Simon saw that his first impression had been correct—not a classic beauty, but attractive enough to draw her share of male attention. No doubt that was why the older lady reacted as she had.

He should offer reassurances that the "black-hearted bastard" had no interest in innocent females. Why should he, when so many others threw themselves in his path? Innocence, in his opinion, was a highly overrated attribute. He'd choose experience any time.

The woman on the floor groaned, and her eyelids fluttered. "Do not fear, Ariel. I will protect you from that dreadful man."

Ariel. Simon grinned. Shakespeare's mischievous sprite. He wondered if she was as impish as her namesake.

Harman arrived with the brandy, and the girl forced the prostrate woman to drink some. Sputtering and choking, she finally sat up, clutching the girl's hand.

"We must leave," the older woman announced.

"There is no need for such foolishness," Simon said, a bit more harshly than he intended. "I offer you safe shelter."

"But . . . but . . ." The woman sputtered.

The girl stood and curtseyed. "My aunt and I thank you for your hospitality, my lord."

My lord. How long had it been since he'd heard that courtesy from a young, sweet miss? This girl *was* an innocent.

"Show them to the parlor," he said to Harman, then abruptly turned to return to the privacy of the library.

If the aunt fainted at the sight of him, what was she going to think when she met the rest of his guests? No doubt she would barricade herself and her niece in their room for the duration of their stay.

A pity. He was almost willing to behave himself for the chance to more closely admire that blue-eyed blond.

As he reached for the brandy, he realized he had not even learned their names.

Simon barely had a chance to fill his glass when Harman was at the door again, an apologetic look on his face.

"There are others outside seeking shelter," he said.

"This is not a coaching inn," Simon snapped. "Why in blazes are people traveling in this weather—haven't they noticed it is snowing?"

He saw his butler's frown and sighed. "How many?"

"Two—a man and his wife. A merchant, I believe."

"We are going to run out of bedrooms," Simon grumbled. Even if he spent most of his nights sporting in Claudia's bed, he preferred to sleep in his own. He did not intend to give up that privilege.

"Any one fool enough to be out in weather like this deserves their fate," he said to Harman. "If anyone else arrives, tell them we have no room."

"Of course," Harman replied. "Shall I inform the cook that there will be four more for dinner?"

"Oh, Lord." Simon raked a hand through his hair. With the girl's companion fainting at the very sight of him, it might prove an interesting meal. "Yes, tell her there will be ten at table tonight."

He had a sudden vision of the scene in the drawing room as the odd assortment of women gathered after dinner, and he laughed aloud. Now *that* would be worth seeing. He set his glass down and followed Harman out of the room. He had better tell the others that they were going to have company.

By the time the butler returned to the parlor and offered to show them to their room, Ariel had succeeded in calming her aunt's fears enough that she reluctantly agreed that they would accept the earl's shelter.

They followed the butler up the stairs. The bedroom he led them to was plainly furnished, but still superior to even the best chamber at the Duck. Ariel hoped this would improve her aunt's disposition.

"I will make arrangements to have your luggage brought up," the butler said. "Would you like one of the ladies' maids to attend you?"

"There are other ladies staying here?" Mrs. Dobson regarded him suspiciously.

The butler coughed. "The earl is entertaining guests."

"No, thank you," Mrs. Dobson retorted hastily.

"Dinner is at eight. I shall have someone escort you to the drawing room at a quarter to."

"I prefer to have meals in our room," Mrs. Dobson said.

The butler bowed. "As you wish, madam."

As soon as he left, Ariel turned to her aunt. "Why did you refuse the loan of a maid? And why should we eat in our room?"

"Trust me, Ariel. If the earl has female guests, they are not the sort of women your brother would wish you to associate with."

Ariel could not resist teasing her aunt. "You mean fallen women? I would like to see one."

"Those are the type of women about whom you should know nothing. Now, help me with my dress. I should like to lie down and rest."

Ariel assisted her aunt and then, while waiting for her to fall asleep, she explored her surroundings. A door off the large bedroom led to a smaller dressing room. There was another door in the far wall of this room, but it was locked.

If only aunt would take a nap. Then Ariel could slip out and explore the house—perhaps even meet some of the disreputable women guests. That sounded far more interesting than sitting in a chair while Aunt napped.

Aunt, however, was not so tired as she claimed, and Ariel was finally forced to read to her to alleviate her boredom. She had just reached the end of a chapter in Maria Edgeworth's latest novel when a discreet tap sounded at the door. It was Harman, and servants with their luggage.

"The earl regrets that due to a shortage of servants, we will be unable to serve dinner in your room," he said. "You are welcome to take a tray upstairs, however."

"Why, I never!" Mrs. Dobson exclaimed.

"We will come down for dinner," Ariel said quickly. Harman nodded and left.

Aunt glared at Ariel. "What do you mean, we are going down to dinner? Absolutely not. We shall eat in our room."

"You can eat here, but I intend to dine with the others."

"You cannot sit in the same room as that man, not without a chaperon."

"Then I guess you will have to come with me, won't you?" Ariel smiled sweetly.

She saw the conflicting emotions flit across her aunt's face—horror at associating with the earl's scandalous companions wavering against her need to protect her niece. Ariel knew which impulse would win out.

"We shall dine downstairs," Aunt agreed reluctantly. "And then immediately retire to our room."

Hiding her grin of triumph, Ariel turned to their trunks. Now, if she could only find a maid to help her. Their clothes were sadly crumpled, and she did not want to dine with the notorious Earl of Milford looking as if she'd just crawled out of a portmanteau.

Chapter 2

For the first time in near memory, Simon dressed for dinner. As he wrestled with his cravat, he began to regret his earlier charitable impulses, for he had no desire to entertain all these uninvited guests according to the rules of polite society. Perhaps he should let them dine by themselves, while he and his friends ate in their usual comfortable informality.

Then he remembered a bright gleam of blond hair and merry blue eyes and decided it would not be *that* onerous to play host, at least for the length of one meal—if that gorgon of an aunt even allowed the chit to come downstairs. He'd deliberately refused to serve them meals in their room in hopes of luring them to the table. He would make it difficult—and obvious—if they intended to shun him. Yet if Harman had reported rightly, the girl, at least, intended to dine with him.

Simon gave an uncustomary, self-conscious glance at the mirror. He wasn't togged out in satin knee breeches, but with waistcoat, cravat, and coat, he looked far more presentable than he usually did—almost like a real earl.

He winced at the thought. He was a real earl, although not one who was accepted in the highest social circles. Which did not bother him one bit—Simon knew just how dull and boring those circles were. After all, he had once traveled among them. He vastly preferred his current state of ostracism.

After giving himself a final, cynical smile in the mirror, he stepped into the hall. With this eclectic mix of guests, there was no telling what might happen when they all gathered together.

He wanted to be the first one to the drawing room, in case he was needed to keep the peace.

To his surprise, Claudia was already there, lounging on the sofa, with more than a shocking glimpse of ankle revealed below the hem of her gossamer-thin dress. No doubt she thought to look enticing for Simon, but he thought she merely appeared common.

"I understand you have some new guests," she said. "Do tell, Simon."

"There's nothing to tell," he said. "Some travelers stranded by the snow. No one of any consequence."

She laughed. Her throaty tones had once enchanted him, but now sounded affected, boring. He really needed to find a new mistress. But until the snow melted, he was stuck with her—and everyone else.

How had he managed to get himself into this fix? He was saddled with four respectable and uninvited houseguests, a mistress who bored him, and companions whose presence he was tired of. And now he had to play the gracious host?

Or did he? It was his home, after all. He could do what he damned well pleased.

With a sense of freedom, Simon ripped off the restricting cravat and flung it onto a chair.

He heard voices coming from the hall and turned toward the door, ready to play host on *his* terms.

"I do not know why I allowed you to talk me into this." Mrs. Dobson twisted her gloves in her hands while she and Ariel waited for a servant to escort them downstairs. "One can only imagine the kind of disreputable people the earl is entertaining."

"Since we are included in that number, I do not think we have to worry overmuch."

"Silly girl. You know to whom I refer. The earl's *invited* guests." Aunt shivered in horror.

"They cannot be too terrible," Ariel said as the awaited tap sounded on their door. "After all, he is an earl."

"Mark my words, we are both going to regret this."

It was not the butler, but one of the footmen who stood outside.

"I am here to escort you to the drawing room," he said.

Ariel took her aunt's arm, and they stepped into the hall. To her surprise, another couple stood there, a middle-aged man and woman. He wore an eye-popping waistcoat of bright yellow, while her deep maroon dress dripped lace. Cuddled in the woman's arms was a fuzzy black-and-brown mop of a dog.

"Blakenose," the man said, a jovial grin on his florid face. "Horace Blakenose, purveyor of fine foodstuffs." He gestured to the woman at his side. "M'wife."

Ariel gently squeezed her aunt's hand to encourage her to respond.

"I am Mrs. Aurelia Dobson," she said at last. "May I present my niece, the Honorable Miss Tennant, sister to Viscount Derring."

"And this is Blinky." Mrs. Blakenose held out one of the dog's paws. "Shake hands with the ladies, Blinky."

Ariel sensed her aunt's suppressed shudder.

"What a cute little doggy." Ariel took the furry, golden-brown paw. The dog let out a sharp bark, and she jerked her hand back. "Will he bite?"

"Oh, no. Blinky never bites. He's just saying hello."

Ariel regarded him doubtfully.

"Was that your carriage we saw out on the road?" Blakenose asked as they walked down the hall. "Looks like you had a spot of trouble."

Ariel nodded. "The wheel broke when the carriage skidded into the ditch. We are grateful the earl offered us shelter."

"Likewise," Mrs. Blakenose said. "We were of a mind to continue to Derby, but I said to Mr. Blakenose that we ought to seek shelter before we ended up like those poor souls in the ditch."

"You are not guests of the earl then?" Ariel asked. "I mean, not a part of his regular house party?"

Mrs. Blakenose laughed loudly. "Lord, no. We don't usually hobnob with the likes of earls and such."

They followed the manservant through the corridor and down the stairs to the entry hall, where he opened the door to what Ariel presumed was the drawing room. Leaving her aunt beside Mrs. Blakenose, Ariel eagerly took the first step into the room. She couldn't wait to see what the lair of a rake looked like.

Milford stood in the center of the room, looking disappointingly presentable in a tailored black coat and pale grey waistcoat.

Ariel wasn't certain what a rake should look like, but Milford's appearance disappointed her. Oh, his hair was worn too long for fashion, but his clothing was elegant and well-tailored. He wasn't paunchy from too much rich food, and he didn't have the red nose of a drinker. In fact, he was extraordinarily handsome.

Yet, as he turned to greet them and she caught the full force of his glinting dark eyes and dazzling smile, she suddenly knew why women found rakes so appealing.

She quickly glanced away.

The room itself was almost a disappointment. Ariel did not know exactly what she had expected, but it certainly wasn't this—a gilded plasterwork ceiling, and pale blue walls hung with framed paintings. Thick carpeting cushioned her feet, and the furniture had the lines of Sheraton. It looked like a very ordinary drawing room.

The woman sitting on the gold upholstered sofa caught Ariel's eye. She was dressed in a gown of green gauze with the most revealing neckline Ariel had ever seen. Was this one of the improper women Aunt so feared? Ariel hoped so.

"Welcome." Milford came forward as they walked into the room. "I am sorry we have not yet had the chance to be introduced. I am Milford."

Blakenose pushed forward and took the earl's hand. "Blakenose, Horace Blakenose. Glad to make your acquaintance, m' lord. Just what was I saying to my wife when we first spotted your house—'I bet there's a nob that's living there, Euphy, if I do say so myself.' She was nearly beside herself at the thought."

"Indeed." A distant smile crossed the earl's face. He bowed low and reached for Mrs. Blakenose's hand, then hastily jerked it back at the sight of the dog in her arms. He turned instead toward Ariel and her aunt.

"This is my aunt, Mrs. Dobson." Ariel dropped a quick curtsey. "And I am Miss Tennant."

"The *Honorable* Miss Tennant," Mrs. Dobson said with as much haughtiness as she was capable.

Milford arched a brow. "Indeed. Your father is . . . ?"

"Viscount Derring is my brother," Ariel replied.

"Derring." Milford looked thoughtful. "Can't say that I have met him."

"I should hope not," Aunt retorted sotto voce.

The blond woman who'd been seated on the couch came up behind the earl, laying a proprietary hand on his arm. "Simon, dear, are you not going to introduce me?"

"This is Miss Claudia Baker," the earl said.

"It is such a pleasure to meet you," she said with a simpering smile.

Ariel tried not to stare too blatantly at the woman, but it was difficult to restrain her curiosity. Was she the earl's *fille de joie*? Judging from her voluptuous proportions, Ariel thought that likely. No wonder Aunt had been so worried about the earl's guests. Ariel glanced at her aunt, who regarded the woman with an expression of pained resignation.

"It is indeed a pleasure to meet you, Miss Baker," Blakenose said with an enthusiastic smile. It faded under the disapproving gaze of his wife.

A loud giggle punctuated the awkward silence that followed. Two new couples stepped into the room. Ariel watched them with avid curiosity, certain they were more of the earl's disreputable friends.

It took little imagination to guess that the two women were of the same status as Miss Baker. Their gowns appeared both fashionable and expensive, but were scandalously low-cut. Ariel thought she caught a flicker of amusement in the brunette's eyes as she surveyed Ariel's demure lutestring dress.

"And here are the others," the earl said with obvious relief. "Harry Bates, and Baron Lynnwood. May I present Mr. and Mrs. Blakenose, Mrs. Dobson and—" his eyes twinkled briefly—"the Honorable Miss Tennant."

Lord Lynnwood, a tall, lean man with graying hair, took Ariel's hand and brought it to his lips. "A delight, Miss Tennant."

Aunt harrumphed loudly, and he quickly released Ariel's hand.

Bates merely nodded, but the bold way his eyes traveled over her made Ariel feel distinctly uncomfortable. *Gentlemen* did not look at ladies in that manner.

Milford turned to the women. "And these lovely ladies are Miss Marguerite LeDeux and Sarah . . . Vining, is it?" The dark-haired woman nodded.

The butler appeared in the doorway. "Dinner is served."

The earl turned to Mrs. Dobson and held out his arm. "May I escort you into dinner, madam?"

Ariel smothered a laugh at Aunt's predicament. By precedent, Ariel should go in with the earl. Would fear for her niece overcome society's rule?

"I hardly think . . . that is . . ." Aunt glanced at Ariel. "I believe that my niece takes precedence, my lord."

Striving to appear nonplussed, Ariel took Milford's proffered arm, and he led her across the hall to the dining room, Aunt following closely on their heels. The earl seated Ariel to his right, with Aunt beside her, then stood waiting for the other ladies to be seated.

Ariel saw a frown cross Milford's face. "Mrs. Blakenose?" he called out.

"Yes?"

"You cannot bring that dog in here."

"Oh, he won't be a problem." Mrs. Blakenose hugged the dog. "Blinky always eats with us."

"The dog must go," the earl said sternly. "Harman, take the creature and put him . . . somewhere."

Mrs. Blakenose tossed her husband a pleading glance, but he shook his head. Reluctantly, she handed the dog to Harman.

"Now, be certain you do not put him in a draft," she warned him anxiously. "And you must cut his food very small, or he will choke."

Harman nodded and took the dog away.

"I don't understand why we don't eat in here every night," Miss Vining complained with an exaggerated pout. "Aren't we honored guests?"

Lynnwood leaned over and whispered something in her ear.

"I find it rather dull to dine formally every night," Ariel said brightly. "While we were visiting my cousins, I often took meals with the children in the nursery."

"A place you've been away from for *so* long," the earl drawled with light sarcasm.

"I am one-and-twenty and have been out of the nursery for quite some time now, my lord," she retorted.

"Forgive me, Miss Tennant. I had not realized you were so advanced in years. Surprising, in an unmarried lady."

Ariel flashed him an annoyed look, then smiled as she saw the teasing expression in his eyes.

"Our family has been plagued with a series of unfortunate deaths in recent years," Mrs. Dobson informed him. "We insist on observing strict mourning, which has severely limited Ariel's opportunities for a Season."

"Then I wish long lives on the remainder of your relatives," the earl said. "It would be a crime to further deprive society of Miss Tennant's presence."

To her chagrin, Ariel felt herself blush.

"Now, I admire a family that observes strict mourning," said Mrs. Blakenose. "Too many these days think that black gloves are enough."

Mrs. Dobson regarded the merchant's wife with new respect. "Exactly," she said.

"Then you intend to go to London this spring?" Milford asked Ariel.

She nodded. "Will you be there, my lord?"

"Perhaps. Although I fear our paths will not often cross. I rarely attend entertainments suitable for young ladies. Although, for you, Miss Tennant, I might make an exception."

He flashed her a wide grin, and Ariel thought it was terribly unfair that a man with such a horrible reputation could be so wickedly handsome.

"They certainly aren't going to let you in at Almack's, Milford," Lynnwood said, smirking.

Milford snorted derisively. "Why would anyone wish to be admitted?"

"Almack's is a place of taste and respectability," Mrs. Dobson said archly. "Two things I fear you do not value."

"Aunt!" Ariel stared at her aghast.

Milford laughed. "Touché, Mrs. Dobson. I confess I am a highly unrespectable fellow."

"Who wants respectability when he can have fun?" Bates

asked. "I'll take a masked ball over some boring dinner party any day."

Miss LeDeux giggled. "Perhaps we should hold one here. It would be rather fun."

"I fear it would not work, Marguerite," Milford said. "There are so few of us—we would soon guess everyone's identity. Isn't the thrill of a masked ball the unknown, the forbidden?"

Ariel felt her aunt's tension rising and feared that if Milford and his friends kept talking like this, she would be banished upstairs before it was over.

She glanced across the table at Miss Baker, who looked bored as she toyed with the food on her plate. Perhaps they could steer the conversation back into more suitable areas.

"Where do you make your home, Miss Baker?"

Aunt pinched her arm, and Ariel yelped.

Miss Baker shot Milford a coy glance. "I have a lovely house in Lisson Grove. Although you might say I live here at Thornhill the moment."

"As do we all," the earl said. "At least, until the snow melts and the roads are passable once again."

"Which cannot come too soon," Mrs. Dobson said under her breath.

Blakenose refilled his wineglass. "Excellent table you set, m'lord. Do you buy all your supplies locally? I'm a purveyor of foodstuffs, myself. Mayhap we can do some business together."

The earl did not look enthused.

Suddenly a loud commotion in the hall startled the diners. Simon frowned. He heard thumping, yelling, the frantic barking of a dog—it sounded like a band of hunters racing though his house.

Harman appeared at the door, an apologetic expression on his face. "There is another group of travelers seeking shelter from the storm."

"There is no room," Simon said.

"Ho, Milford!" A young man, red faced from the cold, stepped past Harman. Melting snow dripped from his many-caped greatcoat. "Could have knocked me over with a feather when we discovered this was your lair. Can you believe it? We almost decided to push on toward Derby, but when we saw the signpost, we could not resist."

"Remind me to tear the sign down," Simon muttered. In louder tones, he asked, "And who are you?"

The young man looked crestfallen. "You don't remember? At the mill in Derby last fall? When the Giant took on Paddy O'Neal? We were right next to you, at the ring."

The earl shuddered, remembering how much money he'd lost on that bout. "How could I forget?"

Two other men, looking to be in their early twenties, crowded in behind the first arrival.

"Good Lord, it looks like a regular party," the taller, dark-haired one said. "Good thing we arrived when we did."

"Anything left to eat?" His companion, a round-faced fellow who was nearly a head shorter, looked eagerly at the table.

Harman cleared his throat and looked at Simon. "Shall I have three more places set?"

"Have I a choice?" Simon shook his head in resignation. "I suppose I must put you three up for the night as well."

"Can't go anywhere now." The first man who had entered pulled out the chair at the end of the table and sat down. "Phaeton's stuck in the ditch, just past the big tree."

"You were driving a phaeton in this weather?" Simon demanded incredulously.

The three friends shared conspiratorial grins.

"It was a bet," the tall one said.

Simon shook his head at their youthful idiocy. "Introduce yourselves to my guests."

"Gregson," the ruddy-faced one announced.

"Townsend," said the taller.

"Mallory," announced the plump one. "And I know one of your guests." He cast an adoring gaze on Marguerite. "I am one of your most fervent admirers."

She smiled. "Why, thank you."

"Couldn't take my eyes off you at Drury Lane the last time you danced," he continued.

"We are an eclectic group," Simon said dryly. "There are other travelers stranded like yourselves. The Honorable Miss Tennant, and her aunt, Mrs. Dobson. Mr. and Mrs. Blakenose. Miss LeDeux you profess to know. Bates, Miss Vining, Lord Lynnwood, Miss Baker."

"Looks like a jolly party." Townsend smiled widely at Claudia.

"Don't forget Blinky," Mrs. Blakenose said. During the commotion the dog had run into the room and jumped onto her lap.

Harman, looking thoroughly unperturbed, took the dog from her again while a footman set plates and silver for the newcomers.

"Couldn't have had better timing, what?" Mallory plopped down in the chair next to Miss LeDeux and heaped his plate with food. "What sort of entertainment have you planned for us this evening, Milford?"

"Don't press your good fortune," Simon said. "Be thankful that you have a roof over your head and aren't sleeping in the snow."

"But surely, these lovely young ladies must have some talents—the piano or singing," Townsend protested. "We know Miss LeDeux can dance."

"My niece and I will be retiring after dinner," Mrs. Dobson said with a firm look at Milford. "I found today's harrowing travel quite exhausting."

"I believe we will do the same," Blakenose said.

The four of them stood and bade them good night.

"Sleep well," Simon said as they departed. He would rather have had that girl stay, but he was glad to see the others go. Ah, well. He'd have a chance to see her again tomorrow.

Ariel, who had not expected that aunt would permit her to remain downstairs after the meal, still felt disappointed. How was she ever going to learn more about the earl and his disreputable guests—even a real opera dancer—if Aunt kept her in their room all the time?

Tomorrow she would find a way to escape from Aunt's overly cautious eye. Ariel knew she'd never again have the chance to mingle with such interesting people, and she did not want to waste a moment of this opportunity.

"I cannot imagine the nerve of that man." Mrs. Dobson spoke indignantly to her niece when they reached their room. "To actually force us to sit down at the same table with those, those . . . *women.*"

"They seemed very pleasant," Ariel said.

"Hmmph. You heard what that nice young man said. That one creature is an *opera dancer*. If your brother knew how you forced me to allow you to dine with those people . . ."

"I really do not think that I am in much danger from an opera dancer."

Aunt gave her a withering look. Ariel responded with an impish smile.

"Oh, Aunt, neither of us are in any danger here. You saw how respectably everyone acted tonight. Why, I find it hard to see why Milford has such a terrible reputation. He acted the perfect host."

"You do not see what goes on behind closed doors."

She feigned wide-eyed innocence. "What does go on?"

"Never you mind. That knowledge is not for your ears."

Ariel sat down in the bedside chair. "If the earl has someone as lovely as Miss Baker to entertain him, he certainly is not going to try to get his hands on me."

"Ariel!"

"Well, it's true. She is lovely. Did you notice her gown? It was the very first stare of fashion. I wager it cost a pretty penny."

"Paid for by the earl, no doubt," Aunt said with a derisive sniff.

"Richard pays for all my clothes," Ariel reminded her.

"That is entirely different. He is your brother. Not your . . ." Aunt's voice trailed off.

"Protector?" Ariel dared to suggest.

"That is quite enough of that," Aunt snapped. "Now help me out of my dress. I ate more than I should have—I must admit that the earl does set a nice table—and I wish to lie down. You can read more of Mrs. Edgeworth to me."

With a sign, Ariel complied, knowing she was in for an excessively dull evening.

To her relief, Aunt fell asleep sooner than she'd hoped. Ariel wanted to slip out of the room and venture downstairs, but some inherent sense of caution stayed her curiosity. It was one thing to face the earl and his friends over the formality of the dinner table. Quite another to burst in on their private party. Who knew what they were doing now?

Having an orgy, perhaps? Ariel laughed softly. Aunt would

surely think so, but she did not think Milford looked that deca-
dent. If she had seen him riding in the park, she would never
have guessed he was a notorious rake.

And, to her great disappointment, he had not leered at her
once. Not like that horrid Lynnwood. Now he looked, and
acted, like a rake.

She would not have minded so much if it had been Milford
who looked at her that way. But with three stunning lightskirts
in the house, why would he bother? She was only plain Ariel,
with nothing exceptional to mark her countenance.

Even a rake like Milford found her dull.

It was far past midnight when Simon finally staggered off
to his bed. In a burst of generosity, he'd allowed the three
young bucks to join his guests in the drawing room for their
after-dinner revelry. The young men had spent the entire time
trying to make a favorable impression on the ladies, with
boastful accounts of impossible exploits and exaggerated
prowess. The women responded with genial flirtation while
he, Lynnwood, and Bates watched the whole thing with
amused tolerance.

To his chagrin, Simon realized he had drunk more brandy
than he had intended, and his steps verged on the wobbly as he
made his way to his chamber.

Claudia's room lay next to his, through a connecting door,
and he realized he ought to pay her at least a short visit, or she
would be unhappy.

He kicked off his shoes and pulled off his jacket, tossing it in
the general direction of a chair, then reached down and undid
the buttons on his pantaloons. He tried to pull one leg off, but
his foot caught and he stumbled, barely catching himself on the
bedpost.

Leaning against the bed, he struggled to remove his pantaloons as the room started to swim around him—not a good
sign. He shook his head, trying to clear his vision. After tossing
his waistcoat atop the bed, he unbuttoned his shirt, before
weaving unsteadily to the wardrobe and reaching for his dressing down.

Simon pulled the maroon brocade from its hook and set it
aside while he struggled with his shirt. The first sleeve slipped

off easily, but the other cuff snagged on his hand. He shook his arm, trying to free himself, but the shirt only flopped about. Finally, he grabbed it with his other hand and pulled free. After shrugging into his robe, he moved unsteadily toward the door.

The damn thing was locked. He fumbled for the key, twisted it in the lock, and turned the latch.

The dressing room beyond was dark. He thought to grab a candle, but reasoned there would be one in Claudia's room. He tacked toward the other door and smashed his hand against the wall while reaching for the knob.

"Damn." He swore loudly and reached for the knob again. He pushed the door open and stumbled toward the bed. He sank down on the edge and shut his eyes, blinking them open again when the room started spinning.

Perhaps if I lie down . . . just for a moment. He stretched out on the mattress. *That was better.* Now, if only that annoying buzzing in his ears would stop.

Buzzing? Simon realized it sounded more like snoring.

Claudia snored? He tried to remember if he'd ever noticed that before. Just one more reason to give her the congé as soon as possible. He rolled over and gazed bleary-eyed at the woman lying beside him.

Something was not right. Claudia never wore a nightcap. And the hair spilling from that cap was . . . grey.

"Damnation."

Someone gasped, and Simon rolled over to look across the room into the shocked eyes of the Honorable Miss Tennant.

He had crawled in bed with her aunt.

Chapter 3

Simon groaned. "Oh, God. What am I doing here?"

"The very question I would ask."

He scrambled off the bed, expecting Miss Tennant to start screaming at any moment. But to his surprise, she only regarded him with a slightly amused expression.

She was wrapped in a voluminous robe that hid every trace of her lithe shape, but her long blond hair was unbound and fell below her shoulders in golden waves that gleamed in the candlelight.

Simon ran a hand over his face, trying to think clearly. "I must have gone the wrong way. Claudia's room's on the *other* side."

"Then perhaps you should go back the way you came and try again," Miss Tennant said.

He looked at her through bleary eyes. "What? Now that I'm here, you don't want me to stay?"

"I certainly do not!"

"Pity. We could have a good time." He took an unsteady step toward her.

"May I remind you that my aunt is sleeping in that bed?"

He slapped himself on the forehead. "How could I have forgotten?"

"Shh. You'll wake her."

"Then you should find a way to keep me quiet."

She glared at him. "I shall do no such thing. You should not be here in the first place."

"You're right." Simon grabbed her hand and pulled her into the dressing room.

"What do you think you are doing?" she demanded.

"You told me to leave."

"I didn't tell you to take me with you."

He squinted at her. "You don't want to come with me?"

"Of course I do not. Lord Milford, you are three sheets to the wind. I suggest you take yourself to bed immediately."

"Good idea." He put an arm around her shoulder and tried to pull her toward the doorway. "Come along."

Somehow, she deftly slipped away from him and pushed him through the open door to his room.

Simon waggled a wavering finger in the air. "This is your last chance." He turned to go, then stopped, his hand on the door-knob. "Are you sure?"

"Good night, my lord." Miss Tennant's voice was firm.

He shut the door behind him, stabbing at the lock with the key, but the damned thing did not want to go into the hole.

Lord, he had not been this drunk in a long, long time.

Finally, with frustration, he pushed the door open and held out the key to Miss Tennant, who was still stood there, watching him warily.

"You lock it," he said and shut the door.

He glanced toward the opposite wall, to the door that led to Claudia's room. But he found he had no desire to go to her room now. He only wanted to crawl into his bed and sleep.

Simon tore off his robe and slid between the sheets, hoping that the room would stop spinning soon.

Ariel stood staring at the door, key in hand, for several minutes after Milford left.

She had wanted to shout with laughter at the look on his face when he realized he'd crawled into bed with her aunt. A rake like Milford trying to ravish Aunt!

Thank goodness he hadn't woken her. Ariel was willing to believe the earl had made a simple mistake; Aunt would not be so forgiving. No doubt she would have raised enough fuss to rouse the entire household. This way, she would never know what had happened.

She'd felt a flash of fear when the earl first stumbled into the room, but that quickly changed to amusement when she realized he wasn't there intentionally. He had not come looking to ravish anyone—he was seeking his mistress. Ariel should have known he was not interested in *her*.

The premier rake of the realm had invaded her bedroom, but only by mistake. Ariel knew that no rake would ever wish to ravish her. She was too ordinary, too plain, too . . . boring. Milford's reaction proved it. He hadn't even tried to steal a kiss.

Ariel awoke early while her aunt still slept. She dressed quickly, eager to slip out of the room. At this hour of the morning, she felt sure she would have the opportunity to explore the house without disturbing the others. Quietly shutting the bedroom door, she listened carefully, but no sounds came from any of the other rooms. Ariel walked quickly toward the stairs.

She was certain the earl would not be about—not after his drunken appearance in her room during the night. If he was anything like her brother, he would not crawl from his bed until late afternoon, at best.

Ariel hoped she might be able to find some breakfast. She peered into the drawing room, but it was deserted, reassurance that she was the only one awake. The sound of china and cutlery clattering across the hall told her that the servants were probably laying the table for breakfast in the dining room, and she pushed open the door.

Milford sat at the far end of the table, buttering a piece of toast. He glanced up at her, and his eyes mirrored her own surprise.

Ariel hesitated, feeling suddenly awkward intruding on his solitude. Should she leave?

"Come in." Milford gave her a cheerful look. "I assure you, I will not bite."

Ariel took a tentative step into the room. "I am not afraid of you, my lord. But if you wish to eat alone . . ."

"If I intended to eat alone, I would have picked another room. I expect my guests to join me here." He gestured to the table, and the plate of food on it. "Take what you like."

Ariel saw a plateful of sliced ham, toasted bread, butter, jam, scones, and coddled eggs. A footman pulled out a chair and she sat next to the earl.

"I am surprised to find you up so early," Ariel said as she reached for the ham.

He laughed. "You mean after my inebriated condition last night? I assure you, Miss Tennant, I have a harder head than most."

"When my brother comes home in a similar state, he rarely ventures out of his room until afternoon, at the least."

"How old is your brother?"

"Oh, ancient," she replied with a saucy grin. "Five-and-twenty."

"A veritable Methuselah," he agreed. "Does he often come home inebriated?"

"Oh, rarely. He is usually very well behaved."

"Unlike myself?"

"Quite unlike you, my lord." She noticed he had made no apologies for his intrusion last night.

"I assume you live with him?"

She nodded.

"And your aunt lives with you, also?"

"Fortunately, no." Ariel smiled. "We have been visiting relatives and Richard insists that I do not travel alone. She will be accompanying us in London this spring."

His eyes took on a sardonic gleam. "Husband hunting, the both of you?"

His remark sent her into whoops of laughter. "I am sorry," she said, wiping her eyes. "But the thought of Aunt on the marriage mart . . ."

"My sentiments exactly." He flashed her a quick grin. "Where do you make your home when you are not in London?"

"In Wiltshire."

"So you still have some traveling ahead of you when the snow melts."

She glanced at the curtained windows. "I have not even looked outside this morning. Is it still snowing?"

In answer, he rose and walked to the window, pulling open the curtains. The landscape outside was invisible behind the wall of thickly falling flakes.

"I don't think it let up at all during the night. No one is going anywhere for a time."

"It is very kind of you to allow us to stay here. I imagine we have put a damper on your party."

"I welcome some new faces. We were growing bored with each other's company."

Ariel laughed. "I only hope you will not say the same of us in a few days."

"Oh, I highly doubt that." Milford grimaced. "Not if your aunt keeps looking at me as something that crawled out from under a particularly loathsome rock."

"You do have to forgive her. She takes her guardianship of me seriously—too seriously."

"Is that why you slipped the traces this morning? She will be horrified to find out that you have dined with me—alone."

"Then we simply shall not tell her." She gave him a conspiratorial grin.

Harman appeared at the door. "Mrs. Dobson is asking after her niece."

Ariel jumped from her chair. "I must go." But it was already too late. She could hear Aunt calling in the hall.

She darted Milford a panicked look.

"Under the table," he said, lifting the cloth. "Quickly."

Ariel dropped to her knees and crawled under the table.

"Sit down," Milford told Harman. "Start eating."

Beneath the table, Ariel tried to scrunch herself as small as possible, her back pressed against Milford's boots. She froze when the dining room door opened.

"Good morning, Mrs. Dobson," Milford drawled in languid tones. "How nice of you to join me for breakfast."

"I am looking for my niece," Aunt replied stiffly.

"Haven't seen her. Harman, have you run across Miss Tennant this morning?"

"No, my lord."

"I am sure she is around here someplace," Milford said. "Now, do sit down, please. Can I get you a fresh pot of tea?"

"I cannot eat a bite until I know where my niece is. What have you done with her?"

"I?" Milford sounded hurt. "I believe, madam, that you are the one who lost her."

"I know the type of man you are," Aunt said, her voice rising. "Seeking any opportunity to prey on young, innocent ladies."

Milford laughed. "Mrs. Dobson, I am crushed. What use do I have for a young, innocent girl? I may prefer women in their first bloom, but I also require them to have a great deal of experience."

Ariel could only imagine the expression on Aunt's face. Milford was lucky he was an earl, else Aunt would be liable to dump a plate of eggs on his head.

"If you have had a hand in her disappearance, I will—"

"Feel free to search my room, or any other room in the house," Milford said. "Harman, take Mrs. Dobson upstairs so she can reassure herself that I have not hidden her niece in my bedroom."

"Please come with me, madam," the butler said. "I am sure we can find Miss Tennant."

Ariel heard footsteps, then the door opened and closed.

"You can come out now," Milford said after a moment.

Ariel crawled out from under the table. "You only encourage her dislike of you, you know," she said as she resumed her seat.

His boyish grin made him look most un-rakish. "I know, but it is so delightfully amusing!"

"Thank you for hiding me. I fear she would have been tiresome if she'd seen us alone together. I did want to finish my breakfast."

"And as I am done, I shall allow you to do so by yourself. In case your aunt returns, we would not wish to be caught in a lie."

Ariel felt disappointed that he was leaving already. She had enjoyed talking with the notorious earl. His sense of humor was refreshing after spending so much time with her repressive aunt.

Milford pushed back his chair. "I trust we will meet again. In the meantime, feel free to make yourself at home in the house, although there is little to provide entertainment for a young lady. I do have a library full of books, and there is a piano in the drawing room if you play."

"Very badly," she admitted. "But I do like to read."

"The library is at the back of the house. But be forewarned— I tend to spend a great deal of time there myself. You might need to fight off an attack on your virtue."

"Then I will come prepared to defend myself." She smiled as he bowed and made his departure.

"Ariel!" Scant minutes after Milford left, Mrs. Dobson scurried into the dining room. "What in heaven's name are you dong down here by yourself?"

"Eating breakfast," Ariel replied, spearing another piece of ham.

"You are a naughty girl, leaving the room without a word. I was worried sick."

Ariel took a sip of tea, trying to look unconcerned. "As you can see, I've come to no harm."

"I consider that a miracle in this house. Your brother will never forgive me if—"

"Nothing will happen—unless I perhaps perish from boredom. Have you looked outside? It is still snowing."

Aunt sat down. "Your poor brother will be frantic with worry when we do not arrive by tomorrow."

"I am sure he will hear that there is snow in the north. He will assume that we are safe and warm in a superior inn."

Mrs. Dobson sniffed. "If he only knew . . ."

Harman entered the room, bearing a steaming pot of tea. "Fresh hot water for the ladies," he said, setting it on the table. "Can I get you anything else? The toast must be cold; let me bring you some warm slices."

Mrs. Dobson beamed at him with gratitude. When she glanced away, Harman gave Ariel a slow, broad wink. She knew he would keep her secret.

Despite what she'd said to her aunt, Ariel knew she was not going to be bored during their stay here. She prayed the snow would continue to fall so they would have to stay for ages. This was the closest thing to an adventure she was ever going to have in her ordinary life, and she wanted to enjoy it for as long as she could. Observing a rake firsthand was turning out to be vastly entertaining.

After breakfast she persuaded Aunt to retire to the drawing room instead of hiding in their chamber upstairs. Ariel ran upstairs to retrieve a book and Aunt's embroidery, and they settled in comfortable chairs by the fireplace.

After reading for a half hour, Ariel wished someone would

come in to relieve the tedium. There were eleven other people in the house—surely, they could not all still be abed? She did not expect to see the earl, of course, but even the Blakenoses and that horrible dog would be welcome right now.

She looked up eagerly when the door opened, but to her surprise it was Miss Baker, dressed in a stylish day frock of patterned muslin that was only slightly less revealing than the gown she'd worn to dinner last night.

Ariel wished she dared to wear something like it.

Furious barking sounded from the hallway; then Mrs. Blakenose's dog came bounding in, followed by his mistress. The dog raced around the room, stopping briefly to sniff each person's shoes before dashing on to the next pair, his yapping growing louder with each newly discovered scent. Mrs. Blakenose seemed oblivious to the disturbance and sat down on the settee across from Ariel.

"Isn't he the cutest thing?" Miss Baker held out her hand for the dog to sniff. "What kind of dog is he?"

Mrs. Blakenose clapped her hands, and the dog jumped up and draped himself across her lap. "He is a Belgian griffon."

"I shall have to ask Milford to get me one," Miss Baker said. "He would look so cute sitting beside me in the carriage when I drive in the park."

"Milford?" Ariel asked with a straight face. "Or the dog?"

Miss Baker laughed. "Why, the dog, of course."

Mrs. Blakenose reached into her reticule and offered something to the dog. "Sweetmeats," she said. "He dotes on them."

"He will be sick all over the carpet," Mrs. Dobson warned her. "Dogs should not be given sweets."

"My little Blinky never has any trouble with sweets, do you?"

Blinky responded with a bored yawn, and Mrs. Blakenose popped another treat into his mouth.

Miss Baker cast a languid look at the window. "I fear this snow will never cease."

"Mr. Blakenose says it will last a good three more days," his wife said. "We'll be here for a long while yet."

"Is your husband a skilled weather prognosticator?" Mrs. Dobson asked haughtily.

"Oh, Lord, yes. Does it by his knees. When the right one

starts aching, it means rain. When the left one twinges, it's wind. And when both knees hurt and his ankle starts throbbing, you can be sure it will snow."

Ariel smothered a smile. "The poor man must be in some discomfort today."

"Oh, he has a wonderful liniment that he applies. Eases his aches in no time."

"Perhaps you would be willing to share some with my aunt," Ariel said, feeling mischievous. "She also suffers when the weather is damp."

"I'd be more than happy to let you try some," Mrs. Blakenose said eagerly and grabbed up the dog. "I will get some for you right away." She dashed out of the room.

Mrs. Dobson gave her niece a sour look.

Ariel smiled. "Well, you did say your fingers were aching this morning."

"I have my own treatment, thank you."

"But it works so well for Mr. Blakenose." Ariel struggled to keep a straight face. "Surely, you should try it."

"Probably made from bear grease and sheep offal," Mrs. Dobson said and sniffed.

"But if it works . . ." Ariel's voice trailed off. "At least she took the dog with her."

"He looks like an ordinary rat-catcher to me," Mrs. Dobson said. "She treats him like a human baby. Some people are so silly about their animals."

"Perhaps the poor woman has no children," Miss Baker said.

Aunt sniffed. "That is no excuse."

Mrs. Blakenose quickly returned with her precious liniment. "Here is the preparation my dear husband uses," she said, holding out a squat jar to Mrs. Dobson. "Open it."

Mrs. Dobson reluctantly took the jar and removed the lid. Ariel wrinkled her nose at the pungent smell. It was not offensive, exactly, but she would not wish to wear it as perfume.

"Go ahead, try it." Mrs. Blakenose's beady eyes watched Aunt eagerly. "Tell me what you think."

With deep reluctance, Mrs. Dobson took the tiniest dab of the ointment and rubbed it over the knuckle of one finger.

"Oh, that is not nearly enough." Mrs. Blakenose grabbed Aunt's hand and slopped a large dollop of the lotion onto the back, then began vigorously rubbing it in before Mrs. Dobson could pull away.

"It makes my hand feel hot," Aunt complained.

"See? What did I tell you? Working already." Mrs. Blakenose grabbed aunt's other hand and began rubbing lotion onto it.

A look of surprised wonder crossed Aunt's face. "Why, I do think it feels better," she said, experimentally flexing the fingers of her free hand.

"Best thing in the world for the joint aches," Mrs. Blakenose said. She held out the jar to Ariel. "Try some."

She shook her head.

A loud thump sounded from the hall, followed by the crash of breaking china. Blinky jumped from Mrs. Blakenose's lap and ran to the door, barking loudly.

"What do you suppose that was?" Mrs. Dobson asked.

"I shall go see." Ariel jumped from her chair.

"Do not let—" Mrs. Blakenose cried, but it was too late. Before Ariel had the door open a crack, the dog pushed through and ran into the hall, his barks turning to excited yelps at the sound of another loud thump.

Ariel heard footsteps coming down the hall. She turned and saw Milford approaching, an exasperated look on his face.

"What in the deuce is going on?" he demanded.

"I don't know." She hurried after him as he strode down the corridor and into the great hall. There was another loud thump, followed by a cry of triumph. Ariel cautiously peered around Milford's shoulder. Townsend lay sprawled on the floor, with Mallory and Gregson grinning down at him. The remnants of a porcelain vase lay in pieces on the floor.

"What do you think you're doing?" Milford demanded.

The men's expressions turned sheepish.

"We were seeing who could leap the farthest off the bottom step." Townsend scrambled to his feet, dusting off his breeches.

"I've got the record," Mallory proclaimed.

"Of all the inane . . ." Milford's voice trailed off.

"It was a bet, you see," Gregson explained.

"I should have guessed as much," Milford said. "If you have so much excess energy, go expend it outside."

"But it's snowing like the devil out there!"

"Unless you intend to find yourself permanently out in the cold, I suggest you find a less bothersome activity to while away your time."

"Doing what?" Mallory asked. "Half the house is still abed."

"Miss Baker is in the drawing room," Ariel announced.

"Really?" The three men dashed down the hall, the dog yapping at their heels.

Milford shot her an amused look. "Thank you for mentioning that, Miss Tennant. I hope she will divert their attention for hours."

"It is rather generous of you to share your mistress's company."

He arched a brow. "Tell me, Miss Tennant, do all young ladies speak so frankly these days?"

Ariel laughed. "Not at all. Aunt says it is my besetting sin."

"I hope you do not listen to her," he said, his eyes teasing.

"As little as possible."

"Claudia knows how to deal with young pups." He grinned. "Unless they choose to show off their athletic prowess again. In which case I will pitch them headfirst into a snowbank."

Ariel laughed. "Really, my lord, you are being a rather churlish host. It is your job to entertain your guests."

"Guests?" His brow furrowed. "I don't recall inviting any of these people."

She had forgotten that for the earl, this was not an unexpected treat, and gave him an apologetic smile. "I realize we are imposing on you."

He regarded her with such a warm smile that it turned her knees week. *Now* she understood the attraction of a rake.

"Some of you are imposing," he said and bowed. "I hope you have an enjoyable afternoon, Miss Tennant."

Once again, she watched his departure with reluctance. Ariel sighed. She would liked him to have joined them in the drawing room, but she imagined that was far too tame a pastime for a rake. She would have to think of some activity that would lure Milford into company. What was the use of being snowbound in a rake's house if you never saw the rake?

She heard more high-pitched barking coming from the drawing room. Sighing, she turned back in that direction. Something had to be done about that dog.

When she opened the door, she spotted Blinky racing frantically back and forth between Townsend and Mallory, who were tossing something between them. Mrs. Blakenose called out, trying to get her dog's attention, but he ignored her while he tried to catch the prize, which looked to be a wadded-up glove.

Mallory tossed it to Gregson, seated next to Miss Baker on the sofa. The dog immediately ran to him. Mallory held out the glove, then jerked it back just as the dog leapt for it. Blinky sat back on his haunches and growled.

"What have you done to my Blinky?" Mrs. Blakenose cried.

"N-nothing,' Gregson stammered. "He . . . he doesn't seem to like me."

Mrs. Blakenose gave him a dark look. "My Blinky is an excellent judge of character. I am going to be keeping my eye on you, young man."

"Now, Euphy." Mr. Blakenose had come into the room while Ariel was in the hall. "He's just an animal. Quit talking as if he's human."

"Many animals are known for their human sensibilities," Mrs. Blakenose said defensively.

"But that dog's not one of them," Blakenose said with a hearty laugh. "Damn thing doesn't have the brain of a flea."

"He's a highly intelligent dog."

"Intelligent?" Blakenose hooted. "Stupid is more like it. And the way you pamper him. Making that poor footman clean up his mess. Throw the dog outside, that's what I say."

"He would freeze in this weather."

"With that mop of fur? Not likely."

Gregson suddenly jumped to his feet and pointed at the dog. "My boot!" he cried. "The damn dog peed on my boot!"

"I must say I enjoyed myself this afternoon." Mrs. Dobson ran a brush through Ariel's hair as they changed for dinner that evening. "It is a rather pleasant company."

Ariel smothered a smile. Aunt had spent the entire afternoon chatting with Mrs. Blakenose, and the two were already as thick as thieves. Their blooming friendship pleased Ariel, for it meant Aunt would be paying far less attention to her niece. Ariel would be able to enjoy herself without having Aunt's dampening gaze on her every moment. She might even be able to chat with Milford without Aunt having another attack of the vapors.

"Milford!"

The loud shout echoed through the hall.

"Milford!"

Mrs. Dobson clapped her hands over her ears. "Goodness, what is going on?"

Ariel dashed into the hall. Bates stood a few doors away, his face livid, cursing and yelling for Milford. Other curious guests came out of their rooms to stare.

"What is wrong, man?" Blakenose demanded.

"My room," Bates sputtered. "A disaster . . ."

A door slammed, and Milford strode toward them, dressed only in shirt and trousers. "What in God's name is going on?"

Bates grabbed him by the arm and pulled him to his door. "This." He flung the door open, and a blast of cold air shot into the hall.

Chapter 4

Milford took one look into Bates's room and started laughing.

The others crowded behind him to see what he found so amusing. Ariel managed to squeeze between the Blakenoses and peered through the open door.

The window on the far side of the room stood open, and a fan-shaped pile of snow spread across the room, coating the chair, the bed, and the carpet in white.

"Forget to shut the window?" Mallory snickered.

Bates whirled on him. "I never opened the damn window. The latch must be faulty."

Milford stepped past him and gingerly picked his way through the ankle-deep snow to the window. He pulled it closed and latched it securely.

"The latch looks all right to me. Are you sure you did not open it?"

Bates snatched his half-buried coat off the chair and shook off the snow. "Someone is playing a nasty prank." He glared at the others, his gaze lighting on Gregson. "You were out of the drawing room for some length of time. Did you do this?"

Gregson gulped. "No, I—"

"If I find out who the culprit is . . ." Bates's dark eyes narrowed.

Ariel took an involuntary step back at his venomous look. It was a mere accident, after all. He had no reason to get so angry.

"The room is like ice," Bates complained. "I cannot sleep here. The carpet is damp, and no doubt the bed is soaked through."

"I will have the servants clean up the mess," Milford said. "Move your things across the hall into Sar—one of the other rooms."

"A damn inconvenience," Bates snapped.

Milford clapped him on the back. "You'll laugh about this in time, my man."

Looking at Bates's scowling expression, Ariel doubted that would be soon.

"Such a fuss over nothing," Mrs. Blakenose said as they drifted back to their rooms.

"Some people just cannot take a joke," Mallory said.

Ariel glanced at him, instantly suspicious. "Oh, you admit that it was a prank?"

"No!" His round face reddened. "I mean—if it was someone's idea of a joke. He's certainly taking it hard."

"As will I if something like this happens again." There was strong warning in Milford's voice as he came up behind them.

"I intend to keep my doors locked," Gregson said. "That fellow seems to want to blame me."

"A good idea," Milford replied and returned to his room.

Ariel went into her room, where Aunt anxiously awaited her.

"What was that all about?" Mrs. Dobson asked.

"Someone left the window in Bates's room open, and snow blew in," Ariel said.

Aunt shook her head. "Why would anyone open a window in this weather?"

"Bates says it wasn't him—he claims someone else did it as a prank."

"Oh, good gracious, that is all we need to make our lives miserable. Must we stay in our rooms to make certain we will be safe?"

"I don't think that is necessary," Ariel said. "Milford made it very clear he did not want any more incidents. If it was a prank, I don't think the culprits will dare try again."

"Hmmph" was all that Aunt said.

Dinner that night went far more smoothly than the previous evening. Even Aunt looked to be enjoying herself. When the ladies rose to leave the men to their port and brandy, Ariel lingered behind for a moment so she could speak with Milford. He joined her outside the door.

"Do you have any plans for our entertainment this evening?" she asked. "You cannot expect us to spend the entire evening talking."

"What do you propose I do, Miss Tennant? We are confined to the house until the snow melts. The possibilities for entertainment are limited."

"There are any number of things you could organize for our amusement. Cards, for example. Everyone must play cards."

"But not all the guests would enjoy a high-stakes game."

"I wasn't suggesting *gambling,* my lord. It is possible to play cards without wagering money."

"But much less enjoyable," he retorted. "Fine, Miss Tennant. You have my permission to organize card play for everyone. Whist, piquet, *vingt-et-un* . . . That should provide enough amusement for one evening."

"Which game do you prefer?"

He regarded her with a lofty expression. "My dear Miss Tennant, I *never* play cards for less than outrageous stakes. My reputation would be in tatters if it got out that I played for mere *enjoyment.*"

"You intend to ignore us for the rest of the evening?"

"Do you honestly think I would enjoy sitting in the drawing room, with your aunt staring daggers at me, fearing she will once again fall into a dead faint if I should dare speak to her or cast a glance in your direction?"

"I see that a rake's life does have its inconveniences," Ariel said.

His expression clouded, and his smile faded. "I shall find playing cards." He turned quickly on his heel and was gone.

Ariel watched him walk away. Such a strange man, she thought—teasing and smiling one moment, cynical and sarcastic the next.

Of course, anyone would be out of sorts with all these strangers in the house. She would do what she could to make sure that they did not bother Milford overmuch—even if he did not truly appreciate her efforts.

*   *   *

When the other men rejoined the ladies, Simon retreated to his library. He knew he was being churlish, but he did not feel like being bored in the respectable atmosphere that was going to permeate his house this evening.

But after a while, curiosity got the better of him. Were they all cheerfully playing cards, or had Miss Tennant's suggestion failed miserably? He ought to find out.

She was an interesting young female, Simon thought, as he walked to the drawing room. Despite her aunt's attitude, she was not at all afraid of him—or afraid to speak her mind. Were all young ladies so candidly refreshing these days? If so, things certainly had changed in society.

But he knew things had not changed enough for it ever to welcome him back. Which suited him just fine.

He entered the room, surveyed the scene, and wondered how long it had been since this house had seen such a tame gathering. The Blakenoses, Mrs. Dobson, and Lynnwood sat at the far table by the window, playing whist. He stifled a laugh. Lynnwood, playing cards with no money on the table? That story would cause amusement among some circles.

Across the room, Townsend hovered over Miss Vining, who appeared to be playing piquet against Bates.

To his surprise, Marguerite and Miss Tennant sat in the corner, apparently engaged in a comfortable chat. *Good God.* Mrs. Dobson was letting her niece talk with Lynnwood's mistress? Things had changed dramatically since yesterday. *He* might be welcome here after all.

Miss Tennant glanced up and smiled warmly when she saw him, patting the sofa cushion beside her.

"There you are, Milford. We were just wondering if you would deign to join our little party. If we can drag Miss Vining's coach away, you can be a fourth for whist."

"I hardly think . . ."

"Capital idea," said Bates, giving Townsend a pointed look. Reluctantly, the young man gave up his place at Miss Vining's side and walked over.

"Come along," Ariel said to the earl. "If you don't wish to play cards, you will have to engage in drawing room chat, and I imagine you would find that even less enjoyable."

"You are most perceptive, Miss Tennant." Simon pulled out

a chair for her at the round table. He could not imagine a duller pastime than an evening of no-stakes whist. He would play one hand, but no more. That should mollify her.

To his surprise, she proved to be an excellent partner—not overly adventuresome, but readily following his lead, and they thoroughly trounced their opponents for three straight games. Her face glowed with delight after each victory.

How innocent, he thought. Displaying such elation over a simple game of cards, when he found less enjoyment in winning hundreds of pounds. A potent reminder of the vast difference between them—a gulf far wider than the ten-year difference in their ages.

From the corner of his eye, he glimpsed Claudia enter the room. She hastened to his side and draped herself over his shoulder while he examined his cards for the next hand. Her perfume smelled cloyingly sweet; her gentle caresses annoyed him, only fueling his determination to send her packing as soon as the roads cleared.

"Would you like to play?" Miss Tennant asked her.

Claudia shook her head and ran a light finger along Simon's nape. "I much prefer to watch."

He wanted to slap her hand away. Instead, he pointedly ignored her and focused on his cards.

Suddenly, Blinky started yapping furiously. Simon twisted around to see who had aroused his ire. Gregson stood in the doorway, a look of unbridled loathing on his face as the dog danced about and nipped at his feet.

"Get that damn dog away from me!" he cried.

Blinky growled and bared his tiny fangs in what looked to Simon more like a sickly grin than a snarl. It was hard to be afraid of an animal that looked like an overgrown ball of fur.

"Worthless animal," Gregson muttered and gave it a swift shove with his foot as he walked over to the piquet table. Blinky let out a yelp and ran cowering to Mrs. Blakenose.

"What have you done?" she cried, picking up the dog and clutching it to her breast. "Did that nasty man hurt you?"

"I would not dream of harming your precious animal," Gregson said between gritted teeth.

"A pity," Milford said in a low tone that only those sitting at the table could hear.

Miss Tennant shot him a reproachful look, and he grinned at her. "You are an animal lover, Miss Tennant?"

"No one could love that beast," Townsend murmured. "Someone should do us all a favor and lock it out in the snow."

"Now, that would be cruel," Miss Tennant said. "It is not the dog's fault that he has been spoiled abominably."

"Then perhaps we should lock his mistress out in the snow with him," Claudia said. Townsend and Simon roared with laughter, causing the rest of the room to turn and glance their way.

Simon quickly subdued his mirth and adopted a stern look. "We are here to play cards, ladies and gentlemen. Let us not forget our purpose."

Miss Tennant regarded him with open amusement. "A change of heart, my lord?"

"For God's sakes, stop calling me 'my lord.' I'm Milford."

"That sounds presumptuous on such a short acquaintance."

"Anyone who plays whist as well as you do can call me anything she wants. Who taught you to play?"

"My father," she replied. "He taught both my brother and me to play as soon as we could make out the suits on the cards."

"He must have been an excellent teacher."

"He was."

Simon heard the wistfulness in her voice and saw the faint hint of sadness in her eyes, then looked away. She'd had a father whose death she regretted. He envied her that.

Simon quickly dealt out the cards.

Countless hands later, Harman entered, followed by two footmen bearing the tea tray and plates of assorted cakes and biscuits.

"Oh, good. Food." Townsend threw his cards down and stood up.

"And just as we were winning again." Miss Tennant looked at Simon with mock regret.

"Think how rich we would be if we'd been playing for money," he said.

"Winning is its own reward," she said, a trace of smugness in her tone. "You have the pride of a job well done."

"I prefer money. It's far more usable."

"Money can't buy everything," she said.

"No, but it certainly makes life far more pleasant."

She arched a brow. "Does it?"

He saw the challenge in her eyes, but shrugged it off. A young innocent like her knew little of life. While he knew far too much.

Simon awoke in the morning feeling cheerful and clear-headed, and hurried downstairs, hoping that he would encounter Miss Tennant again, alone. He liked her intriguing combination of naivety and frankness. It had been a long time since he'd actually enjoyed conversing with a woman.

To his delight, she came into the dining room shortly after he sat down.

"A pleasant morning to you." He gave her an appreciative smile. She was dressed in a pale pink frock, which gave a faint blush of color to her cheeks. She looked fresh, young, and innocent.

Watching her, Simon felt strangely old.

He jerked his head toward the window. "As you can see, the snow has finally stopped."

"It has?"

Simon thought she looked disappointed.

"Don't worry, Miss Tennant. It is not going to all melt away in a day. You will be forced to remain here a few more days, at least."

She filled her plate with sliced ham and coddled eggs. "I am certain you would wish we all left today."

"Not at all," he said. "I look forward to more exciting hours of card play."

"Now you are teasing me, my lor—Milford."

"Only because you are such an easy target. Tell me, aren't you eager to be home?"

"Oh, I am," she said, taking a sip of tea. "But this is rather an exciting adventure. Much more interesting than being stranded at an inn."

"I am glad you are enjoying yourself." He glanced toward the door. "I promise you, if your aunt comes seeking you, it is my turn to dive under the table."

She grinned. "She means well, but her attention is . . ."

"Stifling?"

"Exactly. She feels it is her duty to keep me as sheltered as possible."

He arched a brow. "But isn't that the purpose of a chaperon?"

"My brother, Richard, is much more tolerant. Aunt would prefer that I go directly from his house to my husband's without experiencing anything in between."

"And what do you want?"

An impish smile lit her face. "To see something of life."

"You would do better to follow your aunt's advice," he said. "A great deal of life is ugly and unpleasant."

"But can't I discover that for myself?"

"It is better that you don't." Simon feared what the world would do to her, destroying her innocence, her optimism. Better that she was kept sheltered and safe.

"It is easy for you to say that," she replied, looking at him with an earnest expression. "You can do whatever you want, when you want, without anyone else telling you what to do."

"Total freedom can be as boring as constant restrictions," he said. "Be glad that you have people concerned for your welfare."

"I don't mind their concern. But I would like to be allowed to trust my own judgment, as well."

"Sometimes it is best to rely on the wisdom of your elders."

"Are you offering yourself as an advisor?" Her blue eyes twinkled merrily.

"No, Miss Tennant. I am the last person in the world you should ask for advice." He turned back to his breakfast, deliberately ending the discussion.

Ariel fumed. Milford thought of her as a mere child. How ironic that a man with his reputation could manage to sound like her aunt!

She hastily finished her breakfast, bade him good day, and went to see if any of the other guests were in the drawing room. As she stepped through the doorway, Ariel halted, mouth agape, staring at the scene before her.

All the furniture had been neatly stacked in several towering piles. A delicate porcelain vase sat atop a Sheraton table, which balanced across an Adam chair, which in turn perched on a sofa.

It was almost an artistic arrangement.

Milford would be furious. And after his condescending treatment of her earlier, she looked forward with gleeful satisfaction to seeing the look on his face when he saw this.

Ariel peered into the dining room, but Milford was no longer there. Following the corridor toward the rear of the house, she searched for the library, guessing he would be there. She tapped lightly on the door.

"Come in." He looked up in surprise when she entered. "Ah, Miss Tennant. A pleasure to see you again so soon. Were you looking for a book to read?"

"I think you should come to the drawing room."

"What now?" He was on his feet in an instant and, without waiting for her, strode down the hall. Ariel had to hurry to keep pace with him.

"Aren't you going to tell me what has happened?" he called over his shoulder.

"This is something that you have to see for yourself," she replied smugly.

He pushed open the drawing room door and stood there, staring at the unexpected sight. Then he burst out laughing, just as he had yesterday at the sight of Bates's room.

"I thought you'd be upset," she said, almost disappointed by his amused reaction. "Some of your furnishings may be damaged."

He turned toward her. "The condition of my furniture is of little interested to me, Miss Tennant. I have to admire the mind that went to so much trouble to arrange this display."

"Who would do such a thing?"

A look of puzzlement crossed his face. "Indeed, that is the question. Who would do this? And why?"

"How will you ever find out?"

"I have a plan." He gave the bellpull a vigorous tug. Harman arrived in scant moments.

"Good God!" he said when he saw the room.

"Interesting, isn't it?" Milford drawled. "I want you to assemble the staff and put the room back the way it was, as quickly and quietly as possible. Do not let anyone in here until you are finished."

Harman bowed. "As you wish."

Ariel looked at Milford. "Why are you doing that?"

"Who else knows about this? Only the person, or persons, who did it. If I put the furniture back, they will be burning with curiosity to know if I saw this. My guess is that he, or they, will not be able to resist finding out."

"And hence give themselves away."

"Exactly."

She grinned. "You have a devilish mind, Milford."

He executed a mocking bow, then took her arm. "We must leave the scene before we are spotted, Miss Tennant. Come back to the library until Harman has righted things."

"Better that I go upstairs," she said. "If anyone else is about, I can try to delay them, or steer them to the dining room."

"Good idea." He gave her an ostentatious wink. "You make a good conspirator, Miss Tennant."

Simon returned to the library and sat down, wondering anew about the identity of the prankster—for he was certain that was what he had on his hands, when this was added to the incident in Bates's room yesterday.

The three young gentlemen—Mallory, Gregson, and Townsend—were the likeliest suspects. The two pranks had a certain schoolboy smell to them. He'd have to keep a sharper eye out to make certain that they did not get carried away. Meanwhile, he would find some task to channel their youthful enthusiasm into a more worthwhile endeavor.

He had just the activity in mind.

"Shovel the terrace?" Townsend glared at him after Simon summoned them to the library. "Why should we do that?"

"Because it needs to be done. The ladies would appreciate the chance to take a turn outside in the fresh air."

"But why us?" Mallory demanded. "Don't you have servants to do that sort of thing?"

"My staff is severely overburdened with all the unexpected guests I am entertaining," Milford said with a pointed look. "Which includes you three."

He half expected one of them to ask sly questions about the

drawing room furniture, but they only grumbled and left to do his bidding. If they had been behind the prank in the drawing room, they were giving no sign. He did not know if that was an indication of innocence or cleverness.

Chapter 5

"Look at this!" Mallory yelled to his companions as he took a running leap and slid halfway across the ice-encrusted terrace. "Better than ice-skating."

Ariel covered her eyes, afraid he would crash into the wall. When she dared to look again, Gregson and Townsend had joined him, slipping and sliding across the flagged stones, their arms windmilling as they strove to remain upright.

Smothering a grin, Ariel carefully picked her way across the terrace. Next, they would be making snow forts and bombarding each other. She almost wanted to join them.

She sniffed the clear, crisp air with delight. Ariel suspected her nose was turning red, and she wiggled her fingers to combat the numbing cold that seeped through her calfskin gloves, but it was worth the discomfort to get out of the house for a short while. It had been thoughtful of Milford to arrange this.

Gregson suddenly dashed in front of her, pursued by Townsend with a handful of snow. He caught his friend on the edge of the stairs and dumped the snow on his head.

"I'll get you for that!" Gregson cried.

"You'll have to catch me first," Townsend retorted, ducking back behind the terrace wall as Gregson bent to grab some snow.

A blob of snow landed at Ariel's feet, exploding in a cloud of white that coated the hem of her cloak.

"You dolt!" Mallory yelled. "You almost hit Miss Tennant."

"Sorry," Gregson called from the bottom of the steps.

Ariel walked over to the low wall enclosing the terrace.

Compacting a handful of snow into a tight ball, she turned and threw it straight at Gregson. It caught him square in the chest.

"Hey! You can't do that!"

Ariel laughed and grabbed another handful of snow. "Why not?"

"Because it is highly inappropriate behavior for a young lady of your standing," a stern voice behind her said. "You should be inside, embroidering handkerchiefs or some such thing."

Ariel whirled about to face Milford, who must have just stepped outside. Before he could utter another word, a snowball clipped him on the shoulder.

Everyone went silent, staring with apprehension at Milford. His face looked stern and foreboding as he eyed each of them in return. Slowly, he brushed the snow from his coat, then gave Ariel a broad wink.

"I fear they have declared war, Miss Tennant. Shall we accept the challenge?"

He picked up the remnants of the snowball and flung it toward Townsend, hitting him in the face just as he ducked for cover behind the wall.

"Run, you coward!" Milford cried, throwing another snowball after him.

Ariel couldn't contain her surprise as Milford eagerly joined in the fray. Laughing as he attacked the three men, he looked young, carefree, and not at all like a cynical rake.

"Miss Tennant." His voice broke her concentration. "You are failing me! Where is your help?"

Ariel began pelting Gregson and Townsend with snow. Milford joined her at the wall and threw snowballs as fast as he could make them.

Another snowball hit Ariel in the back as she was gathering more ammunition. She whirled and saw Townsend poised, ready to throw at Milford. She took careful aim and hit his arm just as he threw, and the missile went awry.

Milford took advantage of his surprise and plastered Townsend with snow.

"Good shot," Ariel said.

The earl grinned. "Why thank you, Miss Tennant. You are a fair fighter with a snowball yourself."

"With an older brother, I learned to defend myself at an early age," she said.

Two snowballs came lobbing over the top of the wall from the garden, catching Ariel on the shoulder. Milford lunged toward the wall and shoved a thick clump of snow off the edge.

Hearing the sputtering sounds coming from below, Ariel knew he had hit his target. She leaned over the railing and saw Gregson digging snow out of his collar.

"Not fair!" he cried.

A snowball hit Ariel in the back, hard. She whirled around and saw Townsend at the top of the stairs, a pile of snowballs at his feet. She darted toward the safety of the porch pillars, but her foot hit an icy patch and she started to fall.

Strong arms caught her before she hit the ground, then suddenly jerked her to one side. Ariel heard a loud crash, snow flew everywhere, and she landed hard on her elbow, a heavy male body atop her.

"Good God!" someone exclaimed.

She dared to open her eyes, but all she could see was a pair of boots rushing toward her.

"Are you all right?"

The man on top of her rolled away, and Ariel turned, surprised to find herself staring into Milford's dark eyes, which were filled with concern.

"Are you hurt?" he asked harshly.

She experimentally wiggled her limbs. "I . . . I don't think so."

He sat up and Gregson pulled him to his feet. They each took Ariel by an arm and helped her stand.

"Thank you," she said. "That was rather silly of me, slipping like that."

Milford acted as if he didn't hear her, staring instead at something behind her. She whirled about and saw a pile of crumpled stone lying on the terrace.

"What happened?" Ariel asked.

"One of the stone urns fell from the balcony," he said, pointing to the small ledge atop the porch. "The snow and ice must have cracked the railing. Thank God it missed you."

Ariel stared dumbly at the pile of crushed stone at her feet, then looked up at the one remaining urn on the other corner of the balcony.

"Oh!" She gasped at the sudden realization of the danger she'd been in. Milford had saved her life.

She flung her arms around him and gave him a grateful hug. "Thank you."

Then, embarrassed by her unladylike exuberance, she stepped back and gave him a sheepish smile. A trickle of blood seeped from a cut on his temple.

"Good gracious, you are hurt."

He reached up and touched the cut.

"Merely a scrape," he said. "Probably a shard of stone."

Milford took a step back and craned his neck to get a better look at the balcony. Ariel saw a small gap marking the spot where the ill-fated urn had once stood.

"Good thing you weren't a foot closer," Townsend said. "It would have squashed both of you flat."

"Yes," Milford said, his face growing serious as he glanced at Ariel. "I think your slip on the ice was providential, my dear lady."

He turned around. "Gentlemen, if you would escort Miss Tennant inside, I think she's had enough fresh air for a while. I don't want anyone else out here until I make certain that the other urn won't come tumbling down as well."

Ariel was glad to go into the house. Her knees felt rather shaky at the moment. Not from the cold, but from the realization of just how close she—and Milford—had come to serious injury. If that urn had hit either one of them . . .

It would have made a rather gloomy end to an innocent snowball fight.

Harman reacted with uncharacteristic alarm when Simon told him what happened.

"I cannot understand it," the butler said. "That railing has always seemed sturdy. Those urns have been there for years."

"Well, it wasn't as sturdy as we thought." Simon took the stairs two at a time. "And I want to make sure nothing else is going to fall on top of some unsuspecting person."

He entered the salon at the rear of the house and walked toward the glass doors leading to the small balcony. Simon opened the latch and started to step out, then halted. If the stone at the railing was rotted, might the rest of it be as well?

Glancing down, he saw footsteps in the snow. Someone had been outside recently, perhaps to smoke a cigar or get a breath of fresh air. Did that mean the balcony was sound after all?

Taking a deep breath, he took a cautious step, easing his weight onto his foot, but the surface underfoot felt as sturdy as ever. With Harman hovering at his shoulder, Milford knelt and inspected the railing where the urn had sat. The coping stone was definitely loose, and the surrounding stone did not look too sturdy.

He checked the other urn. The railing here looked solid, but he did not want to take any chances.

"Give me a hand," he directed Harman. With a great deal of effort they lifted the heavy planter off the rail and set it down on the balcony.

"I will warn everyone to stay off the balcony. Be sure that the door is kept locked," Milford told him. "When the weather clears, send for a stonemason to make the necessary repairs."

Harman nodded and locked the door behind them.

From the doorway, Milford glanced back at the balcony and a sudden chill swept over him at the thought of how near they had come to disaster on the terrace. If Miss Tennant's foot had not slipped at just that spot, if he had not jumped to her rescue so quickly, either one of them might have been seriously hurt.

He was not accustomed to rescuing damsels in distress. Yet it had felt rather nice when Miss Tennant threw her arms around him. Well worth the annoyance of that small cut on his temple.

A pity she was the sister of a viscount. He wouldn't mind having her in his arms again.

When he joined the others in the drawing room, Mallory, Townsend, and Gregson were regaling them with the tale of Simon's daring exploits.

"That urn came this close." Mallory held out his hands in measurement. "Another foot or so and—bam!"

Simon saw that Miss Tennant and her aunt were not in the room.

"Where is Miss Tennant?" he asked, afraid that she might have been hurt after all.

"She took her aunt upstairs," Claudia said. "The aunt was quite overset by the news."

"Don't know why the old lady was so concerned," Gregson said. "She wasn't the one who ended up facedown on the terrace with an earl on top of her."

Simon smothered a smile. If that was how they'd described the incident to Mrs. Dobson, no wonder she was upset. Still, he wished to make certain that Miss Tennant was not hurt. He excused himself and hurried to her room.

To his relief, she answered his knock herself.

"I wanted to make certain you were not suffering any ill effects from your fall," he said. "You are all right?"

"Apart from a bruise or two, I believe I am fine."

"And your aunt?"

Her eyes twinkled impishly. "I believe she will recover from the shock. When she does, she will wish to thank you."

"I look forward to that occasion."

"You should get a bandage for your cut."

Milford touched his temple. He'd forgotten all about it. "You're right."

"Thank you again, Milford, for saving me." She flashed him a dazzling smile that would have melted the heart of the most hardened rake. Even Simon felt unaccustomed warmth within. He covered his unease with a laugh.

"It's merely that it's so damnably inconvenient to have one's guest meet an untimely end. I try to avoid it at all costs."

She laughed. "I shall see you downstairs later."

As the door closed before him, Simon had to admit that he was very much looking forward to that.

While waiting in the drawing room before dinner, Ariel stood listening while Gregson expounded on Milford's quick thinking on the terrace. Ariel suspected he was suffering from a case of hero worship.

Suddenly, a hush fell over the room. Gregson turned to see what everyone was staring at, then walked away from Ariel without a backward glance.

Miss LeDeux stood in the doorway, dressed from head to toe in men's clothing.

Mallory was the first to arrive at her side. "What a delightful outfit!"

She giggled. "It is the oddest thing. I went to my room to change and . . ." She paused to make sure she had everyone's attention. "All my clothes were gone! Whoever is playing this little joke took pity on me and left these instead." Raising her arms, she did a slow pirouette.

Ariel wondered whose clothes she was wearing, for they fit her remarkably well.

"Some people," Aunt murmured to Mrs. Blakenose, who nodded her disapproval.

Lynnwood looked around the room. "Someone isn't here—Townsend, isn't it? Maybe he took your clothes."

"If he appears in a dress, we will know," Gregson said with a laugh.

"I hardly think such a juvenile prank is amusing," Lynnwood snapped.

Miss LeDeux lay a hand on his arm. "Now, George, no harm was done. I've always wanted to try men's clothing. It feels so . . . unrestrictive."

"As if those gowns she wears restrict anything," Aunt said with a sniff.

"I think you look lovely," Gregson said. "Perhaps you will start a new fashion."

"Heaven help us if ladies start wearing trousers," Milford said.

"What is so bad about that, my lord?" Ariel gave him a challenging look.

"Women already think they run the world," he said. "Put them in trousers and it will become fact."

"Would that be such a bad idea?"

He opened his mouth to answer, but Aunt interrupted.

"Women were put on earth to be helpmates to their men, to provide a gentle, guiding influence," Aunt said. "No woman wants to live the life of a man."

"Oh, I think there are plenty of women who'd like to act as men," Gregson said. "My sisters are ferocious creatures. I, for one, wouldn't like to face an army of females like them. They're far too mean."

"They'd break into tears at the first loud noise," Bates said with a sneer. "Women are only suited for . . . certain endeavors."

"What do you think, Miss Tennant?" Milford's eyes held a look of amusement. "Do you wish to live like a man?"

"There are some advantages," she said tartly. "Men are not nearly so hemmed in by rules and restrictions."

"Which are only there for your own good," Aunt spoke sternly, and Ariel realized she was being too outspoken.

"Well, I'm perfectly content to let women do whatever they want," Mallory said, casting another appreciative glance at Miss LeDeux. "Especially if it involves wearing trousers."

"If they wore trousers every day, you'd be longing to see them in a dress," Milford pointed out. "Even novelty becomes tiring over time."

"None of this is answering the question of where Marguerite's clothes have gone," Lynnwood said. "I, for one, think we should start a search."

"No doubt because he paid for them," Aunt whispered loudly.

"You are right," Milford said. "If no one is willing to confess, I shall have to instigate a search."

"Let's start with Townsend's room," Lynnwood said. "He's not down here yet."

Milford held up a hand. "This must be done in an orderly manner. I don't want a mob tromping through everyone's bedroom. Miss LeDeux is the most logical person to look, since they are her clothes. I will accompany her."

Just as he turned toward the door, Townsend walked in, a perplexed look on his face. "What the deuce is going on? There's women's clothing scattered all over my room. Could hardly find my own things."

"My clothes!" Miss LeDeux cried joyfully.

Townsend stopped and took a long look at her. "By Jupiter, if you aren't a sight in that rig." He stepped closer. "Hey, isn't that my coat?"

"Another question answered," Milford said. "Townsend, if you had anything to do with this, better tell me now, before I wring your neck."

"Me? I don't know anything about this. I suppose that's my

shirt you're wearing, too." He smiled at Miss LeDeux. "You can keep it if you want."

Harman stood at the doorway, announcing that dinner was ready.

"I'll deal with this after dinner," Milford said. "But I want an end to these pranks. This foolishness has gone on long enough."

"I'm quaking in fear," Ariel said in a low voice as she took his arm. "I feel as if I should confess all my sins."

"You are one of the few people I do not suspect, Miss Tennant."

"Why, thank you, Milford. I am grateful to have your trust."

"Oh, it's not trust. I just know that if you staged a prank, it would be far more clever than the silliness that is going on here." He grinned at her.

Following dinner, while the men gathered over their port in the dining room, Ariel and the other women retreated to the drawing room. She found this an annoying custom. Watching Milford was vastly more entertaining.

Miss LeDeux went upstairs to retrieve her clothing. To Ariel's surprise, when she came down again, she was wearing a dress. Most of the men, who had just rejoined them, looked crestfallen.

Milford came and stood at Ariel's side. "What sort of entertainment do you have planned for us this evening, Miss Tennant?"

"You have a perfectly good piano. Does no one here play?"

"Everyone denies having that skill."

"Then I guess there is no alternative—parlor games it must be."

He groaned. "That sounds intolerably dull."

She gave him an exasperated look. "Do you have another plan?"

He shook his head.

"Well, then, I do not want any complaints."

"What are you planning?"

"Charades."

"I vote for blindman's buff," Townsend said with a glance at Miss LeDeux. "I'll volunteer to be blindfolded first."

"I hardly think that the proper game for *mixed* company," Milford said dryly.

"Oh."

Ariel smothered a smile at Townsend's disappointed look.

"We must have teams," Ariel said. "My lord, would you be willing to lead one?"

"Age against youth," Gregson shouted out.

"Why not the men against the women?" Milford gave her a teasing look.

"Do you think your side will win?" Ariel asked.

"Of course."

"We need to have a theme," Mallory said.

"Famous battles," Gregson suggested.

"Famous women," Ariel countered.

"A splendid idea," Milford said. "Famous men and women. We shall act the ladies, and you may have the men."

Ariel suppressed a giggle. This might prove most entertaining.

The drawing room door crashed open, and an ashen-faced Mrs. Blakenose came in.

"I can't find Blinky anywhere!" she cried. "He's gone!"

Chapter 6

"That's the best news I've heard all day." Milford's voice was pitched low so only Ariel could hear him.

"Hush," she said.

Mr. Blakenose patted his wife's hand. "Now, Euphy, I am certain he is close by."

"I spoke with the butler." She dabbed at her eyes with a handkerchief. "He put Blinky in the back parlor during dinner, and now he's not there!"

"He better not be peeing on my boots again," Gregson said.

"Have you looked upstairs?" Milford inquired. "Perhaps he is in your room."

"I will look." Blakenose rose, a look of pained resignation on his face.

"I suppose it is too much to hope that we'll find the beast frozen in the snow," Townsend said under his breath.

Ariel rapped him lightly on the knuckles. "You should not say such things."

"I don't think anyone here would miss that cursed animal," Gregson said.

Harman came in and spoke quietly with Milford. The earl listened intently, nodded, then dismissed the butler.

Blakenose returned shortly, shaking his head. "He's not up in our room."

"What am I going to do?" Mrs. Blakenose's voice rose louder. "I must have my Blinky."

"I'll organize a search." Milford gave a deep sigh. "He has to be somewhere in the house."

"I'll give a reward to the person who finds him," Mrs. Blakenose announced. "Thirty—no, fifty pounds!"

"That's all the encouragement I need," Townsend said under his breath. "Now, if someone would pay that much to have him disappear . . ."

"We'll separate into groups to search," Milford said. "Lynnwood, you take Townsend. Mallory, go with Bates. I'll take Gregson. Blakenose, do you want to join us?"

"Don't the women get to help?" Ariel asked with a touch of annoyance that he had so summarily dismissed them.

Milford executed a low bow. "My apologies, Miss Tennant. You are more than welcome to join us. As are the other ladies. I thought perhaps that Mrs. Blakenose would like to remain here, in case the dog returns on his own."

"Do stay with me, Mrs. Dobson." Mrs. Blakenose took her hand. "Your presence will be a great comfort in my time of need."

Ariel edged closer to the door. Searching for Blinky looked to be an entertaining adventure. And it would get her away from Aunt's vigilant eye.

Blakenose and Miss Baker opted to stay in the drawing room, while the other two women joined the search.

The searchers gathered in the hall. "You start at the top of the house," Milford told Lynnwood, Townsend, and Miss LeDeux. "Bates, take this floor. Gregson, you and Miss Tennant will come with me to the kitchen and cellars."

Ariel felt a thrill of excitement as he said her name. She liked the idea of being partnered with Milford. She'd glimpsed a different side of him while watching his gleeful participation in the snowball fight this morning. Perhaps she would learn more about this intriguing earl while they searched.

"To the kitchens," Milford said.

Ariel and Gregson obediently followed him to the rear of the house and down the servants' stairs into the vast room below. Ariel had never seen such an enormous kitchen. She wondered if Milford ever threw the kind of lavish banquets it was designed to serve.

"Here, doggy," Gregson called with little enthusiasm. "Nice doggy."

"Perhaps we can lure him with food," Ariel said. "Find something that he likes."

"From what I can tell, that encompasses nearly everything," Milford said.

"Try something sweet," she said. "That seems to be his favorite."

Milford looked helplessly about. "I don't know where anything is."

Ariel sighed. "Don't you ever go into your kitchens, Milford?"

"Not if I can help it," he said. "Harman deals with that sort of thing."

"Well, it's time you learned what is down here." Ariel walked into the pantry, peering into cabinets, searching not only for a tidbit for the dog, but curious to see what was behind all those doors.

Milford trailed behind her, leaning over her shoulder to inspect the contents of the shelves.

"Interesting," he said, scanning a shelf full of jellied preserves. "I had no idea there was so much food down here. We could be snowed in for a month and still not starve."

"As long as you had someone who knew how to cook," she reminded him.

"Can you?"

"Not really," she confessed.

"Then you will be of little use," he said with a wry grin.

"Here's something." Gregson stood in front of a tall cupboard. "Tea cakes. Just the thing. If we leave a trail of crumbs all through the house, he's bound to find his way to the drawing room."

"Along with a herd of mice," Milford said. "Just put a piece here and there in strategic places—the stair landings and such. We'll check the cellars while you do that."

Gregson departed on his mission.

"Do you really think that will lure Blinky out?" Ariel asked.

"No, but it did get rid of Gregson." He gave a mock shudder. "What is wrong with youngsters today? I do not think I was ever that young—or idiotic."

"They mean well," Ariel said.

"No, they don't."

She laughed and took his arm. "Lead on, my lord. We must find Blinky and earn our reward."

They glanced briefly into the other rooms leading off the kitchen—the cook's private parlor and the household offices—but no Blinky. Finally, Milford stopped in front of a heavy oak door.

"Quiet," Ariel said. "Do you hear something?"

She listened carefully, certain she heard a faint barking.

They looked at one another. "Blinky," they cried in unison. Milford pulled open the door and started down the steep stairs to the cellar.

"Stay there," he said to Ariel, but she was already behind him. The barking grew louder.

"He is down here," she said. "However did he manage to get shut in?"

"Sounds like he's in the wine cellar." Milford reached the bottom of the stairs, crossed the room, and opened another door. Blinky came bounding out, jumping in the air, racing around in circles in his excitement, furiously barking, growing more and more agitated.

Ariel reached for him, but he leaped away and raced up the stairs.

"God help him if he's damaged any of my bottles." Milford entered the wine storage room.

Following behind him, Ariel wrinkled her nose at the unpleasant odor the dog had left behind. "That is not spilled wine I smell."

"No," Milford agreed. He set his candle down atop a wine cask and glanced around. "It seems everything is all right. Good thing, too. That infernal dog would no doubt have lapped up anything he spilled."

Ariel wandered through the small room, astounded at the number of bottles stored on the shelves.

"Do you intend to drink all of this yourself?" She lifted a bottle and blew off a thick layer of dust. "How long has this been here?"

"That's fine French brandy." He took the bottle from her and gingerly set it back on the shelf. "Laid down by my father. It's aging. And yes, I fully intend to consume all this—and a great deal more—before I die. With a little help from my friends."

They walked out into the main room again. After the cozy confines of the wine cellar, Ariel thought it seemed darker and damper than it had before. She looked around, her sense of unease growing. Her gaze turned toward the stairs.

"The door is closed!" she cried.

Milford shoved the candle into her hands and bounded up the stairs. He jiggled the door handle, then threw his weight against the door, but it would not budge.

"The damn thing's locked!"

"Locked?" Ariel stared at him confused. "Who would have locked the door?"

He frowned darkly. "Someone who wants to keep us in here."

His words made her shiver. "Why would they want to do that?"

"Why would anyone move Marguerite's clothes into Townsend's room?"

"You mean this is someone's idea of a silly prank?"

He nodded. "I'm afraid so."

Ariel plopped down on the steps. "Someone will come and rescue us eventually. Won't they?" She looked at Milford for reassurance.

"Your aunt will raise a hue and cry the moment she realizes that the two of us are missing."

Ariel smiled at the idea. "She will be beside herself."

"Exactly." Milford grinned at her. "So I do not think we will be trapped here long."

Ariel scooted to one side of the step. "Do you wish to sit down?"

"Thank you." He sat down next to her on the step. In the narrow space, his body pressed against her. "The worst part is, we may lose the reward for finding Blinky if someone has to come and rescue us."

"I certainly hope not," Ariel said with mock indignation. "We found the beast fair and square."

"I'd be happier if I knew who put him down here in the first place. These pranks are getting out of hand."

"At least you can rule out Mrs. Blakenose." Ariel smiled. "She'd never lock poor Blinky into a damp, dark cellar."

"I wish the person who'd locked us down here had her same sensibilities," he said. "Are you cold?"

"A little," she admitted.

He took off his jacket and draped it over her shoulders before she could utter a protest.

"Won't you be cold?" she asked.

"I doubt we shall be here long." He stretched out his long legs. "Well, Miss Tennant, is this enough adventure for you?"

She laughed. "I hardly call being locked in a cellar an adventure."

"Ah, but you are locked in a cellar with a notorious rake." He leered at her in such an exaggerated way that she laughed.

"For someone with such a horrible reputation, you don't seem the least bit rakish, Milford. I own, I am rather disappointed."

"I do hate to disappoint a lady. Would you prefer that I ravish you here on the cellar steps?"

"As if you would even wish to do such a thing."

"I admit, it would be rather uncomfortable." He patted the wooden step. "I prefer to do my ravishing in softer spots."

His frankness made her bold. "In your bed?"

He looked surprised. "A highly inappropriate remark for a young lady."

"I shall never learn anything of life if I don't ask questions," she replied.

Ariel saw the sudden flicker of amusement in his eyes. "Then let me begin your education."

He slid his near arm around her shoulder, turning her toward him. With his other hand, he cupped her chin and tilted her face toward his.

The touch of his lips was gentle. Ariel was not so green that she had never been kissed, but she sensed that this was going to be different from any kiss she'd known before. She leaned closer.

He ran his tongue along the line of her lips. "Open for me," he breathed.

Her mouth formed a small, round "O" of surprise, and his tongue slipped between her lips, warm and wet. It was wildly shocking, and Ariel felt a sudden tightening in the pit of her stomach.

Footsteps sounded overhead. Milford jerked back, releasing her and dashed to the top of the stairs and pounded on the door.

"Anyone out there?"

"Milford? That you?" Lynnwood's voice came through the door.

"No, Lynnwood, it's Prinny himself. Of course it is me. Find Harman and get the key. We're locked in."

"We?"

"Miss Tennant is with me."

Lynnwood laughed. "Are you certain you wish to be rescued?"

"It is damn cold down here, Lynnwood. Get the key. Now."

Ariel stayed in her place on the steps, fingers pressed to her lips. She'd been kissed by a rake—kissed in a shocking, daring manner. And she'd enjoyed every bit of it.

The question was, had he? Or had her ignorance merely annoyed him?

Milford came back down the steps and helped her to her feet, giving her hand a squeeze.

"An interesting first lesson," he said, a thoughtful look on his face. "I wonder if we shall have the chance for another?"

He stepped aside and let Ariel climb the stairs ahead of him. He followed closely behind her, his hand gently pressed to the small of her back. The touch of his hand made her feel flushed.

Rescue had apparently arrived, for Ariel could hear her aunt's shrieks through the thick door.

"Ariel, my poor dear! What has happened? Are you all right?"

"I am all right," Ariel called out to reassure her.

A key scraped in the lock, and the door swung open. Ariel barely stepped through the doorway before Aunt enveloped her in a hug.

"Oh, my dear girl, what a shocking thing. Are you hurt? Just feel you—you are cold as ice. We need to get you in a hot bath to warm you immediately."

"I think a warm drawing room and some hot tea will be fine," Ariel said. "Milford loaned me his coat. It was not that terrible."

"Milford." Aunt gave the earl a dark look. "I wonder how *he* managed to get locked in there with you."

"Purely by accident, I assure you." Milford gave her a cheerful smile.

"We found Blinky," Ariel explained. "He was in the wine cellar. Then someone locked the door while we were down there and . . ."

"Just another silly prank," Milford said. "Of which I am growing extremely tired." He glared at Gregson, Mallory, and Townsend. "If this does not stop, I will shove the lot of you out into the snow."

"You don't think I did it?" Gregson demanded. "I was putting the cakes out for that damn dog, just as you told me."

Harman cleared his throat. "I will see that tea is brought to the drawing room."

Aunt took Ariel firmly by the hand and led her away toward the stairs.

"Did Blinky come back upstairs?" Ariel asked.

"You've never seen such a carrying on when that dog returned!" Mrs. Dobson shook her head. "You would have thought he'd been gone for a week, instead of a few hours."

They walked into the drawing room. Mrs. Blakenose's eyes lit up when she saw Ariel. She held the dog up for her to inspect. "See? My little Blinky is back."

"I know," Ariel replied. "Milford and I found him. He was locked in the wine cellar."

"Locked in the cellar!" Mrs. Blakenose clutched the dog to her bosom. "My poor darling. Who would do such a cruel thing?"

"Who, indeed?" Milford rejoined them.

"Poor Blinky." Mrs. Blakenose cooed to her pet. "Why would some horrible person want to do such a thing to you?"

"I can think of several reasons," Milford said under his breath. Ariel smothered a laugh.

Harman arrived with the tea tray, and Ariel gratefully took a cup, cradling its warmth in her fingers.

Aunt guided her toward the fire. "I don't want you to take a chill."

"I am fine." Ariel wanted to reassure herself as much as her aunt. The memory of Milford's kiss still made her tremble. He had certainly mastered that skill.

"Such a dreadful happenstance." Mrs. Dobson hovered over

her. "My mind will not be at rest until we can be away from this house. And that man."

"You should be thanking Milford." Ariel fingered the jacket that still hung over her shoulders. She glanced across the room and caught Milford looking in her direction. Their eyes locked, and he slowly lifted his glass in salute.

Ignoring her aunt, Ariel walked over to him. "You would probably like to have your coat back."

He waved a hand. "Keep it. You can return it tomorrow." He nodded toward Mrs. Blakenose, who was still clutching Blinky close. "I notice there has been no more talk of a reward for our finding that blasted dog. Somehow, I thought she'd be more grateful for all our efforts."

"A virtuous act is its own reward," Ariel said teasingly.

He laughed. "You sound as if I consider virtue something to be valued."

"I realize for a *rake,* virtue is not highly prized, but those of us who do not wallow in our depravity find it an important value."

He raised a brow. " 'Wallow in our depravity'? Is that what you think we rakes do?"

She gave him an impish smile. "You cannot tell me that you don't enjoy living the way you do. Else you would reform and live a staid, sober existence."

"I do find the life of a rake more enjoyable," he admitted. "No one has ever accused me of having a sober nature. I fear I was born to be a rake."

A rake with a sense of honor, Ariel thought as she returned to her aunt. She refused to believe that Milford was as black as his reputation painted him. Else he would have done more than simply kiss her in the cellar.

But for her, at least, that kiss had been a unique experience.

Chapter 7

When at long last the excitement died down and the guests finally dragged themselves off to their beds, Simon retreated to the sanctuary of his library.

He pulled out the bottle of fine—and illegal—French brandy from the cupboard where he kept it hidden. He felt no need to share this prime vintage with his guests. He poured himself a large glass and took it over to the well-worn leather chair by the fireplace. He sat down and stared into the glowing coals.

Simon was angry about tonight's incident. He felt in accord with whoever had locked Blinky into the cellar—the dog was a damn nuisance. But he did not look with equal charity on the person who trapped him and Miss Tennant in the same place.

She had not been upset by that incident on the terrace this morning, so he should not have expected her to indulge in a maidenly swoon when she found herself locked in the cellar. Still, her cool-headed acceptance of their predicament surprised him. He wondered what it would take to disturb her composure.

She'd also surprised him by not flinching from his touch when he'd first sat beside her on that cramped step. And when he kissed her . . . he had sensed no fear, no revulsion—only curiosity.

Curiosity, he realized, was Miss Tennant's besetting sin.

Simon had honestly thought she would pull out of his grasp. That kiss had been a halfhearted attempt on his part to put some distance between them, for surely his daring would horrify her. But his plan went awry when she hadn't recoiled from his advances.

Worse, and totally unexpectedly, he actually enjoyed that kiss. He laughed aloud. Perhaps there was something to be said for the allure of innocence after all. But if that was the case, he should stay well away from her.

That was easy enough to do. It was going to be more difficult to find out who was behind all these pranks.

He drained his glass. Who was doing this? One person or several? And was there a purpose to their actions, or were they only taking advantage of circumstances?

The glass slipped from his fingers and rolled across the carpet. With a muttered oath, Simon got out of the chair to retrieve it. He bent down and picked up the glass, then paused and looked at it more closely.

Something rough and gritty coated the glass. Simon rubbed his fingers together and brought them to his nose. It smelled like . . . sawdust? He knelt down and examined the carpet more carefully. Sure enough, a thin track of sawdust trailed across the fine Belgian wool.

What in the hell was sawdust doing in the library?

He turned around and slowly scanned the room. Unless someone had taken to chopping wood in here, he did not see where it could have come from. The furniture still appeared intact. Where—

He stiffened. *The furniture.* Had their merry prankster been up to his tricks again? Was a chair or table leg just waiting to collapse?

This was going too far. Someone could be hurt this time. Simon knelt down again and examined the chair by the fire. All four legs were intact. He set the glass on the desk and quickly walked around the room, checking every piece of furniture for some telltale sign of damage, but everything looked normal.

Then where had that blasted dust come from?

His gaze caught the library stepladder standing beside the shelves—right next to where he'd retrieved the glass. With a growing dread, Simon slowly walked over and examined the ladder's rungs.

The bottom three were fine. But as he looked at the fourth step, his heart started pounding. It had been neatly sawed through, right along the edge. He hastily checked the next few steps and they, too, were cut.

His first reaction was pure anger. This went beyond a prank. A tumble from that height could mean a twisted ankle, a strained wrist, or worse. Someone might have been seriously hurt.

Someone—or him? Everyone knew this was his private retreat, knew he spent a great deal of time here. Of all the people in the house, he was the one most likely to use the ladder. This piece of work had been aimed directly at him.

Simon sat down heavily in the chair, fighting back the sudden fear that rose within him. What was going on? These pranks were rapidly turning from mischievous to malicious.

Then he sucked in his breath.

What if that falling urn this morning had been no accident? his heart turned to ice at the very thought. Until he jumped to help Miss Tennant, he'd been standing directly where it landed. He remembered the footprints in the balcony snow and suddenly felt sick to his stomach.

Was someone trying to hurt him?

The thought was ludicrous. Who—why—would anyone want to hurt him? Half his guests were strangers; the other his friends. He had done nothing to anger or injure any of them. They had no reason to wish him ill.

He glanced at the empty glass on the desk and blanched. What if something had been added to his brandy? Poison could already be coursing through his system.

Nonsense, he told himself firmly. Anything strong enough to kill him would have left an odd taste or smell. No one had touched this liquor. He was imagining things.

Simon puzzled over the mystery of who might be behind this. He did not think it was any of the women—this did not have the feel of a woman's hand. No, it was one of the men. But which one? Despite their fondness for pranks, those overgrown schoolboys had no reason to hold a grudge against him. Bates and Lynnwood were among his closest companions. Blakenose? He had not met the man until two days ago.

It simply made no sense.

Of course it made no sense. No one was after him. He was seeing bogeymen in the dark, chasing at shadows that were not there. He had taken a few random incidents, combined them with some simple pranks, and come up with a plot worthy of the most lurid gothic novelist. There was an easy explanation for everything.

He himself had seen the crumbling stone on the balcony railing; the urn simply fell on its own. Sawing the ladder was stupid and dangerous, but not necessarily designed to hurt him. The pranksters had merely gone too far with their antics and needed to be reined in, quickly.

With a rueful grin, Simon sank back into the chair. He was starting to think like Mrs. Dobson, imagining disaster behind every corner. He felt like a fool.

A floorboard creaked in the hall.

Simon froze. There was no need for anyone to sneak around at this time of the night—unless one had nefarious schemes in mind. Was it the person who'd sawed the ladder, coming to examine his handiwork? Or did he intend to prepare a new, even more dangerous trap for Simon?

This might be the chance Simon had been waiting for—the chance to catch the prankster red-handed. There was no time to snuff the candles; the smell would give his presence away. Let the person think his servants were merely careless and had left the candles burning.

With painstaking slowness, he rose from his chair and moved as silently as possible to the tall drapes that hung over the windows and crept behind them. They bulged around his form, but he prayed that in the dim light it would not be noticeable.

He put his eye to the crack and watched, waiting, to see who entered. His breath caught as the door slowly opened. A ghostly, white figure stepped into the room.

He could barely believe his eyes.

Miss Tennant.

Dressed in her night robe, with her golden hair hanging loose and free. Looking far too enticing to be wandering around a dark house at this time of night.

What was she doing here?

The only thing he knew for certain was that she was not here to do him any harm. Quite the opposite, in fact. He posed a far greater danger to her, if she only knew it.

From his hiding place, he watched as she set her candle down on the desk and glanced furtively around her. Then she picked

up his glass and brought it to her nose. Checking on his drinking habits, or was she a secret tippler?

Simon stepped out from behind the curtain. Miss Tennant
gasped when she saw him and dropped the glass, than glared at
him with exasperation.

"Milford! What are you doing? You nearly frightened me to
death."

"I might say the same of you." He bent to retrieve the glass.
"What in God's name are you doing here?"

"I could not sleep."

"It seems to be a common affliction tonight," he said, reaching for the bottle of brandy to pour himself another glass. He
looked at her. "Would you like some?"

Her eyes brightened. "May I? I am rarely permitted to drink
it. But only a small amount—I do not wish to become foxed."

Simon shook his head at his folly. *The curious Miss Tennant.*
He tossed back his head and laughed.

"What is so funny?" she asked.

Still shaking with laughter, he reached for two clean glasses.
"Never mind. I assume you are looking for something to read?"

She nodded. "I want something more interesting than Mrs.
Edgeworth." She started toward the library shelves. "I know
you must have some scandalous novel I will enjoy."

He glanced up just as she was putting her foot on the bottom
rung of the ladder.

"Stop!" He raced to the ladder, wrapping his arms around her
waist and pulling her off. The ladder toppled to the floor and he
fought for balance, his arms still clasped about her waist. Her
feet touched the floor, and that steadied him.

She looked up at him, her eyes round and wide.

"Good grief, Milford, what is wrong?"

He pointed to the ladder. "That is what's wrong. Someone
tampered with it. Most of the rungs are sawed through."

Her face reflected disbelief. "Why would anyone do such a
thing? Someone might get hurt."

"And if I had not been here, it might have been you," he said.
For the second time today, he'd saved her.

She examined the damaged rungs. "Who would do such a
thing?"

"That is what I was hoping to find out."

She looked up at him. "That's why I didn't see you when I first came in. You were hiding!" Then she sucked in her breath. "And you thought that I . . . ?" Her expression turned incredulous.

"What else was I supposed to think when someone came sneaking down here in the middle of the night?"

She stared at him for a long moment, then started laughing. "Oh, Milford, you have a greater sense of drama than my aunt! Why would I want to hurt you?"

"As soon as I saw it was you, I knew I wasn't in danger," he admitted as they sat down in the wing chairs flanking the fireplace. "But there is a prankster on the loose, and someone is going to get seriously hurt if I cannot unmask him soon."

"Aren't you exaggerating?"

"Remember this morning, when the urn fell?"

She nodded.

"I thought it was an accident. But what if it wasn't?"

There was a flicker of fear in her eyes. "Do you mean someone pushed the urn off that balcony? But it was an accident, wasn't it? You examined the stonework afterward."

"Someone had been out on the balcony," he said slowly. "I did not think anything of it at the time; I merely assumed someone had gone out for a breath of fresh air or a cigar."

Ariel wrapped her arms around her as if she were cold. "I can't believe that someone would do such a thing. Why, either one of us might have been killed. That is no prank."

Simon agreed. And he desperately wanted to believe that it was sheer coincidence. The alternative was too frightening to think about.

"Do you think someone was trying to hurt us when they locked us in the cellar?"

He shook his head. "No, I think that was just another innocent prank, like putting Blinky down there in the first place. No one knew we would be the ones to find him."

"Yet all the other pranks have been directed toward a specific person—Bates, and Miss Ledeux."

"You are forgetting the drawing room furniture. Besides, I think tonight's plot centered around Blinky. Our arrival merely presented another opportunity for mischief."

"Then all we have to do is determine who could have locked

us in." She looked thoughtful. "It was your friend Lynnwood who found us."

"I hardly think—"

"He might think it enormously entertaining to trap the two of us together. He even asked if you wanted to be rescued."

Simon considered. It was the sort of thing Lynnwood would find amusing.

"If you eliminate yourself, me, Bates, Miss LeDeux, and Mrs. Blakenose"—she ticked the names off her fingers—"then our prankster must be one of the others."

"Are you suggesting that we consider your aunt as a suspect?"

She grinned at the thought. "My aunt may be horrified by your reputation, but I hardly think she would indulge in silly pranks. And she would never have locked the two of us together in the cellar."

"Perhaps there is more than one prankster."

"If that is the case, then it could be any one of us." She gave him an exasperated look. "We are trying to eliminate suspects, Milford, not add them."

"Let's go back to the original list, then."

"Have you angered your mistress?" she asked.

He laughed. "No."

"Miss Vining?"

"No."

"Then that leaves only the men—Bates excepted."

"I still suspect our three young gentlemen. We only have Gregson's word that he was distributing those tea cakes. He easily could have locked the cellar door."

"None of them have been the butt of a prank yet," she admitted.

"Exactly."

She leaned forward eagerly. "I think we should concentrate our investigation on them."

"*Our* investigation?"

"I intend to help you, of course. I want to discover the truth as much as you do."

"And how do you propose to help?" Simon asked, amused by her offer.

"One of them might slip and say something in my presence that they would dare not say in yours," she explained.

"If only I could devise a trap. . . . But how does one set a trap for an unknown person, with an unknown target? The possibilities are enormous."

"You have to give them a special opportunity, Milford. Make a deliberate production of going out onto the terrace tomorrow," Ariel said. "One of us can hide in the upstairs room and see if anyone goes out on the balcony."

"I thought we decided that the urn was not deliberately pushed?"

"True. If we made it known that you were leaving your door unlocked . . ."

"Our prankster might decide to strike there." Simon nodded slowly. Her idea just might work.

"Exactly. All we would have to do is keep watch on your room."

"And if no one falls into the trap?"

"Then we will have to think of something else."

"I can set myself up to watch," he said.

Ariel frowned. "That might be dangerous for you. You will have to be very careful."

"Are you appointing yourself as my bodyguard, Miss Tennant?"

She smiled. "I think between Harman and myself, we can keep you safe."

"Your aunt will look askance if you are in my company too much."

"Oh, pooh. Aunt is having too much fun gossiping with Mrs. Blakenose. I doubt she would even have noticed I was missing tonight if Lynnwood had not gone running to the drawing room with the tale."

"It would be a damn sight easier if this blasted snow would melt." His expression darkened. "Then I could be rid of the entire lot of you and not have to worry about what is going to happen next."

"Until that happens, we shall all have to be careful."

"And no more nocturnal wanderings on your part," he said sternly. "I'll escort you back to your room. Your aunt would call me out if she found you down here in your nightclothes."

Ariel blushed prettily. "I was not expecting to find you here."

For an instant he remembered the feel of her soft lips against his in the wine cellar, her utter lack of resistance, and he wondered how responsive she could be with further tutelage. Then he felt shamed by his thoughts. She was, after all, a lady, and not for the likes of him.

Simon stood and held out his hand. "Let me escort you back upstairs."

Ariel took his hand, then dropped it. "I almost forgot. I need a book." She walked to the shelves and scanned them, quickly pulling out two volumes.

Simon raised his eyebrow at her selection. *Tom Jones.* "Will your aunt approve?"

"I will hide them under my pillow," Ariel said. "If I have to read one more improving work from Mrs. Edgeworth I will scream. At least when I am at home, I can read anything I wish."

"I will not reveal your secret."

He snuffed out the library candles and picked up the one she'd brought with her. Then he took her hand and led her out of the library, carefully locking the door behind them.

The candle threw ghostly shadows on the dark and deserted hall, and Ariel shivered, thinking about the person behind these pranks. If someone was really after Milford, this would be the perfect time to attack him. The rest of the house was asleep, so no one would come to his aid. Her presence would be no impediment.

"Cold?" he asked.

She shook her head. "I fear your lurid musings are inspiring my imagination."

He smiled. "We decided that's what they were—lurid musings. You are in no danger, Miss Tennant."

"If we are going to be working together, I think you could call me Ariel," she said. "At least when we are in private."

"Your aunt would be horrified," he said.

"She cannot be horrified at something she knows nothing about," Ariel replied.

Milford laughed. "I pity the poor woman once she gets you

to London. She will not have an inkling of half the things you are up to."

They reached the landing at the top of the stairs and started down the corridor toward their rooms. All was silent, deserted, the other guests asleep in their beds.

He halted outside her door. "Try to get some sleep tonight," he said. "We will have a busy day tomorrow if we intend to catch this prankster."

"I will try," she said and looked into his eyes. Would he try to kiss her again? Until this moment, she had not thought about it, but now she desperately wanted him to. But how could she let him know?

"Milford?"

As if he read her mind, he curved an arm about her waist and drew her toward him.

"It is time for another lesson, Ariel." He bent his head and brushed his lips across hers. She uttered a sigh of contentment and kissed him back, pressing against him to let him know that she was eager for this.

To her disappointment, he did nothing more. He pulled away, releasing her and chucked her under the chin.

"Good night, Ariel. Sweet dreams."

She nodded and carefully turned the latch on the door, shutting it behind her. She could hear his footsteps continuing down the hall toward his room.

Lying in bed, she strained to hear some sound of his preparations for sleep through the adjoining dressing room, but all was silent.

Had he left her and gone directly to Miss Baker's bed?

The thought strangely dismayed her.

Chapter 8

Ariel awoke suddenly in the middle of the night, sitting bolt upright in the darkened bedroom. The image of Milford lying sprawled on the terrace, crushed beneath a pile of crumpled stone, loomed vivid in her mind.

She ran a shaking hand over her face, trying to dispel the last vestiges of the dream. This was all his fault. If he had not suggested that someone deliberately pushed the urn, she would never have imagined such a thing.

They had to find the guilty person quickly, or she was not going to have a good night's sleep for the rest of her stay here. First thing in the morning, she and Milford had to investigate in earnest. With the two of them working together, they might solve the puzzle faster.

And it meant she would be able to spend more time with Milford. But her reaction to that horrible dream showed her that Milford might pose a greater danger to her than any prankster. After those kisses, Ariel knew she needed to be wary of the earl. Not because he intended her any harm. He had to be the most harmless rake in the realm.

No, it was her reaction to him that posed the real danger. She found Milford's company far too entertaining. He was intelligent, amusing, charming—so charming, in fact, that she wondered how he had acquired such a black reputation. From everything she'd seen, it was totally undeserved.

When they'd first arrived, he'd done everything to make himself seem as dastardly as his name. She cringed at the thought of that first dinner, or the way he'd invaded her room that first night.

But now she realized that had merely been playacting on his part. The real Milford was the man she'd seen in the ensuing days—the man she'd been with last evening, a man who would be far too easy to like.

Why didn't he fight against his undeserved reputation as a dissolute rake? She could ask him, of course, but she feared that doing so might destroy the fragile friendship that had sprung up between them.

But she could worry about that in the morning. With a yawn, she rolled over and snuggled deeper under the covers and soon drifted into a deep sleep.

After performing his morning ablutions, Simon took a fresh shirt from the drawer and began dressing.

His sleep last night had been troubled. Half his dreams were wild adventures involving falling urns, dank cellars, and furniture that collapsed beneath him. But the more troubling images were those involving Miss Ariel Tennant.

What did he find so fascinating about a green girl only a few years out of the schoolroom? He had his pick of London's exquisites and had always enjoyed the best mistresses money could buy.

He shook his head. It had to be due to his boredom with Claudia. Her jaded experience made Ariel's innocence appear novel. Still, it was difficult to understand why he'd enjoyed that kiss in the cellar far better than the last time he'd visited Claudia's bed.

Was he so bored that teasing an innocent like Ariel Tennant entertained him far more than an hour or two spent with his mistress? Simon realized he had been pretending with her for a long time. Making love to Claudia had become a chore, not a pleasure.

Good God, he was not developing a streak of respectability in his old age, was he? Simon laughed aloud as he pulled on his trousers. Not bloody likely. Perhaps he was only discovering that a life of vice, like any other pursuit, grew dull over time.

As did being cooped up in this house. It was enough to make the most complacent person restless, and Simon had never been the complacent sort. But what would he do if he had the choice? Going to town did not seem the least bit appealing.

It was this blasted weather. Simon directed a scowl at the window. There was something smothering about being snow-bound; the fact that half his companions were comparative strangers only made it worse. Add to that this spate of annoying pranks . . . It would be a relief when the snow melted and they could be on their way. He would not miss a one of them.

Except for Ariel.

And if she showed up in his library in the middle of the night again, dressed only in her nightclothes with her fair hair down around her shoulders and those deep blue eyes sparkling with curiosity, he was not going to be held responsible for the consequences. He was a *dastardly* rake, after all. She could not expect better of him.

But there would be no more nights in the library, at least for the near future, until they uncovered the person behind the pranks. He did not want her wandering around the house alone—day or night—until the puzzle was solved. Just in case his fears were real, and there was a sinister plot afoot after all.

This morning after breakfast he would parade about the terrace, just in case someone wanted to dump the other urn on him. But he would get Harman to help him in this effort, instead of involving Ariel. He did not want her entangled in anything that might prove dangerous. And if nothing happened while he was on the terrace, he could finally be satisfied that the incident yesterday, however frightening, had been merely happenstance.

Then he would redirect his efforts to discovering which of his guests was the prankster. Simon could use Ariel and Harman to keep track of each and every person, to notice when someone left the company of the others, to know who had the opportunity to set up another prank, and so catch the villain in the act.

Simon was not sure what he was going to do when he found the person, or persons, responsible. Until the snow melted and the roads were cleared, he'd have to deal with him here. A day or so spent locked in the cellar sounded like a fitting punishment.

But he had to find the prankster before he could take any revenge. And that would involve careful observation in the days to come.

He smiled. At least he had something to look forward to.

But he was not sure whether he was more interested in catching the prankster, or spending all that time with Ariel.

For a moment, he felt a twinge of regret that he had not known her years ago, before his life had taken the course it had. But that notion was silly—she would have been a mere child then. She would have meant nothing to him. As she meant nothing more to him now than a pleasant diversion.

Or so he told himself.

Simon was forced to wait several hours before the last stragglers finally dragged themselves out of bed and appeared downstairs. He had to make certain that everyone understood his intentions for his plan to work. Simon made a very public announcement that he was going to take a few turns around the terrace. To his relief, and dismay, no one showed any interest in joining him. It meant any one of them could be the one.

He paced back and forth across the terrace for nearly half an hour, slapping his hands together to warm his numbed fingers. Townsend and Mallory had joined him for a short while, but the cold soon drove them back inside. They weren't even interested in a rematch of yesterday's snowball fight.

And no one had tried to shove the other urn off the balcony. Early this morning, he and Harman had restored it to its previous position atop the railing. The butler was now hiding in the front salon, watching for any suspicious activity.

Simon began to feel foolish. He was standing on the terrace, miserably cold, when he could be warm and comfortable inside. It was as he'd said—the urn fell because the stone beneath it was rotten.

He started to walk back into the house when Ariel stepped out the door. Simon smiled in greeting, then remembered the danger she might be in by joining him here, and his expression changed to a frown. He took her arm and drew her away from the balcony.

"What are you doing out here?" he demanded.

"I thought you might like some company," she said. "I imagine it must be rather dull walking out here all by yourself."

"I thought I told you to stay in the drawing room and keep an eye on the others."

"All is arranged. I appointed Miss Baker as my substitute spy."

Ariel and his mistress, conspiring against him. Simon laughed. He watched her as she crossed to the far steps that led down to the garden, then turned to look at him.

"I take it there has been no untoward activities?" she asked.

He shook his head. "I've paced back and forth across this damn terrace all morning, and all I've managed to accomplish is to turn my fingers blue and get my boots damp."

"Well, I for one am glad to find out that no one is trying to harm you."

"So am I," he admitted.

"Unless, of course, the attacker realized you were out here for precisely the reason you are, and knew it would be too risky to try again."

"I find *that* explanation encouraging."

She looped her arm through his. "Come along, Milford. There is no sense in spending any more time out in the cold. Let's go back inside and plan our next move."

Admitting his relief that nothing had happened, he walked with her into the house.

"What do you suggest we try next?" he asked when they stood in the hall, scraping the snow off their boots.

"We must lure the prankster into committing a new act, then catch him doing it."

"Easier said than done."

"I think your bedroom is our best chance. Leave your door unlocked and announce that you are going to be spending a few hours in the library, working on some sort of business matter. That will let the prankster know that your room will be unoccupied."

"And I merely leave the door open and hope he comes by and takes advantage?"

She nodded. "While you hide in the dressing room waiting to catch him."

"Now that sounds like an exciting way to spend a few hours," he said.

"Now don't pout, Milford. You can't expect Harman to do *all* the boring work for you."

"You could stay with me." He flashed her a wicked grin. "I would not find it boring then."

"As if both our absences would not cause comment. No, I will stay in the drawing room and watch who comes and goes. We cannot be certain that our suspect will go upstairs and fall into our trap. He may have other tricks planned. Harman must keep an eye on the rest of the house."

Milford sighed. "You know, if I locked everyone in their rooms, we could stop the pranks for good."

"Yes, but that would be so unkind of you. Besides, we don't merely want to stop the pranks—we want to know who is doing them."

He looked at her with open amusement. "Your curiosity is showing again, Miss Tennant."

"Ariel," she gently chided him. "Do you mean to say that you don't want to know?"

"I do," he admitted. "I hope we can lure the fellow into action again. But if something else happens and we don't catch him, I will think again about locking everyone in their rooms."

"Even me?" She gave him a teasing smile.

"I might make an exception for you—if you ask nicely enough."

"I shall keep that in mind."

They started down the hall for the drawing room, then he paused.

"Ariel?"

"Yes?"

"Remember that this is a game, after all. Do not take it too seriously. I do not want you to anger your aunt with your activities."

"I shall be most circumspect."

"Good." He opened the drawing room door.

"Milford." Gregson hailed him the moment he walked in. "Come here and settle an argument for us."

"Settle your own arguments," Simon said. He did not have time for their foolishness. There was work to be done. He glanced around the room, counting heads. "Where is Bates?"

Townsend glanced around. "Don't know. He was here a moment ago."

Simon edged toward the door, signaling Ariel to remain here while he went in search of his missing guest. He may have told Ariel that this was only a game, but to him it was far more serious. Someone was annoying his guests and Simon vowed to find the culprit.

Ariel took a seat next to Aunt and Mrs. Blakenose, who were comparing various recipes for tisanes, but she could barely contain her excitement. Bates was not here. Was he setting up another prank? Had they found the guilty person at last?

She wished Milford had taken her with him; it would be thrilling to catch the one responsible for the pranks. She had never liked Bates from the moment she met him and would be delighted to discover that he was behind this. Waiting here to find out what was happening was frustrating. It could not possibly hurt if she slipped out for just a minute. . . .

Ariel glanced around the room. Gregson and his friends, along with Lynnwood, were playing cards. Blakenose snored softly in a chair by the window, while his wife chatted with Aunt. Miss Vining, Miss Baker, and . . .

Miss LeDeux. She was not here either! Ariel's breathing quickened. Was it possible that she was Bates's accomplice?

"I'm rather chilly," she said to Aunt. "I'm going to get my other shawl. Do you need anything from the room?"

Aunt shook her head, far more interested in debating the merits of chamomile over peppermint for an upset stomach.

Ariel slipped out of the room and ran down the hall toward the back stairs. If someone was trying to elude Milford, they might come this way.

To her disappointment, she did not meet anyone on the stairs, and the bedroom corridor was deserted. There was no sign of Milford—or the others. She walked quickly to her room and grabbed her cashmere shawl with the knotted fringe. Ariel turned back to the door when she thought to check if Milford was in his room. Ariel walked through the dressing room and tapped softly on the door. Receiving no answer, she turned the key and pushed open the door.

A quick glance told her that Milford was not here, but she lingered, overcome with curiosity about his room. It would not hurt if she took a *small* peek. Who knew what she might discover about the man?

The room sat in the northwest corner of the house and was nearly twice the size of the one she and Aunt shared. The walls were papered in a cream brocade, edged with gold. Ariel found that surprisingly subdued for a rake. Shouldn't his room be done in something more garish? Red flocked wallpaper, perhaps? She grinned at the thought, not able to picture Milford in something that tasteless. The bed was uncurtained, but with a cream-and-gold tasseled canopy that gave it an elegant air.

The rest of the furniture—dressing table, chest of drawers, clothespress, and several chairs—was all dark wood, a matched set. A silver-handled dressing set lay atop the table. Ariel walked over and picked up the hairbrush, then set it down, feeling guilty for touching his things. She really should leave. . . .

Instead, she crossed to the windows that overlooked the back garden. Dark splotches showed where trees and shrubs were starting to throw off their mantle of snow. She imagined in summer it would be a lovely prospect, but now the bland white expanse gave little hint of what lay beneath.

Turning back to the room, she saw the door next to the fireplace—the one that must lead to Miss Baker's room. Ariel moved toward it, then paused. It was one thing to peek into Milford's room—she could argue she had been looking for him. But to enter his mistress's room . . .

She was relieved to discover the connecting door was locked, with no key in sight. It saved her from temptation.

As she surveyed the room again, she realized with a start that there was nothing personal here, nothing that said anything about the man who slept here. The room was neat, orderly, and utterly devoid of the usual personal things that decorated one's room—no paintings of horses, no ornamental treasures on the mantelpiece.

That struck her as odd. Everyone she knew kept personal things in their rooms. Didn't Milford have anything that he treasured? Or did he keep them elsewhere—in the library, where he spent so much of his time?

She heard a noise and jumped, dropping her shawl. Before she could retrieve it, the dressing room door opened, and Milford stood there, a look of surprise on his face, which soon changed to amusement.

"What were you doing in my room?" she demanded haughtily.

He walked in, laughing. "A highly impertinent question coming from *you*, considering your situation. You left your door ajar, and I stopped to check that everything was all right." He stopped in front of her, hands on his hips. "Now, would you care to explain what you are doing in *my* room? I thought I told you to watch the others."

"I came to tell you that Miss LeDeux was not in the drawing room either," she said hastily. "But you weren't here."

"Obviously."

"Did you find Bates? Should we look for both of them?"

He grinned. "I think it can be safely said that neither of them is currently setting up any pranks."

"How do you know?" she demanded.

"Because they are both in her room across the hall." His smile widened.

"In her room? What—" She suddenly realized what he meant and felt her cheeks burning. "But I thought that Bates and Miss Vining . . . ?"

"These are not permanent arrangements," he said with a shrug. "Matters change."

"Do you like having to purchase a woman's favors?" she asked bluntly.

"How do you know they are purchased?" he retorted.

"You provide your mistress with a house and clothing. I would say that is purchasing her company."

"Perhaps I am merely giving gifts to a close friend," he said.

She snorted with derision. "Do not take me for a total fool, Milford. I know a few things about life."

"Such as how inappropriate it is for you to even be discussing such a thing with me? Not to mention being in my bedchamber in the first place."

"I will leave." She started toward the connecting door.

"Ariel."

She turned.

He picked up her shawl. "I believe you forgot this."

Chagrined, she walked back toward him and grabbed for it,

but he held it just out of her reach. "You must pay a forfeit first."

"What?"

"Another kiss."

Ariel's stomach lurched. It had been one thing to kiss him in that damp cellar last night, or later in the darkened hallway. But here, in his room, in broad daylight . . . it was much more deliberate, much more . . . exciting.

"My third lesson?" she asked.

He nodded and pulled her into his arms. "Follow my lead," he whispered before his mouth met hers.

She kissed him as she had last night, with her lips slightly parted, and once again she felt his tongue flick against her lips. Wanting to show him she was not afraid, she touched the tip of her tongue to his.

To her surprise, he groaned softly and tightened his hold on her. His hands, which had been lightly grasping her waist, now moved up and down her back as his tongue moved more boldly, slipping into her mouth, rubbing against hers.

She clasped her hands around his neck as the lump in her stomach turned into a fluttering sensation, and suddenly her knees felt as weak as they had out on the terrace yesterday morning.

And she realized that even an honorable rake like Milford knew a great deal more about kissing than she did. She had no idea something so simple could make one feel so deliciously wicked.

His fingers brushed against the side of her breast, and she gave a gasp of surprise.

He jerked away and stared down at her, his dark eyes clouded. He looked almost angry. Then he shoved the shawl into her hands.

"Go," he said. "Before your aunt comes looking for you."

Ariel fled back through the dressing room, carefully locking the door behind her, then paused to quell her shattered composure. Why had she acted so foolishly?

She'd betrayed her ignorance and given Milford a disgust of her. Now he would think she was no more than a silly schoolgirl.

Milford was right—she was an *innocent*. And no matter how

she argued against it, she had no experience in the kind of things Milford was showing her. He might find her naivety amusing, but it would not make her more appealing to him. If anything, she feared it would drive him away.

And driving Milford away was the last thing she wanted to do. Not now, when she wanted to be held in his arms; to learn more about the wicked way she felt when he touched her, kissed her.

Sighing at her folly, she went out into the hall. To her dismay, Bates stood only a few doors away, almost as if he'd been waiting for her to come out.

"Ah, Miss Tennant. What a delightful coincidence."

She smiled coolly, hoping her cheeks were not as flushed as they felt. "I found the drawing room rather chilly and came to get my shawl." She held it up.

"Let me help you with that."

Before she could protest, he'd taken it from her and draped it around her shoulders.

Was it her imagination, or did his hands linger longer than they should on her shoulders? After being held in Milford's arms, the thought of Bates's hands on her, even for a moment, was unpleasant.

She heard a door close behind them. Bates glanced back over his shoulder, then a smug look flooded his face.

"What a surprise to see *you* here, Milford," he said with a smirk. "Were you feeling a chill also?"

Ariel darted a glance at the earl. His face was impassive as he looked at her.

"Good afternoon, Miss Tennant," he said. "I hope you are not finding yourself too bored today."

"Oh, I doubt Miss Tennant is bored," Bates said now with a cocksure grin as he glanced between them.

Ariel struggled to keep from reacting, but she felt the color creeping up on her cheeks. *He knew.* Knew that she had been with Milford moments ago. And she could not even argue that it had been an innocent encounter. It had been anything but that.

And she knew without a doubt that it was no longer the prankster who posed the greatest threat to her.

If Bates said anything to her aunt about Milford . . . Ariel would find herself locked in her room, without another chance to enjoy Milford's skilled tutelage.

That was an unbearable thought. She must be very careful to keep away from the earl when Bates was about.

Chapter 9

Ariel felt relieved to spend an uneventful afternoon in the drawing room, watching the other guests chat, play cards, or, in the case of the three young men, flirt with the ladies. It was not until they went in to dinner that she realized just how closely Bates was watching her.

She prayed that no one else noticed it. She tried to pass it off as guilty feelings, but every time she glanced across the table, he was looking at her with that same self-satisfied smirk.

He had said nothing to the others about their encounter in the hall, and she soon grew convinced he was not going to alert anyone to his suspicions about her meeting with Milford. But now, she was not so certain. He had some plan in mind, one that could only bode ill for her.

And she had only herself to blame. She should never have been in Milford's room in the first place—and certainly should not have been kissing him like that. Ariel could no longer fall back on innocence as an excuse—not after that kiss. She'd been a very willing participant and enjoyed it far too much.

Would Bates use his new suspicions to devise a way to embarrass her and Milford? If so, she needed to be on her guard, for she suspected he was merely waiting for the chance to catch her and Milford in a compromising situation. Why, she did not know. But she was certain that he did not wish them well.

She turned back to Blakenose, seated on her left. His conversation might not be stimulating, but it was better than trying to avoid meeting Bates's eyes. Something in his look made her feel dirty, ashamed. But honestly, she thought, what was wrong with a few improper kisses?

She certainly had nothing to feel guilty about. She had only kissed Milford a few times—simple, innocent kisses. Except that Ariel knew that they were not from the way she swayed against him when she was in his arms, the way she felt when his lips touched hers. Those delicious sensations that swept from her toes to the tip of her head told her exactly how wrong it was.

He was showing her things she'd never dreamed of, making her feel things she'd never felt, and it was deliciously intoxicating and frightening at the same time.

Which more than anything told her that what she was doing was wrong. But she knew that she would never see Milford again, except from afar, after she left this house. There was no harm in a little bit of flirtation, the chance to gain a bit of knowledge about the mysterious ways between men and women. Ariel knew she was safe with Milford; as a rake, he was harmless.

Unlike that odious Bates. She glanced across the dinner table and caught his gaze on her again. He noticed her looking and flashed her a wolfish grin. Ariel quickly averted her eyes. She did not want him to recognize how much he distressed her.

After dessert, the women retreated to the drawing room. When the men rejoined them, Ariel vowed to sit in a place where Bates could not easily watch her.

But she was talking with Miss Vining when the men entered. Aunt and the Blakenoses immediately lured Lynnwood into a game of whist, and before Ariel could find another refuge, Bates sauntered over and sat beside her on the sofa. It took all of her willpower to keep from moving away from him.

"We need some lively activity," Townsend said, eyeing Miss LeDeux with a hopeful expression.

"Can't dance without music," Mallory said glumly. "Milford won't let us play Blindman's Buff. What else can we do?"

"We never did play charades last night," Gregson reminded them. "Wasted all our time searching for that damn dog."

Bates gave Ariel a knowing look. "I found searching for the dog far more entertaining than playing charades. Did you not find it so, Miss Tennant?"

"You were not locked in a damp cellar," she said coldly.

"But at least you were with an entertaining companion," he said.

"We could play whist," Townsend suggested.

"I'm thoroughly tired of whist." Gregson frowned. "Do you play piquet, Miss Tennant?"

She shook her head. "No."

"Do not worry. I will assist you with the finer points," Bates said, then walked to the small card table and held out the chair for her.

Ariel stood up, scanning the room for a glimpse of Milford, but he had not returned to the drawing room with the others. She didn't mind playing cards with Gregson, but the thought of Bates hovering over her shoulder made her cringe.

But the two men were looking at her, and she did not want to draw attention to herself by causing a fuss. Reluctantly, she slipped into the chair Bates held for her. He pulled up another chair, and sat so close that his leg pressed against hers. She gritted her teeth and tried to ignore him.

Gregson dealt and began to explain the rules. By the end of the third game, Ariel felt that she understood the rudiments of play well enough to have Bates stop coaching her. His shoulder kept brushing hers; when he pulled a card from her hand, his fingers always lingered.

When Gregson went to refill his glass, Ariel glanced toward the door, hoping to see Milford come in, but the door remained closed. *Where was that dratted man?*

"Looking for someone, Miss Tennant?" Bates regarded her with a knowing smile.

"I was hoping the tea tray would arrive soon."

"The tea tray—or our esteemed host?" He leaned closer and lowered his voice. "You and Milford seem to have developed a habit of turning up in the same places together."

She looked at him with cool reserve. "I do not know what you mean."

"Oh, I think you do. But do not worry—your secret is safe with me." He glanced pointedly across the room to where Miss Vining now chatted with Miss Baker. "He's had Claudia under his protection for a long time. He usually tires of them long before this. I do not think she will last much longer."

"Of what possible interest is that to me?" she asked icily.

"I thought you would merely like to know that there is little danger from that quarter."

Ariel stared at him. Was he implying that she had set her cap for Milford? Or worse, that she wanted to be Miss Baker's replacement?

She strove to control her temper, but she was seething within. How dare Bates hint that she entertained the thought of indulging in a liaison with Milford? The thought was appalling. That her own behavior had contributed to his mistaken apprehension made her even angrier.

When she heard the drawing room door open, she jumped. It was Milford, at last. She wanted to run to his side and be safe from Bates, but then she realized that would be the absolute worst thing she could do.

Instead, she focused her gaze on the cards in her hand and tried to pretend that Bates was far, far away. Gregson returned and dealt another hand.

"Well, what have we here?" Milford stepped up behind the younger man. "Luring Miss Tennant into a ruinous life of card play?"

"It's only piquet, Milford," Gregson replied. "No harm in teaching her that."

"She is a quick learner," Bates added. "But then, of course, you know that."

Milford looked puzzled for a moment, then Ariel saw his expression darken as he grasped the meaning behind Bates's words.

"I have a great admiration for Miss Tennant's intelligence," Milford said. "It would never do to underestimate her."

He smiled politely, but Ariel heard the ominous undertone in his voice. She'd wanted to complain to Milford about Bates, to tell him of the man's sly insinuations, but now she wondered if she should. It might lead to more trouble. As long as she kept away from Bates, he would have no opportunity to make more odious comments to her.

Of course, she would have to take equal care about being found alone with Milford in order to smother Bates's suspicions.

Milford pulled up a chair and sat on Ariel's left. "Let us see how much lore you have absorbed from my esteemed friend. Let's hope you will forget it quickly. Piquet was never your strong point, Bates."

"As you wish." Bates stood and bowed to Ariel before he crossed the room to join the others.

"Oh, she's been doing a great job," Gregson said. "Almost beat me on the last hand."

Simon tried to appear calm, but inwardly he was enraged. He'd been afraid of an exchange with Bates ever since that disastrous encounter in the upstairs hall this afternoon. Bates was always ripe for making mischief, and Simon did not want him causing Ariel any distress.

Oh, he'd been very aware of just how many times Bates had glanced in her direction at dinner, and the faint flush that crossed her cheeks when she noticed the excessive attention. But annoying glances at the dinner table were relatively harmless. Ariel could ignore those easily enough. It was what Bates might say—to her, or to the others—that worried Simon.

Simon knew how easy it was to make use of a simple inflection, the arch of a brow, the wave of a hand to convey much more than mere words could express. Bates could blacken Ariel's reputation with a simple look.

And Simon would be to blame. He never should have allowed himself to take advantage of her innocence.

He wanted to keep a close eye on her after dinner, but Harman waylaid him and forced Simon to deal with some pressing household matters. By the time he entered the drawing room, he saw that Bates was firmly ensconced at Ariel's side and judging from the look on her face, she was not enjoying the experience.

So now, instead of spending time trying to determine who was behind the pranks that so bedeviled his guests, he had to protect Ariel from Bates's malicious tongue—protect her from a situation that was of his own making, and for which he could only blame himself. What had he been thinking of when he chose to engage her in a flirtation, however private? He knew his intentions were innocent—and he was certain that she did, too—but it would not look that way to others.

At least, it would not after Bates was through telling his

highly colored version of the tale. And from bitter experience, Simon knew how easily people were willing to believe the worst. He was not going to allow the merest whispered hints to besmirch Ariel's reputation.

Which meant he and Ariel needed to be far from circumspect in their meetings. No more tête-à-têtes in the library, even during the day, when anyone might discover them together. Yet how could they work to unmask the prankster if they were limited to meeting only in full view of the others? They would never find out who was behind these silly antics under those restraints.

Simon did feel cheered by the knowledge that there had not been any new pranks today—or at least none that they had discovered. He had given Harman the task of checking each and every room in the house several times during the day, looking for any sign of mischief—from open windows to damaged furniture—and he had reported that nothing seemed amiss. Perhaps, after failing to cause any stir with his pranks, the person behind them had decided to stop.

Simon sincerely hoped so. He intended to keep a protective eye on Ariel, and a wary one on Bates. He did not need any further distractions.

Ariel was relieved that Milford stayed close to her for the remainder of the evening. Bates had no chance to make any more of his insulting insinuations. And when Aunt suggested they go upstairs to bed, for once Ariel eagerly agreed. She was eager to get away from both men.

She helped Aunt prepare for bed, and in moments Mrs. Dobson was asleep. Ariel thought that had more to do with the several glasses of sherry that Aunt and Mrs. Blakenose enjoyed after dinner, than with any exhaustion on Aunt's part. But Ariel was relieved to have her asleep. It gave her the chance to think.

After gathering up Aunt's discarded clothing, she went into the narrow dressing rooms to repack them in the trunk. Ariel was now grateful that Aunt had insisted on taking all their luggage from the carriage, or she would have already been reduced to wearing the same clothes every day.

She was bent over one trunk, folding Aunt's flannel petticoat, when she heard voices coming from Milford's room. Milford's deep tones were immediately recognizable, but who was the other person? With only a small twinge of guilt, Ariel crept toward the door and put her ear against it.

"I am growing weary of this."

A woman—Miss Baker no doubt. Burning with curiosity, Ariel listened more carefully.

"Nothing is more tiresome than a woman who constantly complains, Claudia," Milford said.

"Even if she has cause?"

"What horrible crime have I committed against you?" he asked.

"You are neglecting me," she said. Ariel could envision the pouting expression on her face. "It has been three nights since you visited my bed."

Ariel felt a strange thrill of pleasure in discovering that Milford had been ignoring his mistress.

"That is my crime?" Milford laughed. "I think that hardly worth such a fuss."

"What am I to think when you ignore me like this? I know I am no longer young, or as beautiful as I once was. I knew that one day another would take my place."

"You are far from being hag-ridden, Claudia." Milford sounded amused. "I suggest that you put all thoughts like that out of your mind. You will still look exquisite when you are eighty."

"Are you tired of me, Milford?" Her voice rose plaintively. "Do I no longer please you?"

"Don't be silly, Claudia. I simply do not find it necessary to come to your bed every night."

"Even one night would be better than none. I wonder why you keep me here. I obviously no longer hold your interest."

"Perhaps with my house full of unexpected guests I have other claims on my attention. To insist that I must live in your pocket is rather absurd."

"You are far more interested in that foolish girl."

Ariel realized with a shock that Miss Baker was talking about *her*. Ariel knew she should leave now, immediately, before she heard more than she wanted to.

But she had to hear Milford's reply.

"What are you talking about?" he asked.

"You heard what I said," Miss Baker replied. "I see the way you make such an effort to be at her side, the way you whisper things to her that no one else hears. Really, Milford, you are sadly mistaken if you think you can lure someone like that to your bed. Girls like that demand marriage first."

A lengthy silence followed, and Ariel held her breath, waiting for Milford to respond.

"Claudia, this is laughable. I am not trying to lure her into my bed. I am merely being a polite host."

"I have rarely heard the term 'polite' used to describe your behavior around women."

"I am rarely around women whose status demands polite behavior."

Ariel smothered a laugh. Milford at his most charming.

"You mean women like me?" Miss Baker demanded.

"Would you rather I treated you like a grand duchess? I assure you, my dear, between the sheets there is no difference between the lowliest street whore and a royal princess. Both are women, pure and simple."

"Treating me as something more than another piece of furniture in your house might be nice."

"If you are so desperate for male companionship, Claudia, throw yourself on one of those overgrown schoolboys. They would think they had died and gone to heaven."

"They cannot afford me."

"And I can? Since I am still paying your bills, I do not think you have any reason to complain. Unless, of course, you would like to end our arrangement here and now."

"No, I do not wish that." Miss Baker lowered her voice and Ariel strained to hear. "But I do wish to understand your actions, Milford. Bates says—"

"Bates says what?"

Ariel shivered at the menace in Milford's voice.

"He says he has seen the two of you . . . together. Alone."

"And Bates is a horse's ass. The only time I have been alone with Miss Tennant was when we were locked in that blasted cellar, and I assure you I made no attempt to make love to her in that miserable spot."

Ariel smothered a gasp. Milford was lying. They had been together several times, and although a few simple kisses could not be construed as lovemaking, he was implying they had no intimate contact. She guessed that a man would not wish to admit even such a minor infidelity to his mistress.

If a man was expected to remain loyal to his mistress.

"You do not wish to be rid of me?" Miss Baker asked.

"Claudia, if I wished to be rid of your company, I would tell you so. If I have not come to your bed these last few nights, it is because I have a great deal on my mind. Do not forget there is that foolish prankster running riot in my house."

"Then I can expect you to join me tonight?"

"I will come to you when I bloody feel like it," he said curtly.

"Please, Simon, tell me what I have done. Tell me what I can do to win you back."

"Stop this groveling, for one."

"I have lost you," she wailed. "You may as well send me back to London tomorrow."

"Since the snow is still covering the roads, you have no fear of that," he said. "And perhaps by the morning you will see things differently."

"I only see that you wish to be freed from a relationship that you now view as an encumbrance."

"I only find you an encumbrance, Claudia, at times like this. Or perhaps this is your way of telling me that you would like to sever our arrangement?"

"No, no. I only wish . . . I only wish to please you."

"Then stop nagging me," he said. "If I wanted a woman to cling to me like a barnacle, I would have taken a wife long ago. Clinging does not become you, Claudia."

"And chasing after young girls does not become you."

"I am not chasing after Miss Tennant," he said. "I merely find her conversation entertaining . . . and amusing."

"You used to say my conversation was entertaining."

"My dear lady," he said. "Do not deceive yourself. It was never your conversation that attracted me."

"What was it then?"

After a moment of silence, Ariel heard the rustle of cloth.

"Was it this?"

"Cover yourself, Claudia. If I wanted you to stand naked before me, I would have asked."

Ariel's mouth fell open at the woman's audacity, then realized it was long past time for her to leave. Carefully, quietly, she stood up and took a cautious step back toward her room.

A board squeaked under her foot and she froze.

"Then I shall go speak with one of those horrid schoolboys," Miss Baker said loudly. "At least they will appreciate what I have to offer."

"You do what you feel you must," Milford said.

"You are willing to share me with one of them?"

"You can sleep with all three of them for all I care," he said. "Lynnwood and Bates as well, if you like. You are not tied to me, Claudia. You are free to do as you wish."

"Then our arrangement is at an end?"

Suddenly, a piercing shriek echoed through the hall.

Chapter 10

Simon jerked open the door and dashed into the hall. What the devil was going on now?

Sleepy-eyed guests peered from their doorways. Simon waved at them to go back inside, but they ignored him. Several people followed him to the room with the still-screaming woman.

Sarah Vining's room. Had the prankster hit again? Bates, wrapped in a robe, shoved passed him and went in. Simon quickly followed.

Sarah stood beside the bed, clad only in a lacy chemise. When she saw Bates, she ran to him and buried her face in his chest.

"The bed," she said, her muffled voice quavering. "Something horrible is in the bed."

Simon walked over to the four-poster and flipped back the covers, then recoiled at the sight.

A foot-wide blob of some blood-streaked substance was smeared over the sheet.

"My God, what is it?" Bates demanded, peering closer.

"I have no idea." Simon was not eager to inspect it. It looked like something that might have come from the inside of an animal. He cringed. Had someone gutted Blinky and left this in Sarah's bed?

He bent closer, sniffing cautiously. Whatever it was, it did not have any distinctive odor, so he felt reassured that it had not come from the unfortunate dog. But what the hell was it?

Others had pushed into the room—Mrs. Blakenose, Gregson,

and Lynnwood—and they gathered around the bed, gawking at the sight. Sarah still stood near Bates, trying to preserve the look of a damsel in distress.

"Ugh," Gregson said. "Looks like something you'd find in a butcher shop."

Sarah let out another shriek at that observation, and Simon gave the younger man a quelling look. Female hysterics were not what he needed right now. Steeling himself, he gingerly poked at the blob. He rubbed his fingers together, feeling the texture of the substance, then brought them to his nose.

The faint smell was vaguely familiar.

He stuck his fingers below Gregson's nose. "What do you think?"

Gregson sniffed, then shuddered. "Damnable stuff," he said. "Forced to eat it every time we was sick."

"What is it?" Simon demanded.

After sticking his finger into the blob, Gregson gingerly touched it to his tongue. "Calves' foot jelly or some such thing," he said. "Don't know what the red stuff is, though." He took another taste. "Jam?"

Simon shook his head. Another prank. Arranged with skill—and planning. It had taken time to mix this concoction, let alone slip it into the bed unnoticed, and keep Sarah from finding it until now. He almost had to admire the skill involved.

Almost.

"I am not sleeping in that bed," Sarah announced.

"That's all right." Gregson stepped forward, smiling. "You can sleep in mine."

Mrs. Blakenose turned and gave him an icy look.

"That is . . ." Gregson reddened. "I meant I will move in with one of the others so you can have my room."

"I think Sarah will be perfectly comfortable with me," Bates said, scowling at the younger man.

Mrs. Blakenose sniffed with disapproval.

"Why would anyone want to put such a disgusting thing in my bed?" Sarah asked.

"For the same reason all these pranks have been committed—to annoy everyone," Simon replied.

"I don't see why anyone should wish to annoy such a lovely

lady," Gregson said. He shot a dark look at Bates. "Especially when there are far more deserving candidates."

"In case you forgot, I have already been a victim," Bates said.

Lynnwood looked at Gregson. "I notice nothing has happened to you."

Gregson flushed. "Perhaps because I am careful about keeping my door locked at all times."

"Or maybe because you are the one behind it all." Bates took a menacing step forward.

Simon held up his hand for calm. "This is not the time or place to accuse anyone of anything. I'll look into this further in the morning. I assure everyone I intend to find out who is responsible."

Frustrated, he stalked out of the room.

To his relief, Claudia wasn't in his room when he returned. That was one problem he did not want to have to deal with tonight. He poured himself a glass of brandy and sat down on the edge of the bed, wondering if he would ever find the person behind these pranks. He'd thought he'd been watching things carefully, and look what had happened. Simple vigilance was not going to be enough.

He looked up when he heard a light tap on the door leading to the far dressing room—the one that connected to Ariel's room. Simon stood and walked to the door, pulling it open. Ariel stood there, wrapped in her quilted robe.

"Another prank?" she asked.

He nodded. "Apparently some concoction of calves' foot jelly and strawberry jam placed in Sarah's bed."

She made a moue of distaste. "How did anyone manage that?"

"That's what I would like to know. You were up here earlier tonight—did you hear anyone prowling around?"

Ariel shook her head. "I heard people in the hall, doors opening and closing, but it all sounded very normal, people retiring for the night."

He glanced over her shoulder. "Did all the hubbub wake your aunt?"

"I do not think anything would wake her tonight." Her smile

grew impish. "Aunt and Mrs. Blakenose were dipping heavily into the sherry after dinner."

Simon motioned for her to enter. "Come in then. No point in you standing in that drafty doorway. You'll take a chill."

He pulled two chairs in front of the fireplace and heaped more coal onto the glowing embers.

"Would you like some brandy?" At her nod, he poured her a glass, and they sat facing each other.

"I am beginning to fear I am never going to discover who is behind these pranks," he said. "But if I can get them to stop, I will be satisfied."

"Perhaps we are going about this all wrong," she said. "We have been trying to think of the most likely culprits. Maybe we should look at the least likely."

"Your aunt?" He smiled at the thought of Mrs. Dobson planting that revolting mess in Sarah's bed.

"What about Blakenose or his wife?"

"She would never lock that dog in the cellar."

"No, but her husband might. He must be tired of having his wife dote on that creature."

"But why bother the others?"

"For amusement." She leaned forward. "Think on it, Milford. He is a food merchant. His luggage could be crammed with jars of calves' foot jelly."

Simon shook his head. "I do not think Blakenose is the type."

"Then that leaves your two friends."

"Nothing has happened to Lynnwood," he admitted.

"And Bates could have left his window open on purpose to divert attention," she said eagerly. "That was the first prank, after all. A masterful way to throw suspicion elsewhere."

"I've never known either of them to be pranksters," he said carefully, thinking. "Why would they start now?"

"Boredom? An appreciative audience? You have to admit that Miss Vining screams quite attractively."

He laughed. "If we want to look at unlikely suspects, why not her, or Marguerite?"

"Or Miss Baker. Nothing has happened to her, either."

Simon thought. The persistence of the prankster troubled him. Why would anyone want to go to such efforts to make his guests miserable? Was it all just a game? There was still the nagging worry that the prankster had a more sinister purpose in mind.

He took a long swallow of brandy. "We could go around in circles like this all night and be no closer to the answer. And no real harm has been done."

"Don't you want to solve the mystery?" she protested.

"You are the one with the insatiable curiosity." He grinned. "You must have been a holy terror as a child."

"Oh, I was very complacent then," she said with a mischievous smile. "I only developed this shameful trait recently."

"How fortunate for your family."

Sitting in front of the toasty fire, Ariel felt warm, cozy, and slightly drowsy. She sipped her brandy and darted a sidelong glance at Milford. A lock of his dark hair fell forward across his cheek, and she fought the urge to reach out and tuck it behind his ear.

It made him look boyish, rather than rakish, reminding her again of the falsity of his reputation. Why was he regarded with such horror by polite society.

"Milford?"

"Hmm?"

"How did you ever get such a terrible reputation? You really are quite nice—and not rakish at all."

His mouth set in a grim line. "I merely lived up to people's expectations of me."

"People expected you to be a rake?"

He remained silent for so long that she feared he was not going to answer her.

"I was the black sheep of the family," he said finally. "My father was a steady sober sort, as was my brother. He was constantly held up to me as a model, one to whom I could not measure up."

"I did not know you had a brother. Where is he now?"

"Dead," Milford said flatly.

"Oh, Milford, I am sorry."

"No need to be," he said. "I killed him, you know."

"What?" She started at him, disbelieving his words. "You are joking."

"It's true. I am responsible for his death, and indirectly my father's, for he never recovered from the shock."

"What happened?"

He stared into the glowing coals. "As I said, I was always the wild one. In my younger years, it was horses and hunting. Then I discovered gambling and drink—and the ladies. After I was sent down for the fifth time from Oxford, my father washed his hands of me."

"Didn't he ever indulge in any youthful mischief?"

"He offered to buy me a commission, but the army was the last thing I wanted to do. So I fell in with some other irresponsible fellows like myself and we tore through life, leaving everything in a shambles behind us."

"Youthful high spirits," she murmured with sympathy.

"My brother—he was three years older, by the way—was affianced to a lovely young lady. I was jealous. Here he was, with everything—my father's approval, the title one day, and now a wife. I had nothing except what I could win at the gaming tables. So I planned my revenge."

"What did you do?" She dreaded to hear his words, fearing what he would reveal, but she had to know.

"I set out to seduce his fianceé."

"Milford! What a horrible thing to do."

"I told you that I was not a very nice person," he said. "Perhaps now you will believe me."

"Did you . . . did you actually seduce her?"

"You mean did I ruin her? No—at least not in the strict sense of the word. But I ruined her chance of happiness with my brother. She fell in love with me, you see. And when he found out what I'd done, my brother came after me and insisted that I make things right by marrying her.

"Instead, I laughed in his face. If I had not been his brother, he would have called me out. Although it would have been foolish on his part—I was by far the better shot."

"What happened then?"

"Both families applied pressure and forced her to go ahead with the wedding to my brother. The night before the ceremony, she came to me, begging me to take her away. I'd been drinking all evening and didn't have the sense to send her home. So I told her we'd elope.

"Somehow, my brother learned she was gone and guessed

what was happening. He knew we'd be heading north, toward Scotland, and shot off down the Great North Road after us."

His voice dropped so low she had to strain to hear him. "Ironically, we left London later than he did. We came upon his carriage in a ditch. The horse had stumbled or a wheel hit a rock—I don't know. He'd been thrown clear . . . and broke his neck."

"How old were you?" she whispered.

"Nineteen."

Nineteen. She remembered how silly and foolish she'd been at nineteen—and she'd had a doting brother and warm memories of loving parents. Milford had acted disgracefully, of course, taking advantage of the poor girl who was no doubt even younger. But for people to say that he'd killed his brother . . . It had been a tragic accident, nothing more.

"What came next?"

He brushed a hand over his face, and Ariel touched his arm, wanting to take away the hurt. For a moment he looked at her, and she saw the raw pain in his eyes.

"No, don't tell me," she whispered. "That is enough. I don't want to cause you any more pain."

He looked back into the fire. "So now you know what a fine, *respectable* person I am. Black-hearted bastard is putting it too fine."

"Don't be ridiculous, Milford. You certainly behaved stupidly, but what nineteen-year-olds do not? Why, you were probably younger than Mallory and his friends and look what idiots they are!"

He flashed her a wan smile. "Thank you for the comparison."

"What happened to the girl?"

"She's a marchioness now."

"So none the worse for her experience. Milford, what happened to your brother was terrible, but it was an accident. It's not as if you shot him."

"I might as well have."

"Is that what your father said?"

He nodded.

"Then I think your father is the most hateful man on earth. If he'd treated you with some understanding to begin with, the whole thing would never have happened. I think most of the blame rests on him."

"Ah, Ariel." He sighed. "What a treasure you are. Why couldn't I have known you back then?"

"Because I was a horrid brat barely out of leading strings." She smiled. "But you have to accept the responsibility for the way you've lived your life since then."

"Oh, I think I've lived an exceptionally scandalous life."

"Nonsense. People expected the worst of you, so you tried your hardest to show them that they were right. You're no black-hearted rake. You have been pretending all these years."

"And doing a damn good job of it. There is nothing pretty about my life, Ariel."

"What have you done that is so awful? Drinking to excess? Hardly an uncommon occurrence. Gambling? What member of the *ton* doesn't? Taking a mistress? You and half the other men in London."

"Ah, but I did it all to such excess."

"Only because you thought you had to. I imagine if you'd been left to your own devices you would have led a remarkably dull existence."

"Sipping sherry and playing chicken-stakes whist," he said with a faint smile. "What a life."

She nodded.

"Your faith in me is remarkable, Ariel." He shook his head. "Too bad it is misplaced."

"It is not my faith that is misplaced, but yours." She rested her hand on his. "You need to have faith in yourself."

"Hah. You speak from your vast years of experience."

"I have seen what you are like these past few days. I've seen through your false facade, Milford. You've a strong streak of respectability in you."

"Oh?"

She nodded. "Look at the way you've dealt with me."

He gave a derisive snort. "Because I have not tried to ravish you?"

"You are not the ravishing type."

"Perhaps I don't find you enticing enough to bother."

She knew it was his pain that caused him to lash out. Ariel leaned closer. "Tell me you don't find me the least bit . . . en-

ticing." With a boldness that shocked her, she pressed her lips
to his.

The contact was electric; her whole body tingled with the
sensation. She reached out and lightly ran her fingers down his
cheek. He broke the kiss and nuzzled at her palm. Then he took
her hand and brought it to his lips and looked into her eyes.

"You are far too good for me, Ariel."

"Is that what *you* think? Or what you think other people will
say?"

"Does it matter?"

She saw the deep sadness in his eyes and realized it was
going to take far more than a simple kiss to persuade him that
he had been wrong, that he deserved to be recognized as the
honorable man he was. And she despaired of ever being able to
convince him.

He stood up and held out his hand. "It is late."

Knowing there was no more she could say to him tonight,
Ariel took his hand and followed him to the connecting door.
He opened it, then stopped and bent to press a gentle kiss on her
forehead. "Don't try to make me into something I'm not,
Ariel."

Ariel crawled into bed beside her aunt, though she knew she
was not going to be able to sleep for a long, long time.

Her heart ached for Milford. He had made a stupid, foolish
mistake at nineteen and had spent the rest of his life punishing
himself for it. What could she do to make him understand that
it was not necessary?

She needed to find a way to dispel his undeserved sobriquet.
Once others treated him well, he would begin to regard himself
in a better light. Once you knew him, it was obvious he was
nothing like his reputation. Why, even Aunt was beginning to
treat him with a measure of respect. It should not be so difficult
to convince others.

This spring, when she was in London, it would be simple to
have him invited to some selected entertainments. Once people
saw him accepted among respectable company, they would forget all about his past.

Of course, that meant Milford had to be in London during the
Season. Ariel feared he might not bother. But surely, she could

devise some way to get him there. Richard would want to thank him personally for sheltering them from the storm. And once she had Milford in London, she could launch her campaign.

Yet what would happen once she succeeded in having Milford accepted by society again? Because of rank and age, he would travel in a far different set than she. Ariel could not imagine Milford going to the balls and dinner parties designed by the matchmakers. She would go to all that work, but get little chance to even see him.

And she wanted to continue seeing him. But why? Friendship? There was not a place for that in either of their lives. Milford would be an amusing escort, but he would not want to take a girl like her anywhere. She was going to London to find a husband, after all. And any man seen with her would be considered a prospective husband.

Ariel realized she was half in love with him, which would never do. Milford was not hanging out for a wife. And even if he was, he certainly would not consider her, when he could have his pick of beautiful heiresses. No, friendship was all she could ever hope to have from him. And even that would be a temporary thing as their lives moved in different directions.

Perhaps she should leave well enough alone and forget about Milford and his reputation. Perhaps he enjoyed having such a black reputation in order to avoid the sort of society events that so many men found boring. In fact, that sounded exactly like Milford. If he was a social outcast, he was not going to be invited to dull dinner parties, overcrowded balls, and poorly acted theater. This way, he could do exactly what he pleased, with his close friends, and enjoy himself.

The more she thought about it, the more she realized that Milford had the better idea. Of course, he was a man, and men could get away with that sort of thing. As a female, she had far less freedom to do as she pleased.

Except while she was here, in this life out of time—where she could sit in a man's room in her dressing gown, talk and sip brandy, and know it was a very special time in her life.

And try to forget that the last thing she saw as she drifted off to sleep, was the errant lock of hair that she wanted to tuck behind his ear.

Chapter 11

Milford awoke to the sound of water dripping from the eaves and gurgling through the downspouts. A loud "whoosh" announced a clump of snow sliding from the peaked roof. He jumped out of bed and ran to the window, pulling the drapes outside. A light drizzle met his eyes. The thaw had come at last. It would not be long now before everyone could be on their way again.

Including Ariel.

After last night, she was the one he most wanted to see leave. He regretted having revealed so much to her. For now she was suffering under the delusion that he was a redeemable man. He'd seen that look in her eyes, the sympathy, the desire to champion his cause.

It had been a mistake to indulge in a flirtation with her—an action he once thought was harmless, but now knew was not. She didn't have the experience to know the difference between a casual flirtation and something more, and he feared she had misinterpreted his interest, or worse, fixed her own on him. The sooner she left, the better for both of them.

Yet with the amount of snow still on the ground, it would be several days before the roads were ready to travel. And their carriage still lay in a ditch on the main road.

That would not be a problem. He could send them home in his carriage and make arrangements to have their vehicle repaired and sent on. There would be no need to delay their departure. He could get Ariel out of his life.

Simon was forced to admit that he was far more attracted to

her than he should be. However, he'd behaved like a perfect gentleman toward her so far—well, maybe not a perfect one, but he had not gone completely outside the bounds of respectable behavior. Yet if she lingered here much longer, Simon knew he would find it harder and harder to restrain his true nature.

Despite her protestation, he knew what he was—a man without honor, a man who'd spent his adult life in an aimless pursuit of pleasure. A man good enough for the likes of a hired mistress, or a bored society matron, but not for an unmarried girl. Continuing the connection with him would only bring ruin and disgrace to Ariel. Or, at the very least, heartache, when she finally realized he wasn't the man she thought he was.

He glanced up at the grey sky, urging it to rain harder, to melt the snow all the faster.

Hoping to avoid Ariel, he breakfasted in his room, and by the time he finally descended the stairs, most of the household was awake. He glanced into the dining room, where the Blakenoses, Townsend, and Mallory were still eating. Relieved not to find Ariel there, he hurried down the corridor toward the library. He'd made it very clear to Ariel that she was not to seek him out alone while the prankster was still at large. He would be safe from her in that room.

Simon halted when he saw the library door standing ajar. He'd told Harman to keep the room locked, and Simon was certain he'd locked it himself last night. With an uneasy feeling, he eased the door open, wary of what he might find inside.

The reek of brandy stung his nostrils as he stepped into the room. A bottle lay on its side on the floor, a dark stain spreading from its mouth, soaking into the Turkey carpet and spilling onto the polished wood floor.

What was the bottle doing out of the cupboard in the first place? Simon had been careful to keep it there ever since the first stranded travelers arrived, wanting to preserve his private stock. He would not have left it out on the desk last night.

Perhaps Harman or one of the other servants had refilled it this morning and left it out in anticipation of his arrival. Had someone looked in this morning, seen the bottle, and dumped his brandy on the floor as another prank?

Simon could not imagine why someone would want to waste

a bottle of good brandy in that manner. Anyone in their right mind would have drunk the stuff.

Of course, that assumed that the prankster was in his right mind, which Simon seriously doubted.

Sighing, he rang for a servant to come and clean up the mess. He was not going to mention this to the others. Whoever had done this would be expecting a reaction from him. Once again it gave Simon another chance to watch for anticipation or apprehension in someone's demeanor.

He heard shouts coming from another part of the house. *What now?*

Simon strode out into the hall. It sounded like the raised voices came from the drawing room. He could make out the loud wails of a woman—Mrs. Blakenose?—and animated male voices.

He walked into the room. "What is going on here?" he demanded.

"My poor Blinky!" Mrs. Blakenose sat on the floor, bending over her dog.

"There's something wrong with the dog," Townsend said, pointing.

The furry beast stood next to his mistress, drool running down his chin. Every few seconds he shook violently.

Mrs. Blakenose wrung her hands. "What is wrong with my Blinky?"

Simon walked over to the dog and kneeled to inspect him. Blinky's eyes dropped low, his breathing was rapid and . . . the smell of brandy overpowering.

"He's drunk," Simon announced. "The damn dog's been in my brandy."

"You shouldn't be putting spirits where the dog can get into them," Mrs. Blakenose said.

"I just found a bottle of my best brandy spilled on the floor in the library," he snapped back. "I wouldn't be surprised to find out this miserable creature was responsible." With a look of distaste, he shoved the dog into Mrs. Blakenose's hands.

"I suggest you force some water on him, then let him sleep it off," Simon said.

She set the dog down on the floor. Blinky took a few wobbling steps toward his mistress then fell on his side, his legs twitching.

"He's drunk all right," Townsend said. "M'father had a hunting dog that liked to take a nip now and then. Acted just like this."

"My poor baby." Mrs. Blakenose knelt at the dog's side again. "You'ums a naughty boy."

"Lots of water," Simon said. "And for God's sake, don't leave him in the drawing room. I don't want any accidents in here."

He started back toward the library, but before he was even out the door, a piercing scream came from behind him.

"He's dead!" Mrs. Blakenose wailed. "My Blinky's dead."

"Dead drunk." Mallory snickered.

That was no doubt the truth, but Simon again knelt beside the dog and put a hand on his furry body.

Odd. He couldn't feel a heartbeat, but with so much fur, it was hard to be sure. He lifted one of the dog's eyelids and saw that the creature's wide brown eye had rolled back into his head. Simon lifted a paw, which fell limply when he released it.

He realized that Mrs. Blakenose was right. The dog was dead.

Simon shot a warning look at her husband. "I suggest you take your wife upstairs."

"No!" Realizing the import of his words, Mrs. Blakenose flung herself on the tiny body.

"If the dog wasn't already dead, he would be now," Mallory whispered. "Crushed flat."

"Is he really dead?" Townsend peered around Simon.

"You check him," Simon said. "I don't know a great deal about dogs, but he sure looks dead to me."

Blakenose pulled his wife away while Townsend knelt and examined the tiny body. Soon he sat back on his heels, shaking his head. "He's dead, all right."

Mrs. Blakenose gave a tiny gasp and collapsed in a faint.

"They say that alcohol's poisonous to some animals," Townsend said. "If they drink enough of it."

"I can think of worse ways to go." Mallory snickered again. "Milford's got damn fine brandy."

"Run upstairs and find Mrs. Dobson," Simon told Townsend.

"Tell her to bring her hartshorn immediately. And have her niece come down, as well."

Blakenose knelt beside his distraught wife, patting her pudgy, limp hand. Simon stood beside Mallory, watching helplessly.

"Be sure not to give her any brandy after she revives," Mallory said.

"Thank you for *that* helpful piece of advice." Simon's voice dripped sarcasm.

Faster than Simon had hoped, Ariel and her aunt came rushing in, with Townsend and Gregson on their heels. Ariel's eyes were wide with alarm.

"What has happened? Townsend said there was a problem with the dog."

"There's been an . . . accident," Simon said.

"Oh, good gracious." Mrs. Dobson noticed the prostrate form of her friend. "Poor Euphemia."

"Mrs. Blakenose has fainted," Simon explained. "Would you be so kind as to attend her, Mrs. Dobson?"

She nodded and hurried to her friend's side.

"What happened?" Gregson asked.

"The dog is dead."

"Oh dear!" Ariel said. "Poor Mrs. Blakenose. She will be heartbroken."

"That's why I called in your aunt. I hope she will be some help in consoling her."

"How did it happen?" Gregson asked. "Somebody step on it?"

"As near as I can tell, the foolish creature drank itself to death. Knocked over a bottle of my best brandy in the library and lapped the stuff up."

As he said the words, the significance of those circumstances suddenly struck him. An icy chill swept up his spine and exploded in a burst of pure panic inside his skull. *His* brandy. A *dead* dog.

He had to get back to that library before the servants cleaned things up.

Trying to keep his voice calm, Simon turned to Ariel. "Which reminds me, I still have that mess in the library to deal

with. Miss Tennant, I would appreciate your assistance there.
Bring the teapot with you, as well."

Without waiting for her answer, he fled out the door and
raced for the library.

He wanted to take a very good look at the brandy bottle and
what was left of its contents. A sudden, sickly fear told him that
Blinky had not died from too much brandy—but what had been
put into that brandy.

Poison. A word that sounded as ugly as that unfortunate rat-
catching dog.

Poisoned brandy—in a bottle that was normally kept tucked
away in a cabinet in the library, and consumed only by him.

He tasted the bile in his throat.

Puzzled by his request, Ariel grabbed the teapot and dashed
after Milford, who was practically running down the hallway.
She felt so sorry for Mrs. Blakenose. The woman had doted on
that dog to ridiculous extremes, and it was a thoroughly ob-
noxious creature, but it did not deserve such a horrible fate.

She smelled the spilled brandy as soon as she stepped into
the library. A dark stain spread across the carpet, and Milford
stood next to it, squinting into a bottle.

"What was that silly creature doing in here in the first
place?" she asked.

"A good question." He upended the bottle over an empty
glass and a few drops of liquid trickled out. He bent and sniffed
the contents.

"What on earth are you doing?" she asked.

He glanced up. "Close the door and lock it, then bring me
that pot of tea."

Ariel did as he asked.

"What are you going to do?" She watched, mystified, as he
filled a glass with tea.

There was a look of gloom on his face as he looked at her. "I
think the brandy was poisoned."

"Poisoned?" She stared at him with rising horror. "Someone
deliberately killed Blinky?"

"I think *his* death was an accident," Milford said.

She glanced into his eyes and saw the confirmation of her
worst fear. "It is your brandy," she whispered. "They were try-

ing to poison you. Oh, my God." She grabbed his arm. "Then
the ladder the other night . . . and the urn . . . Milford, someone
is trying to kill you."

He nodded. "I am afraid so."

Her knees felt suddenly weak, and she sank down into the
nearest chair. "Milford, what are we going to do?"

"I don't know. I still cannot believe . . ." He stuck his finger
in the brandy, then raised it to his mouth.

Ariel jumped out of the chair. "Don't!" she cried, but before
she could stop him, he touched his finger to the tip of his
tongue. Then he grabbed the glass of tea and took a long sip,
swishing the liquid in his mouth before spitting it out.

"There is definitely an odd taste to the stuff," he said.

She watched him anxiously, half expecting him to collapse at
any moment. "Milford, you are mad. You could have poisoned
yourself."

"I doubt such a tiny amount would cause much harm. Remember, Blinky probably slurped up a glassful, and he's a good
sight smaller than I am."

"You could at least be made dreadfully ill."

"I will be fine." He sat down. "This does put a rather different light on things, doesn't it?"

"Who would want to kill you?"

He regarded her blankly. "I don't know."

"Are you certain that it is one of the guests?" she asked.
"Why not one of the servants?"

He shook his head. "They've all been here for years. I trust
them."

"Harman?"

"I would suspect you before I would believe he had anything
to do with this."

"Then it must be a guest." She rested her chin in her hand as
she tried to puzzle out the identity of Milford's enemy. But no
one seemed a likely suspect.

One thing was certain. If it was a guest, then it was critical
that Milford get everyone out of the house at once.

"Now that the snow is melting, you can order everyone to
leave," she said.

He shook his head. "It will take a day or two before the roads are clear enough for travel, and even then they will be muddy quagmires. No one is going to get very far for a while."

"Then you'll simply have to lock everyone into their rooms," she said firmly. "It's the only way to keep yourself safe."

"I'm not even sure that will work," he said. "I'm fairly certain that this room was locked. Which means someone has at least one household key."

Fear stabbed through her. Milford was in real danger. "Then you won't be safe anywhere."

"Oh, yes I will." His expression turned determined. "From this moment on, I intend to see that no one moves an inch without at least one person at their side."

"What if someone still slips away?"

"Then we will know who our prime suspect is, won't we?" He flashed her a smile. "I assure you—after I get done talking with everyone, they will not want to even cross the room without an escort. Either to prove they are innocent, or to preserve their lives."

Her stomach roiled at the thought of what this meant. "This is really happening, isn't it, Milford? A madman is loose in this house."

"Or woman—we cannot afford to overlook anyone, now."

"Can you be certain that you are the only target? What about the pranks directed at other people?"

"I think those other incidents were designed to merely confuse the situation," Milford said.

"We have to find a way to keep you safe for the next few days." Ariel could not bear the thought of something horrible befalling him.

He walked over to the tall cabinet that stood between the bookcases and opened the lower cupboard. He pulled out a polished wooden box with shiny brass fittings. Milford set the box on the desk and flipped open the lid.

Inside, nesting in a bed of white satin, lay a pair of Durs Egg double-barrelled dueling pistols. He lifted one of them.

"I think these will provide me with some protection."

The pistols did not completely allay her concerns. So many things could go wrong. "What about at night—when you are asleep?"

"I can barricade myself in my room—as will you, and Claudia, since my rooms can be accessed through either of yours."

"Aren't you afraid to even eat or drink? How can you know that anything is safe?"

"Unless this person intends to poison the lot of us, I'll be safe enough."

She shuddered. "Now I won't be able to eat a bite."

He laughed. "Perhaps we should revert to the days of the Borgias, when every noble house employed a food taster."

A tap sounded on the door.

"Who's there?" Milford demanded, instantly alert.

"Harman."

He nodded to Ariel. "Let him in."

The butler entered, looking as calm and unruffled as ever.

"I understand there has been an . . . accident regarding that dog? We will no longer be plagued with his presence?"

"The dog is dead," Milford said. "Tell me, Harman, have you been keeping the library door locked?"

"Of course."

"And did you or one of the other servants refill the brandy bottle yesterday?"

"I did so myself," Harman said. "And returned it to the cabinet."

"I found it dumped on the floor when I came in this morning. The dog apparently helped himself to what was there—and the poor creature died for his greediness. I'm convinced the brandy was poisoned."

"Good God!" Harman's imperturbability cracked, and he stared with growing alarm at Milford.

"My reaction exactly. And now I suspect our poisoner has in his possession at least one, if not several, household keys. We must assume that no room is safe from invasion."

Harman's gaze flicked to the pistol box. "Do you know—or suspect—who is responsible?"

Milford shook his head. "I only wish I did; it would make all our lives a damn sight easier. Harman, from this moment on, you are to trust none of the guests, except for Miss Tennant. Take instructions only from one of us. I am going to need to rely heavily on you for the next few days until we discover who is behind this."

"You can count on me," Harman said.

"As I knew I could. Now, I intend only to tell the others that all their lives are in imminent danger and, for their own protection, they should always move about the house in groups. I think we have a better chance to catch this fellow if he does not know how much we suspect."

Ariel nodded.

"I'm also going to have everyone share a bedroom, to prevent mischief during the night," he continued. "Harman, I want you and the servants to help with the moving process."

Harman nodded.

"What if there are two people working together?" Ariel asked. "You might be playing right into their hands if you put the right people together."

"I'm betting that we have only a single criminal here," Milford said. "Pairing him with another might serve to stay his hand for a time."

Ariel listened with a growing sense of dread as Milford discussed plans with Harman. She'd arrived here wanting an adventure, and now she had one—except it was one that she had no desire for, an adventure that was too horrifying to even think about.

She could barely believe that someone was trying to kill Milford. Until they caught the villain, she would be gripped with fear for Milford's life. He may feel safe with those pistols, but they did not reassure her. There were too many ways he could be attacked. Pistols stuck in the waistband of his trousers were not going to keep him safe in every circumstance.

No, he was going to need more personal protection. And Ariel intended to make that her responsibility. She would watch over him, whether he wanted her to or not. She cared for him far too much to let him go through this alone.

Chapter 12

Simon ordered Harman to collect the rest of the guests and bring them to the drawing room. He had to persuade them that their lives depended on doing what he told them. And he intended to do a very good job of it, because they were actually going to be protecting him.

When everyone had assembled—except for Mrs. Blakenose and Ariel's aunt, who remained upstairs—Simon raised his hand for quiet. Instantly, the room fell silent. They had all heard what happened to the dog, and speculation as to the cause ran rampant. Simon knew he was about to shock them even further.

"I am sure you all know that Mrs. Blakenose's dog has died," he began.

"Such a pity," Gregson said, sotto voce.

"This is not the time for wit," Simon told him curtly. "The dog was poisoned."

"Poisoned?" Miss LeDeux gasped. "That sweet little doggie? Who would do such a thing?"

"I can think of several candidates," Townsend muttered.

Simon shot him a dark look. "Perhaps you will be more concerned when I tell you that the poisoning of the dog was accidental." He paused and took a moment to look into each face. "The poison was actually meant for one of us."

Miss Vining let out a muffled shriek. Blakenose and Townsend stared at him with shocked disbelief.

"That can't be," Mallory protested.

Lynnwood eyed Simon suspiciously. "How can you be certain?"

"Surely, the incident must have been an accident," Bates said. "Or at least meant for the dog. Why would you think otherwise?"

"No one could have known it would be the dog who drank the poisoned brandy," Simon said. "No, the intended victim was one of us."

"Who?" Gregson demanded.

"That's what I do not know." Simon spread his hands. "As Blinky's demise shows, no one could be certain who would drink the brandy. The poisoner might not have even cared whom he killed."

"What are you going to do about it?" Mallory demanded. "You must send for the magistrate."

"The magistrate can't travel any more than we can," Simon said. "Until the roads clear, we are trapped here."

"I don't want to be stuck in a house with an attempted murderer." Gregson glanced around uneasily. "Why, it could be any one of you!"

"Could it be the same person who is behind the pranks?" Miss Vining asked.

"I simply do not know," Simon said. "My main concern now is for everyone's safety."

"How do you intend to guarantee that?" Bates sneered. "You don't even know whom to guard against."

"If no one has the opportunity to be alone—for even a moment—nothing more can happen," Simon explained. "So from this moment on, none of you is to go anywhere without another person at your side. Preferably two. It is the only way to guarantee your safety."

"That's going to be damn inconvenient," Townsend said.

"The alternative is worse," Milford said curtly. "And if I find anyone wandering around alone, I will consider it tantamount to a confession of guilt."

"I'll be too frightened to eat a bite," Miss Vining said. "What if the food has been poisoned?"

"What about the servants?" Bates demanded. "One of them could be behind this. It would be easy for them to poison the brandy—or the food."

"I am convinced they are innocent," Simon replied coolly.

"Since I will be eating the same food as you, it will demonstrate my confidence."

"What about nighttime?" Claudia asked. "We could be murdered in our beds."

"As long as everyone locks their doors, you should be safe," Simon said. He did not want to deprive them of that illusion by telling them that he suspected the murderer had several household keys. Besides, if he was right, they were all safe enough. Everyone, except for him.

"Anyone could go sneaking about in the middle of the night," Lynnwood said. "Seems to me that would be the perfect time for skulduggery."

"To solve that problem, no one is going to be sleeping alone," Simon said. "You will all be sharing a room. The servants will help you move your luggage."

"We should be trying to find the guilty party," Townsend said. "What good will all these precautions do if the murderer is still free?"

"It will prevent someone from being killed," Simon said. "And I would rather allow this criminal to go free than have any one of us killed. Wouldn't you?"

Townsend nodded reluctantly.

"What if I have to go somewhere and no one wants to come with me?" Mallory asked.

"You will stay put," Simon said.

"Do we get to choose whose room we share?" Mallory asked hopefully, looking at Marguerite.

"No," Simon replied. "Mallory, you're moving in with Lynnwood. Gregson and Townsend will share with Bates, while Sarah will double up with Marguerite."

"What if my roommate is the murderer?" Mallory scowled at Lynnwood. "He could kill me in my bed and then sneak out."

"I will have servants guarding the floor during the night."

"Fat lot of good that's going to do me once I'm dead," Mallory snorted.

"But you will have the satisfaction of knowing that you helped us identify the criminal." Simon smiled grimly. "If you're so worried, stay awake all night and keep an eye on him."

"Mallory has a point," Townsend said. "One of us here is the guilty one. It could be you"—he pointed at Bates—"or even you"—he slapped Gregson on the back.

"I ain't no murderer," Gregson protested.

"I'm using you as an example," Townsend said impatiently. "I don't think any of us wants to spend our nights locked up with someone we don't trust."

"It's far easier to watch six rooms than twelve," Simon said. "You will share and that is final."

Gregson looked doubtfully at Bates. "What if he snores?"

"Stuff rags in your ears," Simon said. "Now, you are to confine your activities to your bedroom or the drawing room. I don't want you going anywhere else in the house. The dining room will be used only for meals."

"How long are we going to have to keep this up?" Bates demanded.

"Until the roads are clear, and I can be rid of the lot of you," Simon said. "Or until we find the culprit."

"I think we should give the roads another try," Townsend said.

"Anyone who wishes to leave is welcome to go," Simon said. He scanned their faces, waiting to see if anyone was willing to accept his offer. No one did.

"What if we want to visit with someone else?" Mallory demanded. "Do we have to take an escort along, too?"

"Yes," Simon snapped. "I will repeat this one more time. You are not to go anywhere without at least one other person at your side. Or you run the risk of ending up dead."

Harman stepped into the drawing room. "The servants are ready."

"Good." Simon turned to his guests. "Now, go upstairs and we'll get everyone moved."

His harsh words appeared to have had some effect, for they moved to comply without further complaint. Simon followed at the rear of the subdued group, walking alongside Claudia as they mounted the stairs.

This wasn't the ideal situation, but Simon did not know what else to do. His primary interest was in keeping himself alive. And if that meant lying to the others about his real suspicions— that he was the intended victim—he would do it. The guests would be far more alert and watchful if they thought they were in danger.

And if he was wrong, and the poisoner sought to kill indiscriminately, this was the only way to keep all of them safe.

Yet, he still believed that he was the intended victim. Besides the brandy, there were the falling urn and the damaged library stepladder. Three things, two easily fatal, all aimed at him.

But who among the company wanted him dead? Townsend, Mallory, and Gregson he barely knew. He'd never met the Blakenoses. Ariel and her aunt—the thought was ludicrous.

Which left him with his original five guests. Two men, three women. As unbelievable as it might be, he had to accept that one of them was behind this.

Claudia? "Hell hath no fury . . ." After that scene last night, he would have to consider her a candidate. Sarah and Marguerite seemed less likely prospects—what did they have to gain from his death?

Lynnwood? Bates? Simon had gambled, drank, whored together with them for years. It simply made no sense. Why would either of them suddenly want to kill him?

He had to think. He must have done something to bring on this attack. But while Simon ruefully acknowledged he had not led the best of lives, he could not think of any sin he'd committed that was great enough to warrant his death.

Ariel found her aunt still sitting with Mrs. Blakenose, who was now sleeping peacefully after a generous dose of laudanum. They left Blakenose to watch over his wife and retreated to their own chamber, where Ariel quickly explained the situation to her aunt.

"Poisoned!" Mrs. Dobson shrieked. "I knew nothing good was going to come of stopping here. A murderer in our midst! We must leave at once."

"We cannot," Ariel said. "Even if the roads were clear, have you forgotten that our carriage is still lying in the ditch?"

"Milford can provide us with a vehicle." She turned her panic-stricken eyes on Ariel. "I must get you away to safety."

"It will do us no good if we land in another ditch. If we follow Milford's plan, we will be safe."

"I think it's one of those friends of his," Mrs. Dobson said

with emphasis. "That Bates has shifty eyes. And Lynnwood . . .
Well, what can one expect from someone who'd be friends with
the likes of Milford?"

Ariel glared at her. "I thought you liked Milford."

"I cannot like a man who harbors a murderer in his house."
Mrs. Dobson sniffed. "A man's friends are a reflection of himself."

Her words angered Ariel. "You can't hold Milford responsible for the actions of his friends—he would surely disavow
them if he knew one was guilty. Besides, we don't even know
it is one of his friends. Everyone is a suspect."

"Milford himself might be the one," her aunt said. "I seem to
recall that he was accused of killing someone—"

"That is pure fabrication," Ariel said heatedly.

She wanted to tell Aunt how wrong she was—that Milford
could not be the poisoner, because he was the murderer's target. And wanted to tell her how wrong she was to listen to old
gossip—that Milford had not killed anyone, that he had been
more wronged than wrong.

But she could not, because she had promised to keep the
truth about the poisoner secret. And this was certainly not the
best time to explain Milford's unfortunate past to her aunt.
Later, when this was over and they'd caught the criminal, she
could then show Aunt how Milford's quick thinking had saved
them all. That would make her more willing to look at Milford
in a favorable light.

"They do say that poison is a woman's way," Mrs. Dobson
admitted. "And I certainly would not put it past one of *those*
women to . . ."

"Simply because you do not like them is no cause to accuse
them of poisoning the brandy," Ariel said. "For all we know it
was Blakenose who did it to get rid of the dog."

"No husband would do such a cruel thing to his wife."

"Perhaps *I* did it, then," Ariel said.

"Oh, good gracious, do not be ridiculous." Mrs. Dobson
wrung her hands. "Oh, to think I played whist with Lynnwood
when all the time he might have been plotting to kill me."

"I do not think you should voice those kind of suspicions
aloud," Ariel said.

"If more people spoke out, we might be able to come to an agreement on who the guilty party is."

"I don't want you putting yourself in danger," Ariel said. "If you do accuse the right person, he might decide to make you his next victim."

Aunt paled. "Oh, dear."

Ariel hoped that would keep her quiet for a while. She did not want to listen while Aunt speculated about the possible guilt of every one of the guests.

"I do think we should have some sort of ceremony tonight for that poor little dog," Mrs. Dobson said. "Poor Euphemia was so overset. She cared a great deal for that animal."

"I think she would like that," Ariel said. "Why don't you make some plans? I am sure Milford would not object."

"A hymn or two would be nice," Mrs. Dobson reflected. "Something dealing with the Lord's creatures . . ."

Ariel gave an inward sigh of relief. That would keep her Aunt's mind purposefully occupied for a while. Ariel preferred that she devote her energies to the dog's funeral instead of analyzing each and every guest for their possible criminal propensities.

She hoped Milford was doing the right thing by concentrating on protection instead of trying to find the criminal. But what else could he do? They could tear apart everyone's room, looking for poison, but someone as clever as their villain would not be so foolish as to leave that lying around. No doubt he had a hiding place elsewhere in the house. Or he might have even put it into another guest's room, to throw suspicion on that person.

She realized they might never discover who had poisoned Blinky—and who made the other attempts on Milford's life. But as long as Milford stayed alive, she did not care.

While Aunt scribbled her notes for the funeral plans, Ariel peeked out the door. The hallway was a mass of confusion with people and servants crisscrossing back and forth as they moved luggage and even furniture into the other bedrooms. It was a chaotic scene, and she was glad to be out of it.

Harman stood at the end of a hall like a sentinel.

When she looked out again, the hall was empty. Only Harman remained where he had been. Ariel gave him a quick wave, and he winked.

Suddenly Bates shot out of his room and started pounding on Milford's door. "That damn puppy's bolted," he cried.

Milford flung open his door. "What?"

"Gregson. He's not here."

Milford's eyes narrowed in suspicion. "Now, how did he manage to elude your watchful eye, and that of Harman as well?"

"I don't know," Bates said. "He was here and then said he had to go back to his old room to get something, and I haven't seen him since."

"You let him out of your sight?" Milford glared at him as he strode down the hall toward Gregson's old room. "Didn't I tell you not to let him go anywhere without you? And where's Townsend?"

"He's in Lynnwood's room with that other idiot. This must mean Gregson's our criminal," Bates said. "Why else would he lope off like this?"

Ariel started to follow them down the hall, then remembered that she was supposed to stay with her aunt. She'd have to talk to Milford about that. How could she protect him when she was supposed to have an escort with her all the time?

Milford flung open the other bedroom door and peered inside.

"He's not here," he said grimly.

"What did I tell you?" Bates regarded him eagerly. "I knew it was one of those brats causing all this trouble. Gregson knew you were closing in on him and he bolted."

Ariel did not believe that Gregson was behind this—he had no reason to kill Milford. But he surely had cause to get rid of Blinky; he'd made no secret of his dislike for the dog. Maybe he'd only intended to kill the dog, and it was pure chance that he'd used Milford's brandy.

Even so, it was a reprehensible act, killing a defenseless dog. But Ariel could not quite believe it of him. Locking Blinky in the cellar seemed more his style. But deliberately poisoning the dog? And why use Milford's brandy to do that when there was the danger of Milford or another guest drinking it?

It simply did not make sense.

But why else would Gregson have run away? Unless he feared that Bates was the culprit, and he did not want to be trapped in the same room with him.

She'd wondered if Milford had a reason for pairing people up the way he had. To her, it would have made far more sense to put Lynnwood and Bates together; or even pair them with their respective mistresses. That would have created a far more harmonious situation.

Had Milford mixed things up on purpose to stir the pot and see what surfaced? If so, it looked as if his plan had already borne fruit.

While Milford gathered the others to go in search of Gregson, Ariel went back to her room to sit with Aunt. Let Milford and the others look; she would stay here and try to think through the whole confusing mess once again. Perhaps they had overlooked some significant clue, some small thing that would suddenly make everything clear, something that would help her to keep Milford safe.

After watching Aunt busily working on the funeral plans for an hour, Ariel finally announced they both needed a change of scenery. There had been no word from Milford and Ariel was eager to hear about the progress of the search for Gregson. She persuaded Aunt to venture down to the drawing room.

The three mistresses were there, talking quietly among themselves.

"Have they found any sign of Gregson?" Ariel asked.

Milford's mistress shook her head. "They think he left the house; they are looking outside."

"Do you think that Gregson is the guilty one?" Ariel asked them bluntly.

The women glanced among themselves. "We have been talking," Miss LeDeux said. "That is, we do not think he is clever enough to have planned such a thing."

"Although he did not seem to care much for that dog," Miss Vining added.

"No one cared much for that dog," Miss Baker said with a giggle.

Aunt gave her a repressive look, which she ignored.

"I, for one, am glad he is gone." Miss LeDeux looked at Mrs. Dobson defiantly. "He was a pest."

"If Gregson is not guilty, who do you think is responsible?" Ariel asked.

Miss Baker shrugged. "I don't know."

"I still think it is one of the servants," Miss LeDeux said. "We will awake one morning to find ourselves murdered in our beds."

Ariel smothered a laugh at her contradictory remark.

"I am going to be quite eager to leave this horrid place," Miss Vining said. "I've always thought the country was miserable, and this proves it."

"You are lucky," Miss Baker responded. "I will be marooned here until Milford decides to return to town."

Ariel cast her a sharp glance. After overhearing their conversation last night, Ariel wondered if Milford was so eager to have Miss Baker stay. He might send her packing as soon as the roads cleared. Or was that wishful thinking on Ariel's part? Milford was supposedly sharing a room with Miss Baker, after all. Maybe they had settled their disagreement.

Which was fine with Ariel. What did she care if Milford wished to keep a mistress? Many men did. But that did not explain the guilty pleasure she'd felt last night when she'd listened to them arguing.

"Oh, you can leave with us, Claudia, dear," Miss LeDeux said. "I am sure George would not mind. And it will give me someone to talk to on the journey—he always likes to ride alongside. I find riding alone in the carriage so dull."

"I may agree to that," Miss Baker said.

So, Ariel thought, with an unladylike sense of satisfaction. Perhaps Milford and Miss Baker had not resolved their dispute.

Ariel knew she should not care one way or the other. It was not as if she was trying to attach Milford, despite what Miss Baker thought. Ariel knew all she could hope for was to be his friend. Still, she did not mind if he no longer kept a mistress. It made it all the more likely he would come to town later, and Ariel could do what she needed to restore his good standing in society.

So she could continue to see him.

The door opened, and the men trooped in.

Ariel jumped to her feet, eagerly searching Milford's face for a hint of the outcome. But he only looked tired, discouraged.

"Did you find him?" she asked.

Milford shook his head. "He's obviously bolted—his horse is still here, so he's on foot, but there's no way we can follow. The entry lane is slicker than a skating pond, and under water to boot."

"He won't get far," Bates said. "And when I get my hands on him . . ."

"No one is going to do any more searching," Milford said. "If he is the guilty party, I've accomplished what I intended and we are all safe. If not . . . then everyone here still bears watching."

"Well, I for one don't think he's done a thing," Mallory spoke out in defense of his friend. "I think he's gone for help."

Milford looked irritated. "Well, if he has, we'll find out about it soon enough, won't we? Now, I want to get out of these wet clothes. Gentlemen?"

Grumbling, the other four followed him out of the drawing room.

Aunt clutched Ariel's hand. "And I thought he was such a nice young man. Do you think we are safe now?"

"I think it is premature to think there is no longer any danger," Ariel said carefully. "Until Milford gives the word, I think we should all be on our guard."

Chapter 13

The rest of the afternoon passed with nightmarish slowness for Ariel. All the guests sat in the drawing room, eyeing each other with undisguised suspicion. Bates continued to make snide accusations about Gregson's absence, until Townsend threatened to plant him a facer. Milford was forced to stand between them, threatening to lock one or both of them into the cellar, until they moved to opposite sides of the room.

Even the ladies were unhappy. Mrs. Blakenose had come down for a short time, but after overhearing Mallory's comment of "good riddance" when Blinky's unfortunate demise was mentioned, she began wailing again, and her husband took her back upstairs.

If Gregson had run from fear, Ariel began to think he had the right idea. If she was not so worried about Milford, she would be tempted to leave herself. Anything had to be better than sitting here, waiting for the next horrible thing to happen.

It was a relief to move to the dining room for dinner after staring at the same four walls all afternoon. No one bothered to change their dress. In fact, no one had left the drawing room all afternoon. At least they were listening to Milford's warnings not to let anyone out of their sight. If someone so much as moved in his or her chair, all eyes turned that way.

It was a very subdued group that sat down to dinner. Only Mallory and Bates displayed hearty appetites; most of the others picked at their meal. Even Ariel did not feel much like eating, but she forced herself to, hoping to show everyone that she shared Milford's confidence about the safety of the food. He flashed her a grateful smile more than once.

Even the almond custard served for dessert elicited little enthusiasm from any of the diners.

They rose en masse and returned to the drawing room when the meal ended. The men were not going to linger in private over their brandy and port tonight; any drinking they did would be in the company of the ladies.

Ariel watched as Lynnwood and Townsend settled in one corner, huddled around a bottle of port.

"Should we play cards again?" she asked. They needed to do something to relieve the tedium.

"Who wants to play cards at a time like this?" Mallory grumbled.

"It is better than sitting here staring at the walls," Milford said. "I will play with you, Miss Tennant."

"All right," Townsend said. "I'll join you. We need one other person for whist."

Ariel looked at her aunt. "Will you play?"

Mrs. Dobson nodded and took her place at the table, paired with Townsend. Milford won the deal, and they were three tricks into the game when a scuffling sound came from the hall, followed by a loud thud.

Simon was out of his chair and halfway across the room when the door was flung open and Gregson staggered in. Water dripped from his sodden clothes; his face was ashen, and his chattering teeth echoed loudly.

"There is no escape," he cried, before collapsing on the floor.

Milford knelt beside him. Gregson groaned faintly.

"Brandy," Milford called. Ariel quickly brought a brimming glassful. Giving her an approving smile, he raised the shivering man's head, and she held the glass to Gregson's lips, who managed to take a small swallow.

"Townsend, Bates, take him upstairs." Simon snapped out orders. "Strip off these wet clothes and get him into a hot bath. He's deathly cold. And keep giving him brandy."

Gregson's sudden reappearance shocked the others into activity. As soon as the two men left with Gregson, the questions began.

"What does this mean?" Mrs. Dobson demanded. "Is he our culprit or not?"

"How should I know?" Simon asked wearily. "Until we have a chance to question him, you know as much as I do."

"He said, 'there is no escape,'" Claudia said fearfully. "What does he mean?"

"My guess is that he meant escape from this house," said Ariel. "I think he ran out of fear, then found the conditions impossible for travel."

"Especially on foot," Mallory said, nodding in agreement. "I told you he wasn't guilty of any wrongdoing."

"Then that means that the criminal is still here." Ariel said. "But at least we can exclude Gregson from consideration."

"That narrows the field a good deal," Lynnwood drawled sarcastically.

"If you discount Mrs. Blakenose, who would never have done a thing to hurt her dog, we have eliminated two suspects," Ariel retorted with equal sarcasm.

"I know I'm innocent," Mallory piped in.

Simon gave an exasperated sigh. "Does anyone here wish to publicly proclaim their guilt so we can solve the mystery quickly?"

Lynnwood laughed. "As if anyone would. I fear you are going to have to work a little harder to find the poisoner, Milford."

"Who do you think it is?" Ariel asked him bluntly.

"Your guess is as good as mine." Lynnwood shrugged. "Although, I recall things were peaceful until all the uninvited travelers appeared."

"Are you implying that we . . . ?" Mallory, his fists clenched, took a step toward Lynnwood.

"All I am saying is that these incidents started after the lot of you arrived."

"Which proves nothing," Simon said. "And unless—or until—we catch someone in the act, I do not want any more accusations made. Everyone's nerves are on edge. We have to remain calm."

"Don't see why you're so eager to protect a bunch of strangers," Lynnwood grumbled. "I would think your first loyalty would be to your *friends*."

"If you think I'm going to share a room with you after this . . ." Mallory glared at Lynnwood. "I want a new room-mate."

Simon glared at each man in turn. "I would think you'd both appreciate the opportunity to prove your innocence to each other."

"I *know* I'm innocent," Mallory retorted. "He's the one I'm concerned about."

"You're staying together, and I don't want any more argu-ments," Simon said acidly. "Now, if you can manage to control yourselves for a short while, I wish to go upstairs and speak with Gregson."

He gave them both dark looks and started for the door.

"Aren't you forgetting something, Milford?" Lynnwood de-manded.

Simon paused with his hand on the door latch.

"Your guardian," Lynnwood said. "You don't want to endan-ger yourself by going about the house alone, do you?"

Lynnwood was right. Simon had to play by the same rules as the others, or it would arouse suspicion.

"Come along then," Simon said.

Lynnwood at his side, he hastened up the stairs. Although Simon had not really believed that Gregson was their criminal, he half hoped it was true, if only to bring an end to the fear. But Gregson's dramatic return killed that small hope. Simon was no closer to discovering who was behind the attempts to kill him than before. And if Gregson was to be believed, Simon wasn't going to be able to protect himself by sending the lot of them packing in the morning.

A footman stood guard outside the bedroom door. Simon nodded briefly at him and walked in.

Gregson sat in front of the fire, swathed in a robe and blan-kets. Bates and Townsend regarded each other uneasily from opposite sides of the room.

"This is a jolly-looking group," Simon said.

"He thinks I ran off because I killed the dog," Gregson said, pointing to Bates. "I just wanted to get away from here before I turned up dead."

"How are you feeling?" Simon asked.

"Better." Gregson held up his cup. "Hot tea and brandy—just the thing."

"How far did you get?" Simon asked.

"Not far," Gregson said ruefully. "I was trying to cut across the fields to the road, but I think I ended up going in circles. The snow is still fairly deep where it's drifted. Then I fell in that blasted stream . . ."

"You're lucky you made it back to the house," Simon said.

"Some luck," Gregson grumbled. "With a murderer on the loose."

"The only thing dead so far is the dog, and I intend to keep it that way," Simon said. "As long as everyone acts with caution, you will be safe."

He wished he believed his own words. But Gregson had slipped away so easily it showed that he couldn't fully rely on the others for his safety. All it took was one momentary lapse and someone running loose in the house—and Simon would be in danger again.

Although, with Gregson, Townsend, Bates, Mallory, and Lynnwood at daggers drawn, he doubted those five would have the chance to do anything. They'd watch each other like hawks. That left only the women to pose a threat. Simon would pass the word to Harman to watch them even more carefully.

Simon fully intended to come out of this alive.

His plan had only one flaw, he reflected as he and Lynnwood returned to the drawing room. It was not going to be easy to arrange a private meeting with Ariel. He'd have to find a way to meet with her in the library, where they would be well away from prying eyes. Simon did not want anyone else to know that she was working with him. But he had to speak with her, to see if she'd noticed anything he had not.

Ariel was at first puzzled, then pleased when Harman pulled her aside later that evening and explained Milford's plan to talk with her later. She readily agreed to meet the butler outside her room as soon as her aunt fell asleep.

Unfortunately, without the convivial influence of Mrs. Blakenose, Aunt had not been sipping sherry all evening, and it took some time before she fell into a deep enough slumber so that Ariel felt safe to leave. She'd had to put on her nightclothes and lie down in the dark, listening impatiently for Aunt to start snoring—a sure sign she was asleep.

At last, the snoring began, and Ariel knew she could leave. After wrapping a shawl over her robe, Ariel unlocked the bedroom door. As promised, Harman was waiting for her in the hall.

"I am sorry you had to wait so long," she whispered to him as he led her toward the back stairs. "Aunt simply would not fall asleep."

"I do not mind," Harman replied.

The footman stationed at the top of the rear stairs nodded as they passed.

"This must be a terrible burden for the staff," Ariel said.

"None of us mind," Harman replied. "We wish to keep Lord Milford safe."

"How long have you worked for him?" she asked.

"Seven years," Harman replied.

"Is he happy, do you think?"

She felt Harman's curious gaze upon her. "Happy? That's hard to say, miss. I think 'comfortable' might be a better term."

"He is so unlike his reputation," Ariel said. "I find it puzzling. Why would he want people to think so ill of him when he is so nice?"

"I couldn't say," Harman replied.

"Spoken like a loyal butler," Ariel retorted.

"I think he is not beyond . . . repair," Harman said, halting outside the library door. In the candlelight, she thought there was a look of amusement on his face. "If someone cared to make the effort."

He pulled open the door and stepped aside to let Ariel enter, then closed it behind her.

Milford was leaning against the mantel, a drink in his hand, his expression pensive. He gave her a wan smile.

"I am sorry to be so late," she said. "It took forever for Aunt to fall asleep."

"No harm done." He raised his glass. "Some brandy? I assure you, it has not been poisoned. I've been drinking it all evening to no ill effect."

She nodded. "A small glass."

Ariel followed him to the desk. The remnants of a smashed

porcelain figurine lay atop the polished wood. Ariel picked up one shard. A tiny green leaf was painted on the glazed surface.

"What is this?" she asked.

"It seems there is still a flaw in my plan," he said. He handed her a glass and took her by the arm, leading her to the wing chairs by the fire. "Someone managed to get in here again."

"And smashed this figurine? Are you sure? Could it have happened yesterday, when Blinky was in here?"

He shook his head. "I found the pieces on my desk when I came down here tonight."

Once again, she felt a sharp stab of fear. Was there any way to keep Milford safe. "But how could it have happened? Everyone is being carefully watched."

"That is what I thought. But apparently not carefully enough. Someone had the chance to slip away and do this."

"Why would anyone want to smash a porcelain figure? Merely to show you that they were here?"

"No, the person who did this chose this piece on purpose. They meant this as a message." He paused and took a deep breath. "It belonged to my mother."

"Oh, Milford, how dreadful." She put a hand on his arm, wanting to offer comfort.

"It was the only thing of hers I had, you know." He drained his glass, and for the first time Ariel noticed that his hand was trembling. From the brandy—or the shock? "It used to sit on her dressing table, and I remember being fascinated by it when I was a boy."

"What did it look like?"

"It was rather silly, actually. A lady with a lapful of grapes, feeding one to the gentleman at her side. There was a lamb sitting between them. Not a very realistic scene."

"But still, it belonged to your mother. How old were you when she died?"

"Five," he replied.

Only five. Ariel felt that she understood Milford a great deal better now. Losing a mother at such a young age, always playing second fiddle to his older brother, the heir and his father's favorite. It was easy to see now what had led him into such folly at nineteen.

"Perhaps it can be glued back together," she suggested.

He shook his head. "There is no point. The damage is done. Even if it could be repaired, every time I looked at it I would be reminded of what happened. I'd rather toss the thing on the rubbish heap and forget about it altogether."

Ariel's heart went out to him. For just a moment, he looked like a lost and lonely little boy, and she could almost picture the child he'd been, devastated at the loss of his mother.

And she realized, too, that if she had not been in love with him before, she was now. She wanted to draw him into her arms, to hold his head against her chest and comfort him, to let him know that she understood his feeling of loss.

Yet she feared he would laugh at her—or push her away—if she did. And she would find that devastating. Milford had spent long years building up the walls around him; he was not going to let them fall just because she offered a few sympathetic words. She had to be patient, had to gradually work her way through his defenses—until he could admit that he cared for her.

"You are terribly quiet," he said. "I did not intend to bother you with my troubles."

"It is no bother," she said, forcing a bright smile. "It is only that I am worried about you. This shows that the person has not given up."

"In some ways, I'm glad he hasn't," Milford replied. "As long as he keeps trying to get me, we have a chance to catch him."

"Unless he kills you first," she observed dryly.

"I'm too wicked to die," he said.

"Or too stubborn," she retorted. "Have you considered that Gregson could have done this?"

He shook his head. "He had the opportunity, to be sure. But he had no way of knowing that this belonged to my mother."

"Who did?" she asked.

"I can think of several people," he replied. "Lynnwood, Bates, and Claudia knew. Sarah and Marguerite could have learned of it from them."

"I think you have to consider all five of them as your main suspects."

He looked at her, hollow-eyed. "I know."

"Your mistress might be angry with you," Ariel said, then

held her breath, waiting for his response. "Or one of the other men might want her—and need you out of the way."

Milford laughed sharply. "Anyone is welcome to her. No one has to kill me for that."

"Have you two come to a parting of the ways?" she said, trying to sound disinterested.

"It was time," he said, taking another drink. "I make it a rule never to keep the same woman for longer than three months. They grow tiresome if you allow them to stay longer."

"Or do you get rid of them because you do not want to grow too fond of them?" she asked.

He gave her a sharp look. "I am fond of *all* women, my dear. That is why I court variety."

She felt the sting of his words, but tried to ignore it. He was being deliberately crude. Ariel wondered how much brandy he had drunk before she came down. It only showed how shattered he'd been by the destruction of his mother's china figure. Now he was scrambling to rebuild up his defensive wall by seeking to push her away.

"Did Gregson say what the roads were like?" Perhaps changing the subject would dispel his gloom.

"Miserable. He didn't even make it to the road. As near as I can tell, he floundered around in the snowdrifts for hours, fell into a stream, then staggered back here. He's lucky to be alive."

"Then there is little hope of anyone being able to leave tomorrow."

He laughed bitterly. "I wish there were. I've been thinking of leaving myself."

"What?"

"It seems the best solution. I'm the one who is in danger. Once I am gone, the rest of you are safe. And I'll be safe, too."

"But if the roads are that bad . . ."

"I think I can manage on horseback."

A sudden rush of panic filled her. She did not want Milford to leave, not now. She knew if he did, she might never see him again. But if he was in danger . . .

"What if your leaving angers the person even more? You could be putting the rest of us in danger."

He smiled. "Do you really think that, Ariel?"

She lowered her eyes. "No."

He lifted her chin with his finger so she was gazing into his dark eyes. "Remember who I am, Ariel. Even if I thought that my leaving would endanger the rest of you, do you think that would stop me? I'm the 'black-hearted bastard,' after all. Why should I care?"

"Because despite your protestations, you are a man of honor."

He tossed back his head and laughed. "Your faith in me is sadly misplaced."

"Oh, don't give me that tired story, Milford. You're nothing but a fraud."

"A fraud?"

"You're not a disreputable rake. It's all a sham."

"Why would I wish to pretend to be such a thing?"

"It keeps you from being invited to dull dinner parties."

Milford laughed again. "Caught at last, my secret revealed. Promise you will not tell anyone?"

"Now you're being silly. Pay attention. We have to make plans for tomorrow."

"I'd rather make plans for tonight." He leaned forward and put a hand on her knee. "Ariel, my Ariel, what a trusting soul you are. Here we are, alone in the library, with the rest of the house sleeping soundly. No one would hear if you cried out."

"Why would I wish to do that?"

He leaned closer until his face was only inches from hers. "Why, in pleasure, I hope."

Ariel's stomach did flip-flops as Milford gripped her shoulders, pulling her toward him. He boldly thrust his tongue into her mouth, touching hers, daring her to respond.

She met his challenge, teasing at his tongue with hers, opening her mouth to let him in, to fully taste and feel him. Shivers ran up her arms, and she clutched at him to keep from trembling. Heat flowed through her, and she gave a low moan of delight.

Suddenly, he shoved her away, and she sank back in the chair.

When she opened her eyes, Milford was standing by the desk, calmly pouring himself another glass of brandy.

"You're improving with every lesson," he said, his expression sardonic. "You might actually get rather good at this one of these days."

She knew he was being deliberately cruel, saying these things to push her away. He was afraid of her.

He would not be afraid if he did not care. Ariel realized that Milford wore his mantle of rakishness as a suit of armor, a protection against ever being vulnerable to anyone, or anything, again. But now he'd slammed the wall down, and she would get no more revelations from him tonight.

She was surprised that he had let down his guard as much as he had with her. But of course, to him, she was "safe"—an innocent girl who would have no reason to have any future contact with a rake. Once she left this house, he would find it easy to avoid her. This was a temporary alliance, one he allowed precisely because of the differences in their situations.

And she realized that all her plans for him, her wish to push him back into society, to make him respected and accepted again were because she wanted to find a way to keep him in her life. She did not want to leave here any time soon, fearing once she did, she would never see him again. Even if she could persuade her brother to entertain him, she feared Milford would not think himself suitable for her. He'd pretended to be a heartless rake for so long, he considered himself one, even if that description was far from the truth. But he would use it as an excuse to keep her at arm's length.

Her only hope was to persuade him now, while they were still here and the barriers imposed by society were down, that she loved him.

The next time he took her in his arms, she would show him.

Ariel stood and walked toward the door with as much dignity as she could muster. "Good night, Milford."

Harman was waiting outside. Silently, she followed him back upstairs.

The moment she left, Simon berated himself for his boorish behavior. He shouldn't have told her about his mother. By letting her glimpse that weakness, he'd given Ariel another reason to feel sympathy for him. And he did not deserve it.

He did not fear that she would expose him to others; he merely disliked the idea of anyone knowing his secrets. He had kept them to himself for so long it made him feel naked and defenseless, knowing that she knew them, too.

He had to stop confiding in her. But somehow, when she looked at him with those bright blue eyes, something within melted, and he wanted to tell her everything.

And then regretting it, he lashed out at her because he was angry with himself. Like tonight, when he'd so callously made love to her, then deliberately insulted her and drove her away.

He would be on his guard against her in the future—no more intimate discussions. They'd never even talked about the problem of the poisoner, or how they would ever catch the villain tonight. He'd been so stunned at the destruction of his mother's precious figurine that he'd started talking and hadn't stopped until he chased her back upstairs.

He knew he had to gain some control over himself, or he was going to make some dreadful mistake. He did not want to cause her harm.

Chapter 14

In the morning, after breakfast, all the guests gathered in the drawing room for Blinky's funeral service. Ariel contrived to stand next to Milford, in hope she could share a word with him. After last night, she did not know what, or if, he would say to her today.

Mrs. Blakenose had been overcome with delight when Aunt asked her about holding the service, as Ariel had suspected she would be. It was a small thing to do to make the woman feel better.

And perhaps the person responsible would show a flash of guilt as he stood among the mourners—or at least frustration at knowing that the real target, Milford, had escaped.

"This is a solemn occasion . . ." Aunt intoned. Only the "sadly shocking" absence of a prayer book in Milford's house prevented her from reading the Office.

"Occasion for relief is more like it," Gregson said in an undertone.

Ariel stepped on his toe. "Be quiet," she hissed.

"Nobody liked that dog," he protested.

"You can force yourself to pretend for five minutes," she whispered back.

"Children, children." Milford's tone was chiding. "Please maintain the proper decorum suitable to such a solemn occasion."

"And now I would like each of you to say a few words about Blinky." Mrs. Dobson gave them an encouraging smile.

Ariel stared in dismay at her aunt. Didn't she know what a

disaster that would be? Gregson was already ducking behind Milford, hoping to be overlooked.

Miss Baker stepped forward. "He was a cute little doggy. His fur was so soft."

"And brown," Townsend called out. "With a bit of black mixed in."

"And he had such an enthusiastic appetite," Mallory said. Ariel saw that he was struggling to keep a straight face. "He would eat anything."

"Which was his downfall," Gregson muttered.

"He had such a fondness for his mistress," Bates said loudly.

Ariel touched Milford's arm. "Do you think we need to gag Gregson?"

He shook his head. "Let the young man hang himself."

"I notice you haven't offered your words of praise yet."

He grinned at her. "Oh, I'm grateful to Blinky. If he hadn't got himself locked in the cellar, we would have missed that opportunity to be alone together."

She felt a faint blush rise to her cheeks.

Milford leaned closer, whispering in her ear. "I feel I owe Blinky a great debt. That was our first kiss, after all."

"I dare you to announce *that* to my aunt," she retorted.

"Ariel dear?" Aunt was looking at her suspiciously. "Did you have something to say?"

"Blinky was . . . the kind of dog every person would want to own," she stammered out. Aunt nodded approvingly.

"Liar," Milford whispered, then grinned at her. He stepped forward. "Blinky was the kind of dog that was always noticed, wherever he went. He had a . . . presence that could not be overlooked."

"Very nice," Ariel murmured.

"I can be nice—when I try." He winked at her.

After a desultory rendition of "All Creatures Great and Small," which was accompanied by Mrs. Blakenose quietly sobbing in her handkerchief, the tribute to Blinky ended.

Not a moment too soon, in Ariel's mind, for she saw the gleam of mischief in Gregson's eyes and feared he would do something to upset the chief mourner. Blakenose led his grieving wife back to her room, and Aunt accompanied them.

Milford looked relieved when they left. "Thank God that's over."

"Surprised she didn't have the thing laid out on a bier in front of the room," Mallory said. "What does she intend to do with the body? Have it stuffed?"

"I believe the animal will have its final resting place somewhere in my garden," Milford said. "Once the snow melts."

"I bet she'll take it with her," Gregson said. "Can you imagine traveling with a dead dog? She's the type who'd keep it in the carriage with her, too."

Ariel glanced at Milford, who was fighting back a laugh. He caught her gaze, and a moment of shared amusement passed between them. She dared to hope that he was regretting his words from last night and would offer his apologies.

But then he turned away and sought out Townsend in the far corner of the room.

Ariel realized she could not expect Milford to let down his guard in such a public place. She needed to get him alone again. She realized that only then did she have the chance to convince him that he was worthy in her eyes.

Blinky's funeral had provided a grand diversion, but with it over, Ariel feared they were doomed to spend another tension-filled afternoon in the drawing room. She must find something to divert attention from their plight.

"Cards?" she suggested. No one looked enthused. "Charades? Storytelling? There must be something we can all do to keep our mind off things."

"Nothing's going to keep my mind off the fact that there's a murderer loose in the house," Bates said bluntly. "I think we should find out who it is."

"And how do you propose to do that?" Gregson demanded.

"Search everyone's room, for one."

"Search for what?" Gregson asked. "Anyone with half a brain would have disposed of the poison already."

"We might find something suspicious," Bates said. "Enough to show who's behind all this."

"You forget that we all changed rooms," Townsend said. "Everyone's things are all jumbled together."

"Well, I know what was in my room before *he* moved in." Bates gave Gregson a disparaging look.

Ariel didn't think they would accomplish anything by searching, but at least it would give them something to do besides sitting and staring daggers at each other. She glanced at Milford, whose face was set in a dark scowl. Clearly, he did not approve of the idea. But on the mere chance that they might find a clue, Ariel decided to support Bates's suggestion.

"I think it's a good idea," she said. Milford gave her a disappointed look.

"We must do this in an organized manner," Lynnwood said. "Move from one room to the other, in sequence. And search the empty rooms as well."

"I don't think—" Milford began, but he was cut off.

"A good idea," Bates said. "I volunteer to be part of the search committee."

"Me, too," Gregson cried.

Milford held up his hand. "This is ridiculous. There is no need to search anyone's room. You won't find anything."

"We want to search," Lynnwood insisted.

"Even if you find something, how will it prove anything?" Milford asked. "The guilty person could have hidden it among anyone's things to divert suspicion."

"I still say we search," Bates said. "I'll feel a great deal better if we find nothing at all."

"Who is going to conduct this search?" Mallory asked. "Lynnwood can't look through his own things."

"You will have to take turns," Milford said, bowing to the pressure. "Townsend and I can search the room you share with Lynnwood; you three can search Bates's. Miss Tennant, would you and your aunt be willing to help by searching the Blakenoses' chamber? And allow them to search yours?"

Ariel nodded.

"I want to help in this searching," Marguerite said. "I love to look through gentlemen's clothing!"

Milford directed a look at the ceiling. "You and Sarah can help search Gregson, Townsend, and Bates's room, if they do not object."

"Only if they can search our room in exchange," Sarah said with a giggle.

Ariel struggled to suppress a laugh. This was becoming high entertainment, rather than a search for a killer. But it gave everyone the diversion they needed.

"That leaves Claudia." Milford looked at his mistress. "Will you allow me to conduct that search?"

"No," she said coldly. "I want someone else to look."

"What about your room, Milford?" Lynnwood demanded. "Who is going to search there?"

"You can all look if you want," Milford said.

"I will," Claudia said, tossing Milford an acid look.

"What if someone doesn't search thoroughly enough and misses something?" Mallory asked.

"Do you want to personally supervise each search?" Milford demanded sarcastically.

Mallory reddened. "No."

"Then you will have to take that chance," Milford said and stood. "Let's go and get this over with."

They all trooped up the stairs, then split up into groups to conduct their separate searches.

Ariel suggested to her aunt that they should only make the most perfunctory inspection of the Blakenoses' room.

"I thoroughly agree," Mrs. Dobson said. "It's not as if we hope to find anything among their things. I do not wish to disturb Euphy."

"I doubt either she or her husband wish to search our room either," Ariel said. "We can get through the whole process quickly, and then you two can have a nice chat."

Aunt nodded approvingly at that idea.

Ariel wished she'd been among those opting to search Milford's room. She wanted to look through his things.

She feared from the cool way he regarded her today that he was regretting his candor of the previous evening. Why was he so afraid to reveal himself to anyone? Surely, he did not think she could hurt him with her new knowledge? In fact, she found his revelations nearly as painful to her as they must be to him. They only made her care for him more and increased her determination to restore his good name.

Because then he would not think himself unworthy of her.

After their desultory inspection of the Blakenoses' room, Ariel and her aunt stood by while the other two quickly looked around their room. Mrs. Blakenose continually exclaimed her admiration for Aunt's possessions and her excellent taste. Ariel and Mr. Blakenose exchanged a knowing glance. The women would soon be settling in for a comfortable coze.

Ariel heard loud thumping and bumping from the next room and realized the searchers must be in Milford's chamber. It sounded as if they were moving every piece of furniture. *Poor Milford! This must be a sad blow to his dignity.*

She'd seen the glee with which Claudia had asked to search his room. No doubt she'd enlisted several others to help her. She was certainly having her revenge on Milford.

Simon stood by impassively, watching while Claudia ordered her assistants to wreak havoc with his room. Inwardly, he was seething, but was not going to give her the satisfaction of knowing that. He knew his indifference would only infuriate her further.

When order had been restored, they trooped back into the hall.

"Is everyone satisfied with the search?" Simon asked.

"Where's Mallory?" Gregson demanded, looking around anxiously for his friend.

Everyone immediately glanced around, scanning the hall for the missing man.

"He was here just a minute ago," Townsend said. He stared at Lynnwood. "Wasn't he with you? Where did he go?"

Lynnwood eyed Townsend with distaste. "I cannot help it if the young cur eluded me. Maybe *he* is the guilty one and fled."

"Never," Gregson said.

"Might he have decided to try the roads today?" Ariel asked.

Gregson shook his head. "Not Mallory. He hates to go out if there's a light breeze."

"This is the second time we've lost someone," Simon said, his anger growing. "Is anyone taking my warnings seriously?"

"He could not have gotten far," Townsend said. "Let's go look for him."

"I want to help," Ariel said.

Simon smiled at her. She was the one bright spot in this miserable day. He wished he could forget all about poisoners and missing persons and merely sit with her in front of the library fire. But duty came first.

He gave her a warm smile. "You can come with Townsend and me, Miss Tennant. Gregson, you, Lynnwood, and Bates check the main floor. Blakenose, if you would escort the ladies downstairs to the drawing room and remain with them. Everyone stay together!"

As the group split up, Simon could not help but remember the last time they'd embarked on a search like this. Then, they'd found Blinky in the wine cellar. Would they find Mallory in a similar situation, the victim of one more practical joke? Or was he in more serious danger?

They started with Gregson's room. While Simon looked in the clothespress, Ariel glanced under the bed. No Mallory.

It took little time to look in the rest of the rooms, but he was not there either.

"What now?" Townsend asked.

"We'll try the ground floor," Simon said. "Although I doubt he would be down there; the servants would have seen him."

They started down the back stairs.

"Wait a moment," Ariel said when they reached the landing. A small alcove stood off to one side, a door at its end. "What's this?"

"The linen closet, I believe," Simon said. He tried the door, but it was locked. He pulled a ring of keys from his pocket and tried several in the door before he found one that fit. He pulled open the door.

Ariel gave a startled gasp and jumped back as Mallory fell to the floor at her feet.

Simon pressed fingers to the side of his neck. "He's not dead." He ran his fingers through the man's hair, feeling a large knot at the back of his head. "He's been hit on the head. Looks like someone knocked him out and put him here."

"But why?" Ariel asked.

"He probably knows who the killer is," Townsend said excitedly.

"Why would he have left Mallory alive, then?" Ariel asked. "That does not make sense if he could identify the killer."

"Perhaps he was about to spot him and was knocked out to prevent it," Townsend said.

"Or else he was merely an innocent victim put here to create confusion while some other mischief is afoot. Townsend, you stay here with him. Ariel, come with me." He grabbed her by the hand, and they raced down the stairs.

"But everyone is together in groups," she said. "No one will be able to do anything."

"I no longer have any faith in these people's ability to pay close attention to what others are doing. Look how easily both Gregson and Mallory vanished."

"Plus the villain," Ariel said. "He had time to knock Mallory out, stuff him in that closet, and get back upstairs."

Simon stopped briefly at the bottom of the steps and rang the bell for Harman, then pulled Ariel off toward the front of the house. When they reached the main hall, he halted. "Do you hear anyone?"

She shook her head. "Where are the others?"

The entire house was silent. Too silent.

"I want you to go to the drawing room," he said quickly.

"No. I'm not going to leave you alone."

Simon was not going to argue with her now. They had to find the other searchers. He grabbed her hand and hurried toward the rear stairs leading down to the kitchen.

"It sounds like they're down here," Ariel said.

They burst through the kitchen doors, to find Bates, Lynnwood, and Gregson standing around the table, a plate of tea cakes before them. Gregson was stuffing one into his mouth.

"Any luck?" Bates asked.

"We found him," Milford replied grimly. "Knocked unconscious and stuffed in a closet."

"What!" Gregson started to tear out of the room, but Lynnwood grabbed him by the coattails.

"You're not going anywhere," he growled.

"Where's Townsend?" Lynnwood asked.

"I left him guarding Mallory," Simon replied. "I want everyone back in the drawing room. Now."

They all trooped up the stairs.

Simon drew Ariel aside before she went into the room. "Will your aunt be willing to act as nurse for Mallory? I don't think he will need special care, but he should not be left alone."

"Will she be safe?"

Simon frowned. One middle-aged woman was little protection against this determined villain.

"I'll have Blakenose and Mallory's friends sit watch," he said.

"I can help," Ariel offered.

"No, I want you to stay with the others. I need you to watch them when I cannot."

He pulled open the drawing room door and walked in.

"We've found Mallory," he said curtly. "He is injured. Mrs. Dobson, would you be willing to offer your assistance? He needs a watchful eye for a few hours, at least."

"Of course," Mrs. Dobson replied, looking stunned.

"Someone conked him on the head," Gregson announced. "I want to know how he is."

"He was alive the last time I saw him," Milford said. "Which is more than I can promise for any of you if you so much as take a step outside this drawing room. This is not a game. Someone here is trying to hurt us. And unless you fully cooperate and keep together, no one is going to be safe."

He quickly left the room, with Ariel and her aunt following.

"Is the poor boy badly hurt?" Mrs. Dobson asked.

"He's unconscious with a good-size lump on his head," Simon said. "But I do not think it is too serious. In any case, we can't send for the surgeon. We shall have to tend to him the best we can."

They went up the rear stairs. Simon felt relief when he saw Townsend was still sitting beside his friend. He half expected to find some new disaster awaiting him.

"Any change?" Simon asked.

"He's moaned a few times."

"Good—that means he's coming around. I want to get him upstairs into bed. Do you think the two of us can manage him?"

Townsend scrambled to his feet. "Yes."

It was a struggle to get the semiconscious man up the stairs. But at last they reached the bedroom corridor. They half walked, half dragged him to the room. While the ladies waited in the hall, Townsend and Simon stripped the injured man and tucked him into bed. Then Simon called the ladies in.

"There is little you need do until he regains consciousness,"

Simon told Mrs. Dobson. "When he does, ring for Harman immediately."

"How are we going to catch the person who did this?" Townsend demanded.

"Very carefully," Simon replied. "I want you to remain here with Mrs. Dobson. I don't want her and Mallory left alone."

"I want to look for the criminal!" Townsend protested.

"I will see that you are relieved later," Milford said. "I think the Blakenoses will be willing to help with his care. Lock the door after we leave."

He smiled at Mrs. Dobson. "I will see that your niece gets back to the drawing room safely."

For once, the woman was at a loss for words. She merely nodded and took a seat beside the bed.

Simon waited outside the door until he heard Townsend turn the key in the lock. Then he and Ariel started down the back stairs again, stopping at the landing where they'd found Mallory.

"This is as safe a place as any." He sat on the steps and ran a hand through his hair. "This is going from bad to worse."

"Our list of suspects is narrowing." Ariel sat beside him. "Shouldn't Lynnwood have been with Mallory? He could have done this."

Simon shook his head. "In that confusion upstairs, anyone could have slipped away."

"Perhaps when Mallory regains consciousness he might be able to tell us something."

Milford shook his head. "I hope he cannot—else he is in real danger. I suspect he was taken by surprise."

"We have to catch this person," Ariel said. "Before someone else is hurt."

"I am going to set a trap," Simon said. "If I am the real target, using myself as bait will lure our villain out."

"Milford, that's too dangerous! He's already tried to kill you. And poor Mallory shows that he's not concerned about hurting anyone else, either."

"Do we spend the rest of our days cowering in our rooms? We don't have any choice." His mouth was set in a grim line. "I'm the one he wants, and I have to make him come after me."

"How?"

He'd been forming his plan all morning, hoping he would not have to use it. But his hand had been forced. "I plan to announce this evening that I know who the culprit is and will be sending for the magistrate in the morning. He'll have no choice but to come after me."

"Milford!" She grabbed his arm. "He wants to kill you. You can't put yourself in so much danger."

"How else are we going to catch him? Now that he's attacked Mallory, we know no one is safe. We have to get our hands on him."

"What about Mallory? Won't this put him in more danger, too?"

"He will be well guarded," Simon said.

"Milford, I don't think you should say anything. Let this person get away. Don't put yourself in danger."

He shook his head. "I'm not going to let a madman run riot in my house."

Ariel touched his cheek. "Promise me you will be careful."

She spoke as if his life mattered to her. She was wrong, of course, but her concern touched him. He only wished he was worthy of it.

He quickly stood up and pulled her to her feet. "I'm taking you back to the drawing room, and then I'm going to set this plan into motion," he said. "Whatever you do, do not go anywhere by yourself."

"No one is going to do anything to me," she said.

"And I intend to make sure of it." He had to convince her to be careful. "This is no game, Ariel. I'd never forgive myself if anything happened to you."

He put his hands on her shoulders, pulling her toward him for one swift kiss. No matter what happened to him, he intended to make sure that she was safe—even if he had to sacrifice himself to do it.

Chapter 15

The fear that had been growing in Ariel for the last few days held her firmly in its grip. No matter how she tried to push it away, she could not free herself from it. Milford intended to risk his life tonight, and she had to stand by and watch him do it.

Each time he came into the drawing room during the course of the afternoon, her breath caught, fearing he would now make his announcement. But as yet he had said nothing. She watched him for any sign of his intentions, but he looked remarkably calm—far calmer than she felt.

Of course, he didn't want to reveal his plan too soon. The less time the criminal had to plan his revenge, the better it was for Milford. Still, she wished he would give up his plan altogether. It was just too dangerous.

She glanced around the drawing room. Lynnwood and Bates sat huddled in the corner, talking and drinking. The three mistresses had banded together and chatted among themselves. Only Gregson paid Ariel the least bit of attention, and all he could talk about was Mallory, fretting over his condition.

"Why don't we go upstairs and see how he is?" she finally suggested.

"Milford ordered me to stay here with you," he grumbled.

"He only said I wasn't to go anywhere by myself," Ariel replied. "Besides, I want to see how my aunt is faring. She may be weary of sitting at his beside all afternoon."

Gregson stood and darted an apprehensive glance at the two men on the far side of the room, as if he expected them to stop him from leaving. Ariel started for the door, and he scurried after her.

Townsend was just coming out of Mallory's room when they reached the floor.

"How is he?" Ariel asked.

"He's got the devil of a headache," Townsend replied.

"He is awake?" Gregson asked.

"Oh, he's been awake for hours."

Trust Milford not to say a word and let them worry. But Ariel realized he was protecting Mallory from his attacker.

"Did he say what happened?" Gregson demanded eagerly. "Who clobbered him over the head?"

"He hasn't a clue," Townsend said. "Whoever did it crept up behind him and took him down before he knew anything was amiss."

"Is my aunt still sitting with him?" Ariel asked.

Townsend nodded. "She and Mrs. Blakenose are vying among themselves to see who can take the better care of him."

"Poor Mallory." Ariel felt doubly sorry for him, knowing how stifling her aunt's attentions could be.

"We've got to find the person responsible for this," Gregson said.

"I believe Milford has a plan," Townsend said.

Ariel stared at him. Had Milford told him what he intended to do?

"I don't think Milford's that interested in catching the fellow," Gregson mumbled. "He's only trying to protect his friends."

"We still do not know who did this," Ariel said. "It could have been any one of us."

"Mallory didn't hit himself over the head," Gregson said.

"Then he is the one person whose innocence we can be certain of. And Milford."

"And the three of us," Townsend said.

Ariel glanced at him sharply. "Can you be sure? How do you know I didn't do it?"

"But you couldn't . . ." Townsend's voice trailed off.

"Because I'm female?"

"No. You aren't the type of person to do that sort of thing."

"She has to be innocent," Gregson said. "Remember, she and

Milford were locked in the cellar together. She couldn't have done that to herself."

"Thank you for your confidence," Ariel said. "I think we should all go back downstairs. I don't feel comfortable being away from the drawing room for very long. I want to know where everyone is at all times."

"Agreed." Townsend and Gregson fell in step beside her.

They met Milford and Miss Vining at the top of the stairs.

"How is our patient?" he asked.

"Being cosseted and petted by his two nurses," Townsend said.

"Is Blakenose there as well?" Milford asked.

Townsend nodded. "I would not have left the ladies alone."

"Good. Take Miss Tennant and Sarah back to the drawing room; it is nearing time for dinner. I will be down with the others shortly."

"What about Mallory?" Gregson asked. "He isn't going to want dinner."

"That is what I am going to arrange," Milford said. "If the Blakenoses are willing to stay with him, I will have their dinner sent up on trays."

It was obvious to Ariel that Milford was not taking any chances with Mallory; he would be well protected. She only prayed Milford would take the same care for his own safety.

At least he had not come upstairs alone—not that she thought Miss Vining offered him much protection. But as long as he had someone with him, he would be safe enough.

Until tonight.

The tension during dinner that night was palpable. Everyone was on edge; Miss Vining was being openly rude to Miss LeDeux, and even she was ignoring Gregson's halfhearted attempts to get up a flirtation. Lynnwood and Bates merely glared at everyone who attempted to start a conversation with them.

If not for the reassurance of seeing Milford sitting safely at the head of the table, Ariel would rather have dined upstairs with her aunt.

Her own nerves were rubbed raw waiting for Milford to make his announcement. She wanted the chance to watch everyone's faces when he told them his news, to gauge everyone's reaction. She was not naive enough to think that the criminal would give himself away with a look, but she might be able to notice something in a reaction. But all through dinner, Milford carried on in a normal manner. Only a slight tightness around the corners of his eyes told her that he, too, was tense and on edge.

When the others returned to the drawing room after dinner, Simon remained behind in the dining room for a few minutes. He wanted to fortify his courage with a drop of brandy before he set in motion a series of events that he was not altogether certain he could control.

Of Mallory's safety, he had little concern. There were at least two people in the room with him at all times, and the door was locked. No one was going to get into that room without attracting a great deal of attention.

No, Simon knew he would be the only one in danger. And no matter how well he and Harman had planned, there were still numerous things that could go wrong. They could not know for certain what the attacker would do; they could only react to his moves. And if their reactions were off . . . well, the kingdom might soon hold one less earl.

He drank his brandy, set the glass down on the table, and walked toward the door. He may as well get this over with. The longer he waited, the worse he felt. At least once he set his plan in motion, the waiting would be over. And after tonight, he hoped his worries would be as well.

Everyone looked up with alarm when he entered the drawing room, as if the events of the last few days had led them to expect disaster at every turn. He hoped that what he said now would allay everyone's fears—everyone except the person behind it all.

"I have good news," Milford said, trying to force a smile onto his face.

"Mallory is better?" Townsend asked.

"The roads are clear?" Gregson looked hopeful.

"Even better." Milford looked at them all, trying to spot a look of malice or apprehension in someone's eye. They looked expectant and eager, or apprehensive, but not guilty. "I know who is responsible for all the unfortunate events of the last few days."

"What?" Bates jumped to his feet. "Who is it?"

"Where is he?" Gregson demanded, scanning the room.

Simon held up his hand for silence. "Tomorrow, weather permitting, I hope to bring the magistrate here, and I will lay the matter before him."

"Tell us now," Lynnwood demanded angrily. "Do you expect us to spend another night fearing for our lives?"

"I do not think anything else will happen," Milford said. "After all, now that I know who is responsible, I know who to guard against."

"Lock the fellow up until the magistrate decides what to do with him," Gregson said.

"I want to give him a chance," Milford said. "If he is the gentleman I think he is, he will take the opportunity to depart during the night."

"But he'll get away with everything then," Townsend protested.

Simon shrugged. "It is possible that the magistrate will decide that I do not have enough proof to justify my accusation."

Townsend glanced uneasily around the room. "You want him to escape," he said.

If only it were that easy, Simon thought. He'd be overjoyed if the criminal fled in the night. But Simon feared there would be one last attempt to kill him, before he could tell the authorities what he knew. And that was when he would catch the culprit—if he didn't die in the process.

"I think you are being very generous," Ariel said. "He should be charged for his crimes."

"Why do we need a magistrate?" Bates asked. "We could take care of him here, ourselves."

"That is exactly why I am not going to tell you the name," Milford said. "I do not want anyone thinking they can deal with this themselves."

"Does this mean we don't have to go about in groups anymore?" Gregson asked.

"You are probably safe," Simon said. "Although I would still lock your door this night."

"Can we move back to our old rooms?" Gregson asked, giving Bates a dark look.

Simon threw up his hands, as if in irritation, although this was exactly what he wanted them to do. Tonight he wanted the guilty person to have full freedom of movement. Either to flee or to attack. "Do what you want."

"I'll be moving my things then," Gregson said and headed for the door.

"I'll give you a hand," Townsend said.

"I don't know that I wish to sleep alone." Sarah gave Bates a pointed glance. "I am still afraid."

"I will make certain that you are safe," he said.

Perfect, Simon thought. Now everyone was back in separate bedrooms. The stage was set for tonight's adventure. He only hoped it would turn out equally as well as this first part of his plan.

The atmosphere in the drawing room brightened after Milford's announcement. Ariel could feel the tension evaporate with every breath. And the guilty person, whoever he was, looked as calm and relaxed as the others.

Gregson and Townsend must have taken the news to Mallory's room, for after a short while the Blakenoses came downstairs.

"I left those nice young men sitting guard with your aunt," Mrs. Blakenose told Ariel. "She intends to stay with poor Mr. Mallory until midnight, then I will be with him during the night."

"I can help," Ariel said.

"Nonsense. We are managing quite well. It makes me feel useful to have something to do . . . and it is easier to forget my dear Blinky when I am concerned about another."

Blakenose looked at the earl.

"What's this I hear, Milford? You know who's behind these deeds?"

Milford nodded.

"Can't see why you're keeping it quiet," Blakenose said. "Ought to hang the fellow from the chimney."

"I think everything will become clear in the morning," Milford replied.

Harman brought the tea tray and dessert, but Ariel found she had no appetite for sweets. She only wanted this night to be over, to know that Milford had survived it unscathed.

She truly did not care if he caught the person who was trying to kill him. Was that what he was hoping, too, with all his remarks about the culprit fleeing in the night? It would be a welcome end to an awkward situation—and one that wouldn't put him in danger.

While Mrs. Blakenose went upstairs to rest, her husband, Lynnwood, Miss Vining, and Miss LeDeux played a few hands of whist. Ariel could not quell her nervousness, no matter how hard she tried. She was too worried about Milford.

She wished she could go upstairs, crawl into bed, and sleep through the night, to awake and find everything all right in the morning. But she knew she was not going to be able to sleep a wink tonight, wondering and worrying.

At half past eleven, the guests began to drift off to bed. Gregson and Townsend came back down for a short while, to report that Mallory was feeling better, then they left again, followed by Miss Baker and Miss LeDeux. Despite Milford's assurances, Ariel noticed that everyone was still staying in groups.

When Miss Vining and Bates rose, Ariel asked if she could walk upstairs with them. Milford gave her an encouraging smile as she left the drawing room.

Mrs. Dobson was still sitting with Mallory and the Blakenoses when Ariel looked in on her. After saying good night, she and Aunt went to their own room.

"How is he?" she asked her aunt.

"The poor lad has a terrible headache, but he is doing better. He was able to take a bit of broth." Aunt shook her head. "Who would do a thing like that to such a nice young man?"

Ariel smothered a smile. Aunt's opinion of Mallory had certainly improved since he'd been relegated to her care.

She prepared a soothing tisane for her aunt, then sat reading to her at the bedside until Aunt's eyes drifted shut.

Ariel tiptoed around the room, picking up clothes that needed to be put back into their trunks. She carefully folded Aunt's things and put them away, then turned to her own trunk. She undid the latch and lifted the lid.

She gasped. Someone had been in her trunk! All her things were in a jumble. She lifted out the crumpled dress that lay on top, then sank to her knees. The dress had been shredded to ribbons.

Ariel stuffed a fist against her mouth to keep from screaming. This was not some simple prank. It was a cruel, mean attack.

She fought her urge to run into the hall and cry for assistance. It would be of no use; the damage had been done. It would only alarm everyone and no doubt give some sick delight to the person who'd done this.

Hastily, she looked through the rest of her trunk, confirming her worst fears. Nearly every item of her clothing had been damaged, most beyond any repair. Dresses, chemises, stockings were all slashed. Ariel realized that only the clothes she wore were undamaged.

Milford would be livid when he found out. She wanted to run to him, to be held in his arms until he soothed her fears away, but she was too afraid to leave her room. She would wait for him here. Surely, with his plans for tonight, he would be coming upstairs shortly.

Carefully, Ariel unlocked the door that led to his room and peered inside. Everything looked peaceful, undisturbed. She set her candle down on the bedside table and sat down to wait.

Please let him come soon.

"Seems to me that you're taking a bit of a gamble, Milford."

Only Lynnwood and Simon remained in the drawing room, sharing a last glass of brandy before bed.

"Why?" Simon asked.

"Announcing that you know who the fellow is. What's to keep him from silencing you during the night?"

"Luck?" Simon laughed hollowly. "I'm not very worried. I think this man will take off, now that he knows the game is up."

"Oh?"

Simon nodded. "It's the way of a coward, and that's what this fellow is. Mark my words, there'll be one less person in the house come morning."

"I hope you're right." Lynnwood grimaced. "This has been a damnable week."

"Not exactly what we were expecting from a quiet sojourn in the country." Simon lifted his glass in a mock toast. "Here's hoping that matters will get back to normal tomorrow."

"Will you still be sending for the magistrate in the morning?" Lynnwood asked. "Even if the fellow bolts?"

"Of course," Simon said. "Running during the night will only confirm his guilt. If he stays, I'm confident I have enough evidence to lay before the magistrate. This criminal won't be able to brazen it out."

"So everything should be resolved by tomorrow."

"That's my plan." Simon drained his glass and stood. If he expected his man to make a move tonight, he needed to pretend to retire. No one would dare to try anything until he thought the household was asleep.

"I'm going to turn in," he said. "Tomorrow's going to be a tedious day."

"I'll go on up as well," Lynnwood said. "Still don't like going about by myself."

Simon snuffed out the candles, then walked upstairs with his friend, saying good night in the hall. Then Simon unlocked his bedroom door and walked into the room.

Ariel sat on the bed, her face ashen white, a bundle of clothing clutched in her arms. He quickly shut and locked the door and rushed to her side. She wouldn't be here unless something was terribly wrong.

"What is it?" he demanded.

She held up what he recognized as the green dress she'd worn to dinner the previous evening. It was in ruins, the fabric slashed and torn.

Tears welled in her eyes. "Oh, Milford, I am so scared."

He pulled her into his arms. "It is all right," he said in soothing tones. "I won't let anyone hurt you."

He held her tightly until she stopped trembling, then held her longer, because she felt so good in his arms.

"What happened?" he asked finally.

"The trunk . . . all my clothes . . ." Her voice broke. "Everything is ruined."

Simon swore under his breath. This was all his fault. Someone had been watching him too closely, knew that he and Ariel had a . . . a friendship. They had destroyed her things, but the message had been directed at him. Was it meant as a warning— or a threat?

He clutched her tighter. Clothes could be easily replaced. A

human life could not. Simon fought back his anger. He needed
to keep a cool head tonight. His life—and now, maybe hers—
depended on it. "When did you look in the trunk last?"

"Right after dinner. I came up to get my shawl."

"Damn." That meant this had been done *after* he made his
announcement, after he'd claimed he knew the identity of the
criminal. This had been the response. And instead of striking
back at Simon, he'd taken the coward's way and attacked
Ariel—as if he'd known that it would enrage Simon even more.
As if he knew what Ariel meant to him.

Good God, what had he done? He'd never thought to put her
into danger. It was the last thing he wanted. She was too precious, too valuable, too . . .

Simon suddenly found it very difficult to breathe. He felt the
soft, feminine form pressed against him, felt the sudden warmth
that flamed from every point where their bodies touched. He
was suddenly dizzy with need and want for this mischievous
girl who'd delved her way into his heart.

His heart. Simon was not supposed to have a heart. He was
the black-hearted bastard. Women were only meant to be ob-
jects of his lust, not his affection. Affection meant . . . caring.
And caring meant . . . pain.

He realized with sickening clarity that he cared a great deal
about Ariel Tennant. Cared far more than he should—or wanted
to. He had no right. She was all sweetness and innocence—
everything that he was not.

And now, because he'd dared to think that he could care for
her, he'd pulled her down with him, threatening the very innocence he'd fallen in love with.

Love. An emotion Simon had always thought he was inca-
pable of feeling. What bitter irony to discover that he could
love—but a woman he should not, dared not want.

Slowly, regretfully, he released her.

"I want you to go back to your room," he said. "Lock all the
doors and put some furniture—a chair or a table—in front of
them. Make it impossible for anyone to slip in without waking
you."

He felt under the mattress for the pistol he had hidden there
and handed it to her.

Ariel paled when she saw what he held in his hand.

"Do you really think I need that?"

"I would rather you had it and didn't need it, than need it and not have it," he said. "Do you know how to shoot?"

She nodded, and he forced a smile.

"I thought you might. Did your brother teach you?"

Ariel nodded again. "But what will you use to protect yourself?"

"The other pistol is downstairs," he said. "Along with Harman and the shotgun. You needn't worry about me."

"I want to worry about you." Her blue eyes filled with concern.

"I will be all right." He pulled her to her feet. "I want you to get into that room and barricade yourself inside. And do not come out until I tell you it is safe!"

"Where are you going to be?"

"In the library. I've gone to a lot of trouble to arrange this charade. Now I have to see that it bears fruit."

She flung her arms around him, hugging him tight. "Please be careful."

He stroked her hair. He wanted to bury his fingers in those golden curls, to hold her close and stay here in this room, where they were both safe.

But if he intended to keep her safe in the future, he had to go downstairs this night.

Simon stepped back and lifted her chin with his finger. He saw the tears glistening in her eyes.

"Nothing will happen to me," he said, voicing a reassurance he did not truly feel. He planted a soft kiss on her forehead. "Do not worry."

He watched as she retreated to the dressing room and listened until he heard the key turn in the lock. Then he started for the hall door.

Tonight, if all went as planned, he would catch the person behind all of this madness.

Chapter 16

The bedroom corridor sat silent and deserted as Simon closed the door behind him. It looked as if the rest of the household was asleep. But Simon knew there was one other person still awake this night. And after what had been done to Ariel, he knew that it was someone who knew—or suspected—how much Simon cared for her.

And in his mind, that narrowed the list of suspects down to two people. But he could not be certain until someone made a move against him.

It would only take a few minutes to reach the library. Harman waited for him there, armed with the shotgun. Servants hid on the back stairs, ready to nab anyone who tried to sneak down that way. All Simon had to do was get from his bedroom to the library in one piece.

He didn't think he was going to have any trouble—he did not expect an attack until he was in the library. It was too dangerous to try something in the hall, where anyone might see. No, the person would wait until Simon was safely downstairs. In fact, the villain might be waiting for him in the library right now.

Along with Harman. Simon smiled at the idea of two people hiding behind the tall curtains, waiting for his arrival. He'd told Harman to do nothing if anyone came in, unless his life was endangered. The trap would not be sprung until Simon was attacked. He could only hope that he or Harman reacted quickly enough when that happened.

Simon knew he made a perfect target as he walked down the

stairs, candle in hand. The flickering light illuminated him clearly for anyone who might be looking. But it was even more foolhardy to stumble around in the dark.

And he was glad he had brought the candle, for there were none burning in the hall. Simon felt a growing unease as he descended the last of the stairs. Why hadn't Harman left the hall candles alight? The entire floor was in darkness; everything beyond the pale glow from his single candle lay cloaked in deep shadow.

Simon stepped onto the marble floor. Despite attempts to reassure himself, the hairs on the back of his neck rose as he imagined someone watching him, waiting. Was someone lurking in a shadowed doorway, or beneath the stairs, hidden from his sight?

It was the merest whisper of sound, a faint scrape coming from his left, but on hearing it, Simon dove to the floor, pinching the wick on his candle. As the hall plunged into darkness, a deafening shot tore through the room.

Ariel followed Simon's instructions, locking the doors to her room and barricading them with chairs. No one was going to catch her unawares tonight.

There was no way she was going to sleep, however. Not with Milford sitting downstairs, deliberately hoping to be attacked. She would sit awake all night if she had to, until she heard him return and knew that he was safe.

She hated the thought of him risking himself like this. She had not liked his plan from the moment he proposed it, and now that he had set it in motion, she was more concerned than ever. He'd assured her that there was little danger; that Harman and the other servants were on guard, but that did little to ease her fear. All it would take was a single misstep, and Simon could be grievously hurt—or killed.

A muffled noise startled her from the chair.

A gunshot. That had been a gunshot.

Ariel dashed to the door, shoving aside the chair and wrenching the key in the lock. Clutching Milford's pistol in her hand, she ran out into the hall and listened carefully. All was quiet.

Had she imagined the sound? No, she was certain she'd

heard something. Perhaps Milford's trap had worked, and he was already trussing up his prisoner.

Or had Milford been the one caught in the trap?

She knew she should go back to her room, lock the door, and remain there until Milford told her it was safe to come out. But what if he needed her? She had to go downstairs and make certain he was all right.

Ariel started toward the rear stairs when she heard the unmistakable sound of a gunshot. Ariel skidded to a halt. What was going on downstairs? Was Milford chasing the villain through the house? Or was *he* chasing Milford? She knew the situation was fraught with danger; she had to be very careful. Yet she had to help Milford.

She ran toward the front hall, the direction from where the noise had come.

As she left the bedroom corridor, darkness enveloped her. No candles lit the way, but it would take too much time to run back to her room and get one. She put her hand against the wall and used it to guide her steps. Not until the wall fell away did she realize she'd reached the top landing. The smell of gunpowder was acrid in her nostrils, dispelling any doubts about what she had heard.

She prayed with all her heart that Milford was safe.

Ariel clutched the pistol more firmly, grateful that her brother had taught her how to handle a gun. She grabbed the stair railing with her other hand and slowly crept down the stairs in the darkness. If Milford needed her, she wanted to be ready.

Simon lay sprawled on the cold marble tiles in front of the stairs, hardly daring to breathe. In the darkness across the hall, the man with the pistol couldn't see him, any more than Simon could see who was shooting at him, but that gave him little comfort. Darkness was no protection against an armed man.

Where in the devil was Harman? He must have heard the shots. Why wasn't he here? One blast from the shotgun and it would all be over.

Then Simon realized that the butler was not going to have an easy time of it. Harman dared not risk a light, or he would become a target himself. No, he would have to wait until the shooter fired again and revealed his location.

Meanwhile, here Simon was, lying in the middle of the hall with a madman shooting at him.

Simon knew he had to crawl toward a more protected location, which would make noise and give his attacker a target to shoot at. But that would, in turn, give Harman—if he was here—a target of his own.

Simon had intended to be the bait in his little trap, but he had not intended to be quite such exposed bait. He'd underestimated his opponent, and now he was paying the price.

His heart was pounding so loudly he feared it must give his position away. Taking a deep breath, Simon braced himself on his hands, then rolled quickly to the left, toward the stairs.

He saw the flash of powder, heard the deafening roar, then waited anxiously for Harman to return fire. But only echoes reverberated through the hall.

Then at last he heard the sound of running footsteps.

"What's going on here?" Harman cried. Another shot ran out, then a loud cry, the sound of something—the shotgun?—clattering to the floor.

Harman must have fallen behind Simon, just beyond the edge of the stairs. If Simon could make his way there, he could retrieve the shotgun and strike back. Except the man shooting at him would expect him to do that. He'd surely marked the spot where Harman had fallen and would be waiting for Simon to move for it and would shoot at any sound.

Simon could lie in the middle of the hall and hope that someone else would come to his rescue. But if guests weren't streaming down the stairs by now, it meant that they hadn't heard the shots.

No one was coming to his rescue. He would have to save himself.

Slowly, carefully, Simon started inching backward, toward the stairs and his sole chance of escape.

Ariel jumped as the shot flew across the entry hall. She lost her grip on the railing, her foot slipped, and she went down hard.

She sat there, stunned, yet trying to hold her breath, trying to hear what was happening below. Only an ominous silence met her ears.

Ariel wanted to throw down the pistol and race back up the stairs, race back to the safety of her room and hide behind her locked door until everything was over.

Then she thought of Milford, who might be lying on the cold marble tiles of the floor below, bleeding, needing her help, and she knew she had to go on.

Taking a deep breath to steel herself, she rose again, grabbed the railing with new determination, and continued to stealthily make her way down the stairs. After each step she paused, listening, but heard nothing.

Had everyone fled the hall? Or were they all dead?

She sensed rather than felt the railing curve to the left and realized she had reached the bottom. Her fingers gripped the knob at the rail's end, and she extended her foot out and down, feeling for the floor. *There.* That had to be it.

Or was there one more step?

She inched forward, fearing that she'd judged wrong and would tumble down the final step. But her feet remained on solid ground. She was standing on the marble floor of the entry hall.

She halted, relieved, and listened again. Did she heard something coming from her right? She listened again and was sure she heard a noise. It was faint, barely a whisper—cloth, brushing over tile.

Was someone crawling across the floor?

Who was it? Milford, or the enemy?

Someone was coming down the stairs. Simon strained to listen. Whoever it was, was being very careful. Had someone heard the shots after all and come to help?

Or was it his enemy? Had the attacker slipped from the hall, circled around to the back, raced up the rear stairs, and now came down behind him? No, there had not been enough time for that. Simon assumed that whoever was approaching so stealthily had come to help.

Thank God.

He continued sidling to the side and rear, desperate to reach Harman—or the shotgun.

Simon's foot hit something hard, and he realized he had reached the stair. He could sense, but not see, the person standing less than ten feet from him. And unless his brain was totally befuddled, the person smelled like . . . roses. *Roses?*

Damn. In his anger, he almost swore aloud. It was Ariel. He wanted to jump up and throttle her for putting herself in such danger. But he did not dare, for it would announce her presence and make her a target, too.

He prayed that she'd had the foresight to bring the pistol with her.

Simon slid sideways once again. He did not dare risk even a whisper, and he hoped she would not scream or cry out when he reached her. But she remained as still as a statue, making no sound at all as she stood there. Only that tantalizing wisp of roses gave her presence away.

He reached out and touched her ankle.

She gasped, and Simon grabbed her around the legs, pulling her down atop him, expecting to hear the loud report of a shot, afraid he would be too late to save her.

Instead, there was only silence.

Her body was rigid, stiff, but as the seconds passed, he felt her relax. Had she realized who he was? He wanted to make certain she was all right, that he had not hurt her when he pulled her down, but he did not dare. The shooter would be waiting for any sound to confirm their position. Instead, he ran his hand down her arm, seeking the pistol he hoped she held.

His fingers closed around the polished wood of the butt, and he breathed a silent sigh of relief.

Good girl.

Now, he had to get her out of here so he could go after the attacker. Carefully, he inched down so his mouth was next to her ear. "Run. Left," he told her in the barest whisper, praying she understood.

If he could get her out of the way, he had a chance. Two shots. One to draw the other's fire and locate him; the second to hit him. It was a slim chance, but the odds suddenly looked better than they had a few minutes ago.

He squeezed her arm. "Go."

She rose to a crouch and raced around the far corner of the

staircase, while Simon rolled in the opposite direction and fired toward the far side of the hall.

This time there was an answering shot.

The man was between the front door and the dining room. Simon squeezed the trigger again and rolled left this time.

No sharp cry rang out, no loud thud sounded as if a body had hit the floor. Simon had missed, and his pistol was now empty. The other man might still have one shot left, or he might be reloading at this very moment. Simon could not. He had to reach that shotgun.

How long would it take for Ariel to raise the rest of the household?

Then all hell broke loose.

Something heavy crashed noisily onto the tiles to his right. Simon raced for the side of the stairs, seeking safety in their shadow. A pistol fired, but to his surprise was answered with a shot from the stairs above. Then the deafening roar of the shotgun directly behind him nearly deafened Simon. He heard the faint sound of a man crying out, and then it was suddenly eerily silent again.

A hand pressed against his back. He whirled around. It was Harman, his form the merest shadow. In his hand he carried a shuttered lamp, which gave off just enough light to outline his shape.

"I thought you were hit," Simon whispered.

"Only my pride," Harman said.

Simon peered anxiously into the shadows behind the butler. "Where's Ariel?" he demanded.

"She's safe. I brought the light so we can see who we're shooting at."

"Or who is shooting at us," Simon said. "Who the devil fired that gun from the stairs?"

"I have no idea," Harman replied. "But I think he's on our side."

"Where's the shotgun?" Simon asked.

Harman shoved it into his hands, but Simon gave it back. "Keep watch," he said. "I'm going to try and see what's happened."

He crept forward to the edge of the stairs with the lantern. Pointing the opening against the wall, he slid back the cover, then gingerly held the lantern at arm's length and reached around to set it on the bottom step, expecting to have his arm blown off at any time.

The lantern's light was not bright, but it seemed noonday light after the earlier pitch blackness. As his eyes adjusted, he began to make out shapes in the gloom—the front door, the table beside it, the dining room door.

A man slumped on the floor next to it.

Had that shotgun blast hit its mark? And who in the hell had fired that other pistol?

"Milford!" A voice cried out from above.

"Who's there?" he demanded.

"Townsend," came the reply. "I think we got him."

Townsend? Townsend was the other man with the gun?

"What are you doing here?" Simon demanded.

"I heard all the shooting and came down to see what was going on." Townsend bounded down the stairs and joined Simon. "Sounded like you needed some help."

"I'm grateful," Simon said, taking his hand. "Although you might have said something. You're lucky I didn't shoot you."

The man by the dining room door groaned.

"Harman, keep the shotgun trained on that fellow." Simon strode out from behind the stairs and marched across the hall to the man slumped on the floor.

He did not need any more light to tell him who it was.

Lynnwood.

Lynnwood was the one who'd wanted him dead? But why?

He knelt beside the groaning man. "Bring the lantern," Simon called. "He's wounded."

Harman reached his side and examined Lynnwood none too gently. He groaned every time Harman touched him, but did not open his eyes. The light in the room grew brighter, and Simon guessed someone had relit the candles. From the corner of his eye, Simon saw Townsend walk up behind them, Ariel at his side.

Relief washed over him at the confirmation that she was safe. Relief that was rapidly being replaced with a growing anger when he remembered how she had disobeyed his orders.

He stood, stepping toward her, and she flung herself into his arms.

"Oh, Milford, you are all right! I was so scared."

Simon found he could not help himself; he hugged her tightly, letting relief wash over him again for a few brief moments. They were both alive.

Over the top of his head, he saw Townsend looking at them, a silly grin on his face.

"Looks like Lynnwood's got a good load of buckshot in him," Harman said, giving Ariel a quick smile.

"Good shooting," Simon nodded to Harman.

"Thank you," Ariel replied.

Stunned by her acknowledgment, Simon let his arms fall to his sides and stepped back a pace, glaring at her. "You fired the shotgun?"

She nodded.

"Are you mad?" He made no effort to restrain his anger. "Didn't I tell you to get out of here? What could you have been thinking of, to put yourself in danger like that?"

"I was trying to help you," she said, her head held high with pride. "And I think I did a rather good job of it."

"Better than I did," Townsend said with a rueful look. "I missed him completely."

"Miss Tennant is an excellent shot," Harman murmured.

Simon scowled at him. He was going to have a long talk with him later.

"What's going on?" a voice called from the stairs. "Who's shooting up the place?"

They all whirled around. Gregson stood there in a garish dressing gown of green and red.

"Just a little target shooting," Townsend called back. "We were a bit bored."

"You've found the poisoner! Who is it?" Gregson eagerly rushed over, then halted suddenly as he recognized the man on the floor. "My God, it's Lynnwood."

"So it appears," Milford said dryly.

"Always thought he was a rum 'un," Gregson said. "Is he dead?"

"Unfortunately not," Simon said. "It would make matters a lot easier if he were."

Harman coughed. "We should tend to his wounds. I will get water and some bandages."

"Ariel, there is no need for you to stay down here." Milford gave her a stern look, hinting of the blistering scold he was going to give her later. "Go back to bed."

She opened her mouth to protest, but a loud voice came from the rear of the house. "Let go of me! I've done nothing wrong! Let me go!"

Simon looked skyward. *What now?*

Two servants came from the kitchen hall, holding a struggling Bates between them. His face broke into a relieved look when he saw Simon.

"Milford! Thank God. Tell these fools to let me go."

"We found him on the rear stairs, m'lord," the first servant said.

"Sneaking around," the other added. "We nabbed him, just like Harman told us."

"Of course I was moving quietly," Bates sputtered in indignation. "I heard pistol shots. I didn't want to run headlong into a pitched battle."

"Release him," Simon said. "I'm afraid you're too late, Bates. The excitement is over."

Bates glared at Gregson. "What's he doing here?"

"Same thing as you," Gregson retorted. "We both missed out on the fun."

"You found your man?" Bates demanded. "Who is it?"

Simon stepped aside and Bates peered around him.

"Is that Lynnwood? My God, he's hurt! Did your villain do this?"

"Lynnwood *is* the villain," Gregson said.

"What?" Bates stared at Simon. "I don't believe it. Is that what this young puppy told you?"

"Lynnwood told me," Simon said. "In a manner of speaking. While he was trying to shoot my head off."

"Lynnwood was shooting at you?"

Simon examined his friend warily. After Lynnwood's betrayal, he wasn't sure if he wanted to trust anyone again. But Bates's shock looked genuine.

"Even I don't know why," Simon said. "I hope to make him explain himself."

Lynnwood's wounds were not serious, and he regained consciousness before Harman finished dressing them. When the injured man opened his eyes and saw Milford looking at him, he groaned.

"Either I've failed, or we're both in hell," he said.

"I'm not planning on ending up there for a long time," Simon said. "You, on the other hand . . ."

He should question him, should find out what was behind all this, but he almost did not want to know why a man he once counted as his friend had been trying to kill him.

A wave of exhaustion swept over Simon, and he shivered, thinking how close he—all of them—had come to dying at this man's hands tonight.

"What are you going to do with him?" Gregson asked eagerly. "I'll volunteer to stand guard."

"I plan to put him in the cellar for the night. He'll be safe enough there," Simon replied.

"You can't put me down there," Lynnwood protested.

"Oh?" Simon's look quickly silenced his objections.

He conducted a swift search of Lynnwood's pockets, coming up with several keys that probably belonged to the house, but nothing else that would be of any use to him.

Simon looked at the others. Ariel, damn her, was still here. He wiped a hand across his brow. "It's been a long night. I suggest the rest of you repair to the library for some much-needed restorative. I will join you after I've asked Lynnwood a few pertinent questions."

Ariel gave him a questioning look.

"Yes, you may stay." He took her hand and gave it a sharp squeeze, then followed behind Harman as the servants dragged Lynnwood toward the kitchen stairs.

Chapter 17

Ariel gratefully sank into one of the library's comfortable wing chairs. She did not think her quivering legs would support her much longer. Bates grabbed the decanter of brandy and poured out glasses for everyone, and she eagerly accepted the one he handed her.

She felt an enormous sense of relief at being able to sit here and know that Milford was safe at last. She didn't know what she would have done if he'd been killed tonight.

For she knew that she was helplessly, hopelessly, head over heels in love with him. It was the only reason she'd acted with such disregard for her own safety; why she'd grabbed the shotgun from Harman and deliberately pointed the barrel at Lynnwood. He was trying to kill Milford, and she intended to stop him.

"I want some answers," Gregson said.

"So do we all," Townsend said. "We're going to have to wait for Milford to join us."

"It was lucky you arrived when you did," Ariel told Townsend, giving him a grateful smile. "Where did you get that pistol?"

"Oh, I never travel without a sidearm," he said. "One never knows when it will be needed."

"It's a wonder no one found it when the rooms were being searched," she said.

"I hid it well," he said with a modest smile.

"Who cares about Townsend's pistol?" Bates restlessly paced the room. "What in the hell was Lynnwood about? And why didn't anyone tell me what was going on until it was all over?"

"Because you were a suspect," Townsend said. "As were all of us."

"Hmmph." Bates flung himself into a chair. "You'd think Milford would have more faith in his friends."

"Lynnwood *was* one of his friends," Ariel pointed out.

Bates reddened. "Damn fool. What was he thinking?"

Gregson looked at Ariel with curiosity. "Were you really the one who shot him? I should have liked to have seen that."

The library door opened, and they all jumped. Milford walked into the room.

He looked exhausted, and Ariel felt a rush of sympathy for him. How horrible to know that a person you once counted as a friend was not one—was, in fact, your enemy. It had been a night of disillusionment for Milford. He'd already had enough of that in his life. Ariel wanted to go to him, to wrap her arms around him, then lay his head against her breast and hold him until his pain was gone.

But here, in the library, in front of the others, she could not. She realized already she had made a mistake in flinging her arms around him in the hall, but she'd been so relieved that he was safe that she had not stopped to think.

Simon poured himself a glass of brandy, drained it in one gulp, then refilled his glass and sat down in the empty chair beside Ariel.

"Well?" Gregson regarded him eagerly. "What happened? What did he say? Why was he trying to kill you?"

"I haven't the faintest idea," Milford replied, his expression clouded. "He would not tell me."

Gregson jumped out of his chair and started for the door. "I'll get the answer out of him. He owes us an explanation. And I won't take no for an answer."

Milford waved him back. "Lynnwood's not going anywhere tonight. I plan to speak to him again tomorrow before I turn him over to the magistrate."

Ariel regarded him curiously. "Did you suspect it was Lynnwood all along?"

He shook his head. "There were too many possible suspects.

It wasn't until I talked with you tonight that I put two and two together and realized he was one of the likeliest suspects."

"Because of what happened to my clothes?" Ariel asked.

He nodded.

"What's this about Miss Tennant's clothes?" Gregson asked.

"Someone destroyed the contents of Miss Tennant's trunk earlier this evening," Simon said. "After I announced that I knew who the culprit was."

"Why would anyone want to hurt Miss Tennant?" Gregson asked. Townsend gave him a sharp jab with his elbow.

"That was the question I asked myself," Milford said. "And the answer pointed to Lynnwood."

"Did he admit to it?" Ariel asked.

"He was responsible," Milford said, "in a manner of speaking. He enlisted someone else to do the work."

Who? she wanted to ask, but she realized that Milford was not going to be forthcoming about details in front of the others. When they were alone, she would find out.

"What *I* would like to know," Milford said, glancing sternly at Townsend and Gregson, "is who was behind the other mischief that has been going on around here. Lynnwood admitted responsibility for some actions, but he denied committing others."

Townsend and Gregson exchanged guilty looks.

Gregson turned to Milford, red-faced. "I admit that I had a hand in . . . one or two of them."

"We meant them as a joke," Townsend said sheepishly. "We just wanted to liven things up a bit."

"The window in Bates's room," Ariel guessed. "And Miss LeDeux's clothing."

"I opened the window," Gregson admitted. "But we didn't touch her clothes." He looked wistful. "Wish I'd thought of it, in fact. I wouldn't have left her anything to put on. Although she did look dashing in Townsend's clothing."

"What about the furniture piled up in the drawing room, and the dog locked in the cellar?" Milford ticked off the pranks on his fingers.

"I rather liked what we did with the furniture," Townsend said. "Damn disappointing that no one saw it. Your servants are too efficient."

"You can blame Miss Tennant for that," Milford said. "She discovered your handiwork and brought it to my attention."

"What about the stepladder?" Ariel asked him.

Bates looked at Milford, puzzled. "What stepladder?"

"Lynnwood damaged the library stepladder," Milford replied. "Hoping to hurt me, most likely."

"Did he poison the brandy, too?" she asked.

He nodded. "The stuff he put in the brandy probably wouldn't have killed me, but I'd have been deucedly ill. Enough so that he could have finished me off with ease."

"Did he knock out Mallory?" Townsend asked.

Milford nodded. "Lynnwood admitted there was no particular reason for that—he was only trying to confuse matters. He was afraid that I'd realized by then that I was the intended target."

Bates shook his head. "I've known Lynnwood to be involved in some rum deals, but nothing like this. Makes a man wonder about his friends."

"At least I know I still have some I can trust," Milford said, holding Bates's gaze for a few seconds before the other man nodded, then looked away.

Ariel blinked back tears at his words. She feared that this experience would have discouraged Milford, made him bitter, and even more cynical. He had suffered so much already in his life; she wanted him to know that not everyone would betray him.

Townsend rose and set his glass on the desk. "Well, I'm off to bed. There's time for a few more hours of sleep this night."

"What are you going to do with Lynnwood tomorrow?" Bates asked.

"If I can persuade someone to brave the roads, I intend to send for the magistrate," Milford said.

"I'll go," Gregson said eagerly.

"Me, too," Townsend offered.

"Good. Come to me when you're ready to leave—I'll send a note along explaining matters. I'm hoping you'll be able to bring him back and he can take Lynnwood off our hands."

"Then I better get some sleep, too," Gregson said, and the two said good night.

Ariel glanced at Milford. There was so much they needed to say to each other. She suspected he was still angry with her for not having stayed in her room tonight. She resolved to listen patiently to his scolding before she pointed out that without her aid, he might still be in that freezing hall exchanging shots with Lynnwood.

She darted a sidelong look at Bates, who showed no signs of leaving. Should she go upstairs and wait for Milford there? She smiled to herself. He would not be able to berate her too loudly in his room, for fear of waking her aunt.

But she wanted to stay here, where they could talk without fear of interruption. Couldn't Bates see that they wanted to be alone? Or was he too obtuse to have recognized that?

To her surprise, Milford solved the dilemma.

"I have a few matters I need to discuss with Miss Tennant," he told Bates.

Bates gave her a startled glance, and a wide grin spread over his face. "I see." He rose and headed for the door, then paused. "Next time you intend to have a gun battle in the front hall, I'd appreciate it if you would call me."

"Since I have no intentions of ever going through that again, I'll make no such promise," Milford replied. He rose and escorted him to the door. "Good night, Harry."

Ariel sat patiently in her chair, waiting for Milford to speak.

"You know I want to ring a peal over your head, don't you?" he asked at last.

She nodded.

He slammed his glass down on the desk and stalked over to her. Ariel thought it was grossly unfair of him to glower at her from his towering vantage point. The least he could do was sit down—or allow her to stand. He looked far too intimidating when he glared down at her like this.

"What on earth possessed you to come downstairs?" he demanded.

"I was worried about you."

"And your response was to put your own life in danger?" He ran a hand through his hair, a gesture Ariel knew he only made when very frustrated.

"You needed my help," she said simply.

"That's beside the point," he snapped. "Did it ever occur to you that your presence put me in greater danger? Because I had to worry about you, as well as myself?"

She looked down. "I had not thought of that."

"I see."

Ariel glanced up at him. "But I would do the same thing over again, Milford, if I knew your life was at risk."

"For God's sake, why?"

She hesitated, unsure if she should tell him, fearing yet wanting to hear his reaction.

"Because I care a great deal about what happens to you. I could not bear the thought of you being hurt, or killed."

His eyes widened with surprise and . . . was that dismay she saw as well?

"You silly little fool." He reached for her hand and pulled her to her feet. "You silly, brave little fool."

He enveloped her in his arms, and she clung to him as she had not dared to in the hall, cherishing the undamaged body that felt so good beneath her fingers. She leaned her head against his chest, listening to the soothing, steady beat of his heart.

He was alive.

His hand stroked her back, soothing, caressing.

"Ah, Ariel, I never meant for this to happen."

His voice was so low that she barely heard him and wondered if he even realized he'd spoken aloud.

"I love you, Milford," she whispered against his chest.

She knew he'd heard her, for he suddenly went rigid. Ariel waited with inheld breath for him to respond, to say something, anything, but he only stood there, holding her in his arms.

For now, it was enough. At least he had not thrust her aside. She would give him time to think about her declaration.

Ariel was not sure how long they stood there—seconds, minutes—for time seemed suspended.

"You should go back to bed," he said at last. "Before your aunt wakes and finds you missing."

He loosened his hold, and she took a step away from him, looking up so she could see his face. He looked so tired, and a little sad. She wished she could take on all of his pain, to wipe the lines from his brow.

"Harman should be waiting outside," Milford said. "He will take you upstairs."

Ariel felt a stab of disappointment that Milford was not going to walk up with her, but she forced a smile.

"Then I shall see you later today."

He nodded. "Later." Milford bent his head and briefly brushed her lips with his, then stood back and looked into her eyes.

"Thank you for trying to save me," he said. "Even if it was a foolish act."

Ariel patted him gently on the cheek. "Foolish in your eyes, perhaps, but not mine." She walked into the hallway, where Harman was waiting for her and accompanied him upstairs.

Somehow, she had to convince Milford that it was all right for her to love him. And to break through the last remnants of the barrier he'd thrown up around himself to get him to admit that he cared for her, too. She knew it would not be an easy task. But she had to do it, for his sake as well as hers.

Simon stared at the door long after Ariel had gone. He knew as soon as he moved he would destroy this fleeting moment of peace and calm.

Finally, with a long sigh, he slowly turned back to the desk and poured himself another brandy before easing himself into the chair. He could not afford to indulge in maudlin sentimentality. There was too much to do.

He had been lying to himself about Ariel for several days now, and he had to bear the responsibility for what had happened. He knew she was falling in love with him, had seen it in her eyes, the timbre of her voice, the way she looked at him when they were alone. He could have stopped it with a word. But he hadn't.

Because he was selfish. He had wanted to pretend, for a little while, at least, that he was an ordinary man, the kind of man who deserved her love. The kind of man whom proud fathers beamed at, mothers doted on, and society described as "a good catch." The kind of man who could love her in return.

But he was none of those things. And knowing that, he should never have allowed matters to go as far as they had. He should have made it clear to her days ago that their connection would cease to exist once she left these four walls.

If he was brutally honest with himself, he should never have spoken a word to her from the first moment she stepped under his roof. Her aunt had been right—she should have kept far away from him. That she had not was entirely his fault, for he'd encouraged her, yes, even deliberately lured her to him. Solely for his own amusement—at first.

But amusement had quickly changed to appreciation—and admiration. He wanted to be with her, and thought, however foolishly, that he could love her, too. He'd fallen under her spell, and he hadn't given a single thought to how she would react to his attentions.

Yet now he had to face the consequences of his actions. And he had so little time to repair the damage he'd wrought—two, three days at the most. Three days of excruciating pain in which he had to undo everything he had done, in such a way as to leave her as undamaged as possible.

For he did not want to hurt her. And he deeply feared that he already had.

His actions only confirmed what everyone said about him—he was a "black-hearted bastard." What other kind of man would have toyed so carelessly with an innocent girl's heart?

Now he had to make amends, so that when she went to London later in the spring, she would be able to look for the kind of man she deserved—one society approved of, one who was worthy of her.

Not a man like him.

Tomorrow, or later today, actually, and all the days after until he could send her away from here were going to be excruciatingly painful. But he had to make certain that when she left, it would not be with regret, but relief.

His own feelings did not matter. Her happiness was the most important thing. And Simon knew that it did not lie with him.

Simon drained his glass and stood. He had one more matter to take care of tonight before he went to bed, one that he almost looked forward to. He may not have been able to get many answers out of Lynnwood, but at least Simon knew who'd destroyed Ariel's clothes.

He only wished the roads were in better shape, so he could

order Claudia to leave immediately. He had no intention of allowing her to remain under the same roof with Ariel any longer than necessary. And as long as she was, he intended to keep her under lock and key.

No one was going to have the chance to cause Ariel any more distress—except him. He felt an enormous sense of guilt that she'd risked her life for him tonight. He did not deserve such sacrifice—as she was going to discover.

But by the time he reached his room, he realized he was too exhausted for a confrontation with Claudia. It would have to wait until morning. He stripped off his clothes and climbed into bed, then tried in vain to forget how wonderful Ariel had felt clasped in his arms.

As soon as he awoke in the morning, Simon unlocked the door and walked into Claudia's room. She was still sleeping, but he roughly shook her awake.

"I want you to unpack your belongings," he said.

"Whatever for?"

"Because I want to see if there is anything in your wardrobe suitable for Miss Tennant to wear. As you well know, she is rather short on clothing at the moment."

She looked at him sleepily. "What are you talking about?"

"Lynnwood told me all about your little project."

"You are not going to give my things to *her*," Claudia exclaimed defiantly. "They are mine."

"Who paid for them?" he reminded her coldly, noticing she had not even bothered to deny the charge.

"Milford, you are a beast. I only did this out of jealousy. Because I knew I was losing you."

"You had nothing to lose, Claudia. Our arrangement was always a financial one. You knew it would end one day."

"Very well then." She sat up in the bed. "Help yourself. I am not going to do the job for you."

Swearing under his breath, Milford went to the wardrobe and flung open the door. He knew that most of her gowns would not do for Ariel—they were cut far too low for a respectable young lady. Mrs. Dobson would never allow her niece to be seen in such scandalous dresses. But he recalled there were one or two gowns that might be suitable, with some minor alterations.

He finally pulled out two dresses, one a dinner gown of blue silk that matched Ariel's eyes, and a day dress of patterned muslin that would be presentable with the addition of a shawl. He then rummaged through the dresser, taking several pairs of stockings and a chemise.

Finally satisfied, he gathered up the clothing and started for the door.

"I expect Bates will be leaving tomorrow, or the following day," he said to her. "I will ask him to take you with him. I do not expect to return to London for a fortnight, at least. That will give you plenty of time to make other arrangements for yourself."

He ducked as she tossed a slipper at him.

"I hate you, Milford. I wish Lynnwood had killed you."

Simon made sure he locked her door. He was not going to give her the chance to get near Ariel again.

He gave the clothing to Harman, who waited in the hall, then went quickly downstairs. Harman would deliver the clothing so Simon would not have to speak with Ariel.

It was a cowardly act, but he knew he did not have the strength to deal with her today. Tomorrow, after he'd had a decent night's sleep, perhaps he would have more control over himself. But right now, he was far too vulnerable to her charms. If he saw her, his resolve would flee.

To Ariel's relief, she'd been able to slip back into her room during the night without waking Aunt. Ariel waited until breakfast to tell her aunt what had transpired in the downstairs hall.

"You did what?" Mrs. Dobson stared at Ariel in horror.

Ariel feigned calmness as she buttered a slice of toast from the tray Harman had brought to their room.

"Someone had to help Milford," she explained. As she'd feared, Aunt was furious about Ariel's involvement in capturing Lynnwood, and she had not even told her the whole of it.

"You should have gone to one of the men for help."

"But how could I know whom to trust? For all I knew, more than one person was after him."

"Stuff and nonsense," Aunt said. "You wanted to be in on the adventure. I've told you over and over, Ariel, that your penchant for mischief was going to get you into trouble one of these days. You could have been killed."

"But I wasn't," Ariel pointed out. "And neither was Milford."

"If your brother ever hears of this . . ." Aunt shook her head.

"He never will unless *you* tell him," Ariel said.

"I could not lie to him."

"I am not asking you to lie," Ariel said. "Merely to not mention it to him."

"It's nearly the same thing." She gave Ariel, a long, hard look. "You are far too accustomed to having your own way. It is an unseemly characteristic in a young lady."

Ariel smiled brightly. "Then you won't say anything to Richard?"

Aunt shook her head, but Ariel could tell that she would not betray her. "I do not know why I allow you to talk me into these promises."

Ariel gave her a swift hug. "Because you know it is for the best. Now, let me tell you what a hero Milford was! Why, after he grabbed the pistol, he—"

"If those young gentlemen are going to go to the village today, we need to send a letter to your brother. Surely, the Mail will be running by now. He is no doubt sick with worry."

Ariel did not like to even think about leaving. But Aunt was right, Richard would be worried; she should allay his fears. "Tell him we are both safe and that we will resume our journey after the carriage is repaired."

"I believe we should ask him to send another carriage. It might be faster."

"Nonsense," Ariel said. She had no intention of leaving Milford before she had to. "How would we get the other carriage home? We must wait. I don't imagine it will take above a week to have the repairs completed."

"A week?" Aunt eyed her suspiciously. "I would think you would look forward to going home. You have been away so long."

"Oh, I do, I do. But the roads could be nasty for days. And there will be so many other stranded travelers trying to make their way again. By the time the carriage is ready, we should have no difficulty."

She watched anxiously as Aunt considered her words.

"You may be right," Aunt said. "Still, we should consult with our host. He may not wish to be burdened with our presence for longer than necessary."

"Oh, Milford won't mind," Ariel said blithely. Every minute she stayed in this house was one more minute she could use to persuade Milford that he was worthy of her love—and could dare to love her in return.

"I will write to Richard, then, and tell him we will be on our way once the carriage has been repaired."

Ariel gave her a broad smile. "Be sure to give him my love."

. Chapter 18

Ariel hovered over her aunt while she wrote the letter, fearing Gregson and Townsend would leave before it was finished. The moment it was done, Ariel dashed downstairs. The two men were still eating breakfast and promised to mail it for her when they went for the magistrate.

Satisfied that she'd gained at least another week with Milford, Ariel went back upstairs. Aunt had gone to join Mrs. Blakenose in Mallory's room, and this was a good time for Ariel to look through her trunk. She did not think there was going to be much she could do, but she wanted to see if anything could be salvaged from her ruined clothes.

Most of her dresses were fit only for rags. There was one gown that could be patched up enough to wear. And with a bit of clever sewing she could salvage one chemise. All she could do with the rest was unstitch the lace and trim for use on other garments.

She smoothed out the fabric of the blue kerseymere that she wore. Ariel knew she would be thoroughly sick of both her dresses by the time she finally had something else to wear.

Worse, at a time when she wanted to appear attractive in Milford's eyes, she was stuck with what had to be the two drabbest gowns in her wardrobe. Why couldn't she have been wearing her green silk last night?

At least the kerseymere was warm. If she had been wearing the green silk, she would have to spend most of her days swathed in shawls to stay warm. She didn't think that would create an alluring picture for Milford.

After gathering up her sewing supplies and her torn chemise, she went downstairs to the drawing room to await Gregson's and Townsend's return. She wanted to talk with Milford, but she didn't want to bother him until the business with Lynnwood was finished.

It was a relief not to have to worry about him anymore. They could all relax their guard. Yet she would not feel fully secure until Lynnwood was out of the house.

To her surprise, Mallory was in the drawing room, chatting cheerfully with Blakenose and Bates.

She greeted Mallory with a teasing smile. "How did you manage to escape your guards?"

He returned her grin. "I climbed out of bed and threatened to dress in front of them. They scattered quickly enough."

"Have Townsend and Gregson returned?" she asked.

Bates shook his head.

"Has Milford talked with Lynnwood? Has he learned anything more?"

"I haven't spoken with Milford this morning," Bates said. "Spent all my energy soothing the ladies. They were quite overset at the news."

"I can imagine," Ariel said dryly, although she did feel a twinge of sympathy for Miss LeDeux. "It must be rather frightening to discover that your protector is a murderer."

"Poor girl," Mallory said. "Perhaps I should try to comfort her."

"I doubt you have pockets deep enough to provide the kind of comfort she wants," a voice drawled.

"Milford!" Ariel whirled around. He'd entered the room so quietly none of them had heard his approach.

He sat in the chair facing her, and she examined him carefully. Dark circles under his eyes made him look as if he had not slept at all last night. Her heart went out to him.

"It's true," he said to Mallory." "I don't even think *I* could afford Marguerite."

"I've got plenty of blunt," Mallory protested.

"Then by all means, try your luck," Milford said.

Mallory looked at him as if disbelieving his words, but then his face brightened. "I think I will do that." He jumped from his seat and bolted from the room.

"You shouldn't encourage him," Ariel said.

"If Marguerite is willing to accept an offer from him, who am I to stand in his way?" Milford regarded her with a distant expression. "I feel I owe her *something* after depriving her of her protector."

"Lynnwood is the one who owes her, not you," Ariel said. "Have you spoken with him today?"

Milford nodded.

"What did he say?"

"Nothing suitable for your tender ears."

"Milford! I *shot* the man. The least you can do is tell me why he was trying to kill you."

She saw the faintest flicker of pain dance across his face before he resumed his impassive look. "It is a private matter between myself and Lynnwood."

Ariel felt disappointed that he was not willing to confide in her, then realized it was probably the presence of Bates and Blakenose that stayed his tongue. Surely, Milford would tell her when they could finally talk privately.

Harman appeared at the door. "The young gentlemen are back. They have brought the magistrate with them."

"Good." Milford jumped to his feet. "If you will excuse me, I need to get this business over with."

Time crawled while Ariel waited for Milford to return. The magistrate called in first Bates and then Blakenose to take their statements, but did not even ask to see her. Blakenose had not even been downstairs during last night's adventure! *It simply was not fair.* Ariel wanted to march into the library—for that was where the magistrate was doing his work—and demand that he talk with her, but she realized it would only make her look foolish.

But she was certainly going to have a few words with Milford. If he was, as she suspected, trying to keep her name out of the proceedings in a wrong-sided desire to protect her, she needed to tell him a thing or two. *Protect her! When she was the one who'd protected him last night.*

In frustration, she went upstairs to her room. Ariel gasped

with surprise at the sight of two dresses lying on the bed. She walked over and inspected the blue gown. Wasn't this one of Miss Baker's? Milford must have explained Ariel's plight to her, and she'd generously offered to loan some of her clothes.

Ariel should thank her. She went into the hall and tapped on the other woman's door.

"Miss Baker?"

"What do you want?" came the querulous reply.

"I wished to thank you for the loan of the dresses."

"Loan? Ha! Milford is giving them to you."

Ariel sucked in her breath. Miss Baker was not being generous at all. This was entirely Milford's doing. She smiled. It showed Ariel that he did care.

"That is not necessary," Ariel said. "You may certainly have them back."

"*He* would not allow it. They are yours forever, Miss Tennant. As is Milford. I hope he is as horrid to you as he has been to me."

Ariel took an involuntary step back at the venom in her words, clear even through the closed door. Miss Baker was furious with Milford. Ariel felt a smug sense of satisfaction at that knowledge.

Then she remembered Milford's words from last night: "He enlisted another to do the work."

Had Miss Baker been the one who destroyed her clothes?

The more Ariel thought about it, the more sense it made— especially after the argument she'd overheard the other night. Now she understood why Milford had given her the dresses, and why Miss Baker was so angry. A tit-for-tat exchange.

Ariel went back to her room. She fingered the fine silk of the blue gown, more expensive and elegant than any dress she owned. It would feel odd, wearing a dress that had once been worn by Milford's mistress. But perhaps wearing this gown would make Milford regard her in a new light.

And at least there was no harm in seeing how the dress looked on her.

She took off her dress and donned the blue gown. The silk felt cool and slick against her skin. It was not a perfect fit— Miss Baker was taller, and she certainly had a more ample bosom. But with a little judicious hemming and tucking, Ariel knew she could make it fit well enough.

Did she want to?

Ariel looked at her plain kerseymere dress lying across the bed, and that decided her. She would wear this silk dress to dinner one night. She wanted to look elegant and beautiful for Milford at least one time while she was here.

Simon went down to dinner that night with the feeling of an enormous weight having been lifted from his shoulders. After the tension of the last several days, there was almost a giddiness to that night's dinner. At the end of the meal, Simon convinced the men to eschew their private port and brandy and gather at once with the ladies in the drawing room. Only Claudia was absent—Simon had forbade her to set foot out of her room. He explained her absence as an indisposition. He did not know if she had told the others the truth of the situation, nor did he care. He only wanted to keep her away from Ariel.

"The roads were not that bad," Gregson said when Bates asked him about their journey earlier that day. "Some of the puddles were pretty deep, but carriages could get through."

"I think we shall attempt to leave in the morning then," Blakenose said, glancing at his wife. "Will that suit you, Euphy?"

"I cannot wait to get away from all these dreadful memories," she said. "But to think that I have to leave Blinky behind . . ."

"You can take him with you," Gregson offered.

Mrs. Blakenose paled, and her husband glared at Gregson.

"Have you no decency, boy?"

Gregson reddened. "I just thought she might—"

"Blinky is welcome to make his permanent resting place here," Simon offered. "I assure you, Mrs. Blakenose, his grave will be carefully tended."

She nodded and dabbed at her eyes with her handkerchief. "You are so kind, my lord. It will be a comfort to know that Blinky is resting in such noble surroundings."

"There is no reason for me to linger either," Bates said.

"Would you take Claudia and Marguerite with you?" Simon asked. "I think they would both prefer to be away from here."

Bates frowned. "That's going to be difficult in the phaeton. It won't take four people."

Damn. Simon had forgotten that Bates and Sarah had arrived in that small vehicle.

"I will hire you a carriage then," he said. "I've already promised my traveling coach to Miss Tennant and her aunt." He dared not look at Ariel as he said that; he had not even discussed the matter with her. But he knew it was imperative that he get her out of this house as quickly as possible. Before he did something he—and she—would regret.

"Oh, please, let Bates use your carriage," Ariel said. "I already wrote my brother that we would wait here while our carriage is being repaired. It shouldn't take long—only a few days."

A few days that he did not want to wait.

"Nonsense, you must be eager to get home." Simon smiled at Mrs. Dobson. "I will see to the repairs and have the carriage sent on."

"We would not wish to burden you with that chore," Mrs. Dobson said. "It is far simpler for everyone if we wait for it to be fixed."

Simon gave Ariel a suspicious glance. Somehow, he suspected this had been her plan all along, a way to delay her departure as long as possible.

Well, if she and her aunt insisted on remaining, he could not stop them, but if Ariel thought that she was going to spend the intervening days alone with him, she was sadly mistaken. He intended to avoid her as much as civility allowed.

"Then perhaps you will wish to delay your departure," Milford said to Bates. "We can continue our little party."

Bates shook his head. "If it were up to me, I wouldn't mind staying, but I know Sarah is eager to return to London."

Simon turned a pleading look on Gregson and his friends. "Surely, you will continue to avail yourself of my hospitality."

Townsend shook his head. "I think it is time for us to leave."

"You just want to be the first to bring the news to London," Gregson said. "Just because you were in the thick of things."

Simon grimaced. He had forgotten that there was no way he

was going to keep this incident quiet. Better that the actual par-
ticipants were the ones to spread the news, even though he
knew before long it would become distorted and embellished
with each retelling.

He glanced at Ariel. "I fear you ladies will be sadly bored
without any company."

"We expect you to make up the deficit, Milford," Ariel said
with a teasing smile.

That was what he feared. But he was not going to let her
bully him into doing anything he did not want to. If she insisted
on staying here, she would have to make her own entertainment. He intended to ignore her.

But would he be able to maintain his resolve for the several
days it would take for the carriage to be repaired? It might be
worth paying extra to get the job done quickly.

He had to be strong. If he was alone with her again, he might
weaken. Because she had a way of making him think, if even
for a moment, that it might be possible for him to deserve her
love, and to love her in return. Then he remembered who he
was, and what he had done, and the hope vanished like a wisp
of smoke.

She deserved far better than him. He did not deserve her at
all.

Ariel awoke early the next morning, determined to find Milford alone so she could talk to him. There were so many things
she had to ask him—had it really been Claudia who'd destroyed her clothing? And most important, why had Lynnwood
been trying to kill him?

She realized that Milford had spent the previous day deliberately avoiding her. Had her declaration that night in the library
frightened him that much? That meant she had to work all the
harder over the next few days to persuade him that she wanted
him, that his past did not matter to her, that he was an honorable and worthy man she was proud to love.

Milford was not in the dining room, although breakfast was
laid out for the guests. She quickly ate a piece of toast, and then
went down the hall to the library, where she knew he would be
hiding.

She entered without knocking and found him sitting at his

desk. Papers were piled in front of him, but he was gazing out the window, a frown on his face.

"I've found you alone at last," she said cheerfully, sitting down before he asked her—to make certain that he would not order her away.

"Yesterday was rather hectic."

"What did the magistrate say about Lynnwood? Will he be charged with attempted murder?"

"That is up to the magistrate, but he seemed to think that Lynnwood's behavior was criminal."

"Did he ever tell you why he wanted to kill you?"

Milford looked at her for a long moment, then nodded. "It has to do with a business venture we were involved in. Apparently, it was failing and Lynnwood thought my death would save him."

"Whyever would he think that?"

Milford sighed. "He owed me a great deal of money. I originally put up the funds to get things started."

"What did the business involve?"

"It was a canal boat company. A complicated matter—Lynnwood proposed to buy the boats, then lease them to the boatmen and take a commission both for the use and a percentage of the goods shipped. It sounded like a reasonable proposition."

"What happened? How did it fail?"

"I don't know. As far as I knew, everything was going well. The time was coming for the loan to be repaid and Lynnwood never indicated there was a problem."

"Didn't he have the money to pay you back?"

Milford shook his head. "He lost it—every cent, plus all the money put up by other investors—at the gaming tables."

"Killing you wasn't going to bring that back."

"No, but if he was unable to pay me, once the word got out, the other investors would soon be demanding their funds as well."

"But Milford, he was your friend! Why didn't he just tell you that he'd lost the money, and ask for more time to pay you back?"

"Debts are a matter of honor," he said.

"And murder is the answer? He must have been mad."

"I think you are right." Milford regarded her with a sad expression. "I think there must be a streak of insanity running in his veins."

"Didn't he think anyone would guess that he was the one out to kill you?"

"People might be suspicious, but there would be no proof unless he was caught in the act." He laughed wryly. "I have to give him credit. Once he decided to do this, he was very clever. He made certain there would be at least one other suspect."

"Who?"

"Claudia. He encouraged her to ruin your clothes—to hint that she had a reason to want me dead as well."

Ariel shivered at the memory of how close Milford had come to that fate. Only a darkened hall and Lynnwood's poor shooting had saved him.

"He admitted that the idea to kill me only came to him when he was here," Milford went on. "When all the stranded travelers arrived, he thought he'd have a perfect chance to do me in without being caught."

"Well, I think he is a horridly despicable man and he deserves the worst fate the magistrate can assign him."

"He is a baron, remember," Milford said. "The whole thing could become a legal nightmare."

"He won't go free, will he?"

"It is possible. But he will not be long in England. Lynnwood is definitely looking at an extended stay abroad."

"But Milford, I—" She swallowed the rest of her words when Gregson stuck his head through the doorway.

"We're ready to drive away," he said.

Milford rose and Ariel knew that she was not going to be able to talk with him again until everyone had left. He'd take pains to stay out of her way for the rest of the day.

But later tonight, when Aunt had gone to sleep, she was going to find him again.

After Gregson and his friends left, the Blakenoses began their own preparations for departure. Aunt and Mrs. Blakenose made their teary farewells, with promises of letters and visits in the future.

Ariel caught only a glimpse of Miss Baker in the hall as

Bates and the others prepared to leave. Miss Vining and Miss LeDeux gave Ariel a warm farewell, although they all knew that were they to meet again in London, Ariel could not acknowledge knowing them. That saddened her. She had rather enjoyed their company, finding them far more refreshing and entertaining than the usual bland society ladies.

As she expected, Milford disappeared as soon as the last guest departed. That was fine with her—she still had some sewing to do in order to get the blue silk dress to fit. She had tried it on once again and realized that Aunt would probably swoon if Ariel dared to wear it to dinner tonight. Ariel decided she would wear the muslin instead.

But later, when Aunt was asleep, and Ariel went in search of Milford, she was going to wear that luscious blue silk. The very thought of wearing his mistress's dress emboldened her. Tonight, she intended to show him that if he thought he was not good enough for her, that she was quite willing to bring herself down to his level. She would not allow him to push her out of his life because of his mistaken belief in his own unworthiness.

Ariel kept Aunt's sherry glass refilled after dinner, to make certain that she'd fall asleep quickly and sleep soundly that night. When they went upstairs to the bedroom, the sherry did its work, and Aunt's snoring began barely minutes after her head touched the pillow.

Ariel hurried into the dressing room and changed into the silk gown, then tiptoed out the door. Milford was not going to hide from her any longer.

She quickly descended the stairs and made her way to the library. Outside the door, she paused, listening. No sound came from inside, but light shone under the door. She knew he was inside.

Taking a deep breath, she reminded herself why she was here. Then she pushed the door open and walked in.

Milford was sprawled in one of the wing chairs in front of the fire, a half-full glass of brandy held carelessly in his hand.

"Harman, what do you—" He started out of the chair as he recognized her. "What are you doing here?"

"You've gone quite out of your way to avoid me these last

two days, Milford. I decided I was going to have to come to you."

"You should be in bed," he said.

She walked to the desk, took a glass, and poured herself some brandy, then took a long sip. The strong liquor burned, but it gave her courage. She walked toward him, letting her shawl slip off her shoulders as she did. She saw the reaction in his eyes as he saw the dress.

"Pull up your shawl," he said harshly.

"Why?" Ariel let the shawl fall to the floor. "Don't you like this dress?"

"It is not . . . suitable for you."

"You gave it to me, after all."

"That was a mistake."

"Oh?" She looked down and smoothed her hands over the skirt. "I thought it looked rather . . . nice."

"For God's sake, Ariel, go away. You have no business being here."

She stepped closer, standing just to his left. "But I want to be here, Milford." She placed a hand on his shoulder. "Do not tell me that you don't want me here."

"I don't."

He studiously avoided her gaze, but his breath was coming more rapidly. She caressed his cheeks, letting her fingers trail across his skin. She liked the feel of his rough, unshaven chin.

"Stop that."

She laughed lightly. "Don't you like me . . . touching you?"

He grabbed her hand, his grip tight on her fingers. "Leave me alone, Ariel."

Ariel took another step so she now stood in front of him. She took the glass from his other hand and dropped it on the carpet. It hit with a dull thud, the brandy spilling out.

"We haven't finished my lessons," she said. "I think there is more I need to know." She sat down on his knees and leaned toward him, her lips nearly touching his ear. "Show me, Milford," she whispered. "Show me the other things I need to know."

With an anguished cry, he took her in his arms.

Simon's pulse pounded as he breathed in her familiar rosy

scent. His lips trailed kisses across her forehead, and down her cheek before he captured her mouth.

She was so enticing, a budding woman seeking to emerge from girlhood innocence. He must let her go, must send her away.

In a few minutes, he told himself. Let him pretend for a little while that this was right and proper and what they both deserved.

He kissed her tenderly, telling himself that he would hold his passions firmly in check. A few more kisses and he would release her. Just a few, simple kisses. Nothing more.

Her tongue brushed against his lips, and he was lost. His mouth moved over hers, his tongue seeking hers, exploring her mouth, seeking to taste her, to touch her.

Ariel's hands were wrapped in the hair at his nape, holding his mouth against hers. Simon stroked her bared arm with one hand; the other lightly grasped her waist as she balanced on his knees. *Only a few kisses.*

The heat creeping through his body was not coming from the fire, or the brandy he had drunk. He shifted in the chair, but all he accomplished was moving Ariel more firmly onto his lap, pressing against his throbbing groin.

He looked at her through slitted eyes. The short capped sleeve of the dress had slipped down her arm, baring her creamy white shoulder—as if she was not displaying an enticing amount of skin already. Simon tore his mouth from hers, trailing kisses down her jaw, her neck. Ariel tilted her head back, exposing her collarbone. He ran his fingers along the delicate bone, tracing slow circles across her heated skin.

He dipped his head, and his lips followed the path of his fingers, skimming across her pale flesh. His hand curved over the swell of her breast, and she moaned softly and arched into his hand.

Simon nuzzled along the neckline of the dress; he grabbed it in his teeth and pulled it lower.

She wasn't even wearing a chemise.

That was his last coherent thought before his mouth closed over her breast. He ran his tongue back and forth over her nipple, feeling it harden and rise to his touch. She was so responsive, so sweet. He could not wait to bury himself into her woman's core, to find the mind-numbing release he craved. His hand crept under the folds of her skirt and inched its way past her knee, caressing her thigh.

"Oh, Milford," she whispered.

The sound of her voice shook him from his trance.

What in God's name was he doing?

Chapter 19

Simon jumped from his chair so fast that Ariel slid off his lap onto the floor. Breathing hard, he looked down at her. She sat in a crumpled heap, her skirt ruched up around her knees, one breast exposed, a stricken look on her face.

"Cover yourself," he said harshly. He stepped over her and retrieved the shawl she had dropped by the desk and flung it into her lap.

Those deep blue eyes were filled with pain as she looked at him.

"Milford?"

"You little fool. You weren't even going to stop me, were you?" Without waiting for her answer, he picked up his glass from the floor and refilled it from the bottle on the desk.

"I thought . . . I thought you wanted me."

Simon composed his face into a sneering mask. He would break her of this insane idea once and for all. "Wanted you? Really, Ariel, you flatter yourself too much. I find virgins exceedingly tiresome."

He glanced at her, which was a mistake, for he saw the tears welling in hurt blue eyes. He quickly looked away.

"I don't care what you say, Milford. You care for me. I know you do." Her voice was soft, trembling, and stabbing at his heart.

"In a moment of madness I may have *lusted* after you. Until I remembered what you were. As I said, virgins are far too much trouble. I prefer to keep my arrangements with women on a strictly business level. Then I know I will receive value for my money."

She swiped at her eyes with the back of her hand.

And she still had not made a move to cover herself.

"You look like a little girl playing dress-up," he said scornfully. "That gown doesn't even fit you."

At least that made her pull up her sleeve. He struggled to keep his face impassive as she wrapped the shawl around her shoulders, then rose from the floor, shaking her skirts out. He let out a deep breath. All he had to do was get her out the door and he would be safe . . .

He had almost fallen under her spell, almost succumbed to the lure of her innocence—thinking that by loving her, he could somehow recapture what he himself had lost. But he knew that once he touched her, that innocence would be forever gone, and she would be as tainted as he. He could not let that happen to her.

Because he loved her—loved her so much that he was willing to be cruel to drive her away. He wanted her to hate him. Wanted to drive all the feelings she had for him completely out of her mind, so she could then bestow her heart on a man who deserved it—and her.

Tears stung Ariel's eyes as she struggled to her feet and fled from the library. He'd succeeded in making her feel ashamed. What more did he want?

To make her hate him. The answer was so simple she almost laughed, except she couldn't because the hurt was still so raw. Once again, he'd pushed her away because she'd gotten too close.

She'd proved that he wanted her physically; he hadn't been able to hide that. The dress and her bold actions had succeeded there. Now she had the greater challenge to convince him that he wanted her in his head and heart as well.

Because he still did not think he was worthy of her, she realized. Because he had lived so long with other people's wrong opinion of him that he no longer believed in himself, no longer believed that he deserved to be happy and loved. Somehow, she had to make him believe again.

Or else abase herself to the point where he no longer thought her too good for him. She had been well on the way to accomplishing that tonight before he'd been stricken with an attack of conscience and pushed her away.

Now she must try a different tack. And she had little time to succeed. The carriage would be repaired in a few days. If she had not persuaded Milford by then, she never would, for once she was gone, Milford would take great pains to stay away from her.

Tomorrow, she'd have to find another way to convince him he was wrong.

For the first time in days, a pale sun shone in the morning sky, but its bright rays did nothing to cheer Ariel. How was she going to persuade Milford to confess that he needed her, wanted her?

She was eating breakfast alone in the dining room when Harman walked in. "There is a gentleman to see you, miss."

"To see me?" She stared at the butler, confused. "Who would be here to see me?"

"Who do you think?" A tall blond man in a dark greatcoat pushed past Harman into the room.

"Richard!" Ariel jumped out of her chair and ran to her brother. He crushed her in his arms. "What are you doing here? You couldn't possibly have received my letter."

"Did you think I was sitting calmly at home waiting to get word from you? I've been worried sick for the last week. The minute the roads were clear I started out to look for you, guessing you were holed up in some inn."

"However did you find out we were here?"

"Apparently, the goings on here are the talk of the neighborhood." He squeezed her again. "I couldn't believe it when I heard! I rushed here immediately to take you away."

Ariel suddenly realized what Richard's arrival meant to her—and to Milford.

"Oh, pooh, no one is in any danger now." She smiled sweetly. "Sit down and have some breakfast. Aunt is still sleeping."

"There is not time for eating," he said. "I intend to have you out of here within the hour."

Ariel broke away from his embrace and returned to her chair.

"You may do what you wish—I am going to finish my breakfast."

"But Ariel! You cannot appreciate the danger you are in. What could Aunt have been thinking to let you seek refuge here?"

She gave him a cold glance. "Are you perhaps referring to our host?"

"Of course I'm referring to that . . . that libertine. This is no roof for a young lady to be under."

"Milford has been a most gracious host," she replied. "And I think you owe him a great debt. Without him, Aunt and I would surely have died in the storm."

"What ever possessed you to seek refuge here in the first place? Why didn't you go to an inn?"

"We had an accident with the carriage. This was the closest haven."

"But just look what has happened! Murder and mayhem. We shall be lucky if the entire story isn't spread all over London."

"None of that was Milford's fault," she protested. "In fact, he acted quite heroically through the entire thing. He put his own life in danger to lure the criminal into the open."

Richard looked unimpressed. "That may well be, but it is still not the type of incident you should be associated with."

Ariel thought it best not to tell him just how involved she had been. She would save that for a later time, when he was in a more charitable mood.

"Ariel, I want you to prepare to leave. We can be home tomorrow if we set out soon."

"There is no hurry," she said. "If you've been racing about the countryside looking for me, wouldn't you rather rest for a while before going home?"

"I am not going to allow you to spend another night under this roof. It will be a miracle if we can salvage your reputation as it is."

"He is right, you know." Milford stepped into the room. "The sooner you are gone, the better it will be."

She stared at him, balling her fists in frustration. She'd intended to have several more days to persuade him, to get him to admit that he did love her. Now, with Richard threatening to carry her away within the hour, she was suddenly out of time.

"Derring, I presume?" Milford held his hand out to Richard, who took it reluctantly.

"I am grateful that you provided shelter for my sister and aunt," Richard said with stiff formality.

Ariel wanted to jab him in the ribs and tell him to behave himself.

"I only regret that their stay was marred by such unfortunate events," Milford said.

"Indeed."

The two men stood there, regarding each other in an uneasy silence. It was too much for Ariel.

"Both of you are being silly. I am not a child to be ordered about by either of you. I intend to leave here when I am good and ready, and not one moment before."

She pushed her plate away, stood up, and stalked out of the room.

Grinning wryly, Simon shook his head. "My sympathies are with you, Derring, for having to put up with her. She's a minx."

"I fear she's terribly spoiled," the younger man admitted. "I hope she has not been a difficult guest."

"Not at all," Simon replied, although it was the furthest thing from the truth. Miss Ariel Tennant was the most difficult woman he'd ever met—because she wanted to redeem him. And in his weaker moments, when he held her soft form close, he wanted to believe it was possible. But then his senses returned, and he knew it wasn't.

"Still, I am eager to take her home," Derring continued. "I will talk to her—it may take a bit of persuading, but I assure you we will be on our way today."

"I will help in any way I can," Simon replied. "Your sister has been treated in an honorable manner while she was my guest, but I appreciate your concerns about her presence here. It is best that she is gone."

Derring gave him a surprised look, as if he didn't quite believe that Simon agreed with him.

Simon gestured at the table. "Please, avail yourself of some breakfast. My staff will do everything possible to make your stay here pleasant. Your aunt will be awake soon—perhaps she can reason with the girl."

Derring nodded. "Thank you."

Simon bowed and left the room.

He let out his breath in a long, drawn-out sigh. He was going to get his wish; Ariel would soon be gone from his life. And if her brother couldn't make her see reason, Simon would willingly carry her, kicking and screaming if she insisted, out to the carriage and out of his life.

Despite her protestations, he and her brother knew what was right for her. And it was not the "black-hearted bastard."

Ariel headed for the rear stairs, where she could sit and think undisturbed. She pressed her fingers to her temple. What was she going to do now? Richard wanted to take her home, and Milford agreed with him. She was desperate to find a way to change his mind.

"Excuse me, miss." She looked up and saw Harman looking down at her. "Is something wrong?"

"Everything," she said. "My brother is here to take me home. And Milford wants me to go as well."

"I see." He regarded her with a sympathetic expression, then cleared his throat. "Sometimes my lord does not always know what is best for him."

She gave him a wan smile. "My thought *exactly*. But what can I do, Harman? I've only a few hours at most to make him change his mind."

"Perhaps after he has some days to think . . . ?"

She shook her head. "That won't do, Harman. The moment I am out of this house he is determined to forget me."

"Then you must find a way to delay your departure."

"But how? Locking myself in my bedroom will not accomplish—Oh!" Ariel's eyes gleamed with delight as the idea formed in her mind. "That's it, Harman! Quick—do you have the key to Milford's room?"

He pulled out his ring of keys and removed one.

"Locking myself in my room will not solve a thing," Ariel said. "But if I lock myself in with Milford, he will be forced to listen to me. Will you help?"

He nodded.

"Give me five minutes. Then tell Milford he must go to his

room. Say it is some sort of emergency. Once he arrives, I will lock the door and get rid of the key."

"And when he asks me to free you, I will plead ignorance as to the whereabouts of the key."

Ariel jumped up and hugged the butler.

"Five minutes! I'll be waiting!" She dashed up the stairs.

Simon had retreated to the library again, but he no longer found any comfort within its walls. There were too many memories of Ariel here to allow him to sit in peace—the night she'd slipped down here in her nightclothes, and for one moment he'd thought she was the one trying to kill him; the day he told her about the poisoned brandy, and they realized their worst fears were true; the night they'd captured Lynnwood and celebrated their victory.

And finally he remembered last night, when he'd nearly destroyed her innocence in a moment of lust.

Pushing her away had perhaps been the one noble act of his life. But instead of feeling good about it, he only felt worse. Worse, because he never should have put her in such danger to begin with. Worse, because despite his protestations to both her and himself, he still wanted her as much as ever. He wanted to be the one to take her innocence, to be the first to show her the joys of being a woman, to hear her cries of pleasure as he awakened her to the wonders of love between male and female.

He laughed harshly. *Love.* What did he know about love? He knew only about lust. Sex was something that one paid for; emotion played no part in it. For him, it was only a business arrangement, nothing more—purchased pleasure.

Ariel viewed him as a hero out of a romantic novel, not the worthless fellow he really was. He could not give her what she wanted, and the sooner she recognized that, the sooner she would be able to get on with her life and find the right sort of man—an honorable man, untainted by a scandalous past, a man her family would be proud of.

He heard Harman clear his throat. He glanced up. The butler stood in the doorway, a look of concern on his face.

"What is it, Harman?"

"There is a matter upstairs that needs your attention," Harman said.

"Involving the ladies?" Milford set down his glass and stood. *Was Ariel creating a fuss?*

"No, it is in your room, actually. A small matter, but one that needs to be dealt with. The footman will explain matters."

As long as it did not involve Ariel, Simon didn't care. He went up the stairs and pushed open the door to his room.

Where was the footman? He didn't see anyone here. Simon walked to the far door to check the dressing room.

The hall door closed behind him. He whirled just in time to see Ariel turning the key in the lock.

"What are you doing?" he demanded. "Give me that key, Ariel."

She gave him a smug smile. "No."

Before he could grab it from her, she dropped it down the front of her dress.

This time her smile was blatantly saucy. "Unless, of course, you wish to retrieve it yourself."

He rang the bell for Harman. There was no need to panic. He would be out of here in a few minutes.

"I really do not think your brother would be pleased to discover you were here," Simon said.

"Oh, I agree." Ariel walked toward him, and he took a step backward. There was something about the look on her face that made him nervous.

"Just what do you think you are doing?"

"Trying to get you to see reason, Milford. I didn't think I would have to resort to such drastic actions, but Richard's sudden arrival ruined my other plans."

"This is silly." He glanced at the door that led to her dressing room. Was her aunt there? Could he persuade Ariel to return to her? "You should be helping your aunt pack."

"Aunt is breakfasting with Richard," Ariel replied. "Downstairs."

Harman should be here at any moment, he thought. All he had to do was keep her talking for a few minutes longer.

"Really, Ariel, what is the point of this? I told you last night that this has been an amusing interlude, but nothing more."

"If I believed that was true, I would not be bothering you like this," she said. "But I know it is not, and so do you."

He laughed with forced sarcasm. "Ariel, you have a great

deal to learn about men. Just because they respond to a pretty face does not mean they are going to throw themselves at your feet and pledge their undying love."

She giggled. "I have to admit I find the idea of you doing that rather difficult to imagine. You do not have to fling yourself at my feet, Milford. Only admit that you care for me."

"I care for you," he said impatiently. "Will you let me go now?"

He heard footsteps in the hall and turned with relief to the door.

"Harman?"

"Yes?"

"I seem to have locked myself in my room. Could you please unlock the door?"

An ominous silence followed.

"Harman?"

"I fear I do not have the key, sir."

"What?" Simon darted a suspicious glance at Ariel, who was watching him with a look of bland innocence.

Simon realized that his butler and this chit of a girl were conspiring against him!

"Harman, I want you to find a way to get me out of here."

"Do you wish me to break the door down? I can bring the axe."

"No!" That would only draw the curiosity of everyone in the house. He did not want Derring to discover that Ariel was in here.

"There has to be another key. Try the connecting doors. Just get me out of here!"

"Very good, sir."

Ariel sat on the edge of the bed, swinging one foot. "I assure you, I have the only key."

"Then perhaps I shall have to take it from you after all."

He took two steps toward her, then halted. That was what she wanted him to do. And once he grabbed her dress . . .

"I suppose you will go crying to your brother that I attacked you? He won't insist that I marry you. Most likely he'll shoot me. That won't do you any good."

She acted as if she hadn't heard him, reaching down and slipping off her shoe. Then she hiked her skirt up to her thigh and began untying her garter.

"Ariel!"

Ignoring him, she started rolling the stocking down her shapely leg. She pulled it off and flung it toward his dressing table, where it landed atop his hairbrush. Then she switched to the other leg.

He leaned back against the wardrobe and crossed his arms over his chest, determined to remain unaffected by her little display.

"I have seen women's legs before."

But not ones that belonged to a woman he was desperately in love with. Simon swallowed hard, trying to remain calm.

After she'd removed her other stocking, she stood and walked toward him, draping it around his neck. Then she began to undo the buttons of his coat.

He batted at her hands. "Stop that."

Her face was solemn as she looked at him. "You wouldn't make love to me last night. I'm going to make love to you instead."

He could have stopped her. He was bigger and stronger and could have picked her up and set her down on the bed, the chair, anywhere away from him. Instead, he stood there, trying not to tremble, as she fumbled with the smaller buttons of his waistcoat. Then she pushed her hands beneath it and shoved it and his coat off his shoulders in one fluid movement.

She ran a finger lightly down the front of his shirt, and he sucked in his breath, then let it out again in a short gasp when she touched her lips to his chest. His skin felt scorched through the thin linen fabric.

He dared not look at her, or all would be lost. Everything depended on his being able to maintain control over himself.

It would have been a damned sight easier without the memories of last night still vivid in his brain. He recalled the satiny smoothness of her skin, the weight of her breast in his hand, the taste of her in his mouth.

Her fingers touched the buttons on his trousers, and he let out an involuntary moan.

"Enough," he said, grabbing her hands in his.

She pressed her mouth against his chest again. His nipples hardened, and she nipped at one with her teeth.

He wanted to scream from the sweet pleasure of it.

"What do you want from me?" he groaned.

"Admit that you don't want me to go," she whispered as her mouth closed over the other nipple. "Admit that you love me."

He gritted his teeth, letting her hands slip from his, his arms hanging limply at his sides. *Restraint,* he told himself. *Restraint.* She began tugging at his shirt, pulling it free from his trousers, shoving her hands beneath the fabric and running them across his bare chest.

Simon was close to breaking. She could not know what she was doing to him, teasing, tormenting his flesh.

Or maybe she did.

Her hands went for his waistband once again, and Simon realized he had no choice. Either he made his confession, or she'd strip him naked. He was only a man, after all, and he did not have the desire to resist her any longer. It was all wrong—he shouldn't give in like this, but he was tired of lying to himself, lying to her.

Simon wrapped his arms around her and crushed her against his chest.

"I love you, Ariel," he whispered against her hair. "God help me, but I do. And I don't ever want to let you go."

She melted against him.

"But I am not the kind of man you need, or deserve."

"Shouldn't I be the judge of that?" she asked.

He lifted her chin, so he could look into those blue eyes. "You saw how your brother regards me. You cannot wish to throw yourself away on that kind of man."

Her lips curved into a smile. "I've told you, Milford, you are a good, honorable man. It is only your reputation that is black, not your soul."

"But reputation is all that society concerns itself with."

"Then damn society!"

He sighed and pulled her close. If she was not willing to listen to reason, how could he argue with her?

"I suppose I have to marry you now," he said.

She leaned back and looked into his face, her expression suddenly serious. "You do not have to marry me, Milford. I will live with you, if that is what you wish."

"Live with me?" He gaped at her. "What are you thinking of? Of course we're getting married."

She wrapped her arms around his waist. "I always said you were a fraud, Milford. A *real* rake would want to ruin me."

"I fully intend to ruin you," he said with a grin. "But not until we're legally bound. Then I intend to show you all the terrible ways of a rake."

Her eyes twinkled mischievously. "Promise?"

"Promise," he said as his mouth came down on hers.

"They will come looking for us soon," Simon said much later, reluctant to let her out of his arms, but knowing he must if he had any hope of persuading her brother to consent.

Laying her head against his chest, Ariel sighed. "You are right."

"Can I help you find the key?"

She laughed. "I thought you meant to wait to ruin me?"

He grinned. "Oh, I don't intend a full-fledged ruination. Just a hint."

She stepped away and turned her back on him. When she turned around again, she held the key in the palm of her hand.

"You better put your stockings back on," he advised. "I don't think bare feet will impress your brother."

"And you should tuck in your shirt. And put your coat on, at least."

She offered to let him help with her stockings, but Simon gallantly refused. He did not wish to tempt himself too much; not with the threat of discovery increasing with every moment. He would grit his teeth and think of the numerous objections her brother would raise, instead of her deliciously curved calves.

When their clothes were once again in order, Simon unlocked the door, took Ariel by the hand, and led her downstairs. Before entering the dining room, he tossed her a pleading look.

"Tell me this will go well," he said.

"It will," she promised.

He pushed open the door and they walked in. Mrs. Dobson

and Lord Derring were still at breakfast. Derring frowned the moment he saw Simon, then turned his irritated gaze on Ariel.

"Are you ready to go?" he demanded.

"I have no intention of ever leaving," Ariel replied.

Simon looked at her. "I do not recall we ever discussed *that*."

She looked back at him. "I am not going to give you the chance to change your mind. If I leave, you will come up with all sorts of noble excuses to wiggle your way out of your promise. I'm not going to let that happen."

Simon grinned at her fondly. "Curious *and* determined."

"What in the devil are you talking about?" Derring demanded.

Simon took in a deep breath. "Your sister has done me the great honor of consenting to become my wife."

"What!" Derring jumped to his feet, oversetting his teacup. "Are you mad? Ariel, come here at once."

"No," she replied in an even tone. "I do not think that I will."

Derring cast a despairing look at Aunt. "Tell her, Auntie. Tell her what a mistake this is."

"Mistake?" Mrs. Dobson regarded her nephew with dismay. "Richard, he is an *earl*."

Simon smothered a laugh at her unexpected support.

"I don't care if he is a royal prince, I am not going to allow my sister to marry this . . . this libertine."

"I can marry whomever I wish," Ariel said. "And I wish to marry Milford."

"He's ruined you, hasn't he? You have to marry him?"

She shook her head. "I tried to get him to, but he refused. He insists that he will not touch me until we are married."

Mrs. Dobson was nodding her head in agreement.

Derring cast a desperate glance from his aunt to his sister, and back again. "Have the two of you gone mad? Nothing good could ever come of this."

"They say that there is no better husband than a reformed rake," Mrs. Dobson announced.

"And who says Milford is reformed?" Derring demanded.

Ariel laughed. "Oh, Richard, he's no more a rake than you are."

Simon coughed gently.

"Well, maybe a slight bit more. But his reputation is totally undeserved. People unfairly blamed him for his brother's accident and they've been saying horrible things about him ever since. Horrible things that aren't even true. Why, he's one of the most honorable men I've ever met. He's had all sorts of opportunities to ravish me and he hasn't."

"A hearty recommendation," Simon murmured. He turned to Derring. "I understand your reservations. I would feel the same way, in your position. But I assure you that I honor and revere your sister. Her happiness is the most important thing in my life, and she seems convinced that she must have me to achieve that."

"But . . . but . . ." Derring sputtered.

"Oh, Richard, do stop babbling. Think what a coup this is for your sister! The girl who tamed the black-hearted bas—earl." Mrs. Dobson beamed at her niece.

"I will marry with or without your consent," Ariel told her brother. "I am of age and can do as I wish. But I would like to have your approval. Once you come to know Milford, you will discover just how wonderful he is."

Simon almost blushed. He'd never heard the adjective "wonderful" applied to him before. He found he rather liked it.

Of course, Ariel could call him a worthless lout and he would still worship at her feet. Because she had made him believe, at last, that he had the right to love her. And to accept her love in return.

"A spring wedding would be so lovely," Mrs. Dobson mused. "I can just picture the church filled with flowers and—"

"Special License," Ariel said.

"Banns," Milford retorted. "We don't want to encourage any talk."

"Everyone is going to talk," Derring protested.

"Let them," Ariel said.

"But it will take months to get your bride clothes together," her aunt protested.

"One month," Milford said. He took Ariel's hand and looked into her eyes. "It will not be so very long, my dear. We will both have plenty to do in that time."

She smiled back at him and nodded, and he ached to gather her up in his arms again and shower her with kisses. Instead, he brought her hand to his lips.

"Well, Richard?" she asked, not taking her eyes off Milford. "Am I to be married from home?"

"If Aunt agrees."

"Of course I agree." Mrs. Dobson said firmly. "A highly suitable match."

Ariel's eyes brimmed with laughter as she looked at him. "And to think that she fainted at the sight of you only a week ago."

Simon shook his head. "Stranger things have happened. Like you falling in love with me."

"I do not find that strange at all," she replied and stood on tiptoe to kiss his cheek. "Only the most wonderful thing in the world."

Simon caught her up in his arms and held her tightly, knowing he was going to love her madly until the end of his days.

DILEMMAS OF THE HEART

☐**THE SILENT SUITOR by Elisabeth Fairchild.** Miss Sarah Wilkes Lyndle was stunningly lovely. Nonetheless, she was startled to have two of the leading lords drawn to her on her very first visit to London. One was handsome, elegant, utterly charming Stewart Castleford, known in society as "Beauty," and the other was his cousin Lord Ashley Hawkes Castleford, nicknamed "Beast." Sarah found herself on the horns of a dilemma.   (180704—$3.99)

☐**THE AWAKENING HEART by Dorothy Mack.** The lovely Dinah Elcott finds herself in quite a predicament when she agrees to pose as a marriageable miss in public to the elegant Charles Talbot. In return, he will let Dinah pursue her artistic ambitions in private, but can she resist her own untested and shockingly susceptible heart?   (178254—$3.99)

☐**LORD ASHFORD'S WAGER by Marjorie Farrell.** Lady Joanna Barrand knows all there is to know about Lord Tony Ashford—his gambling habits, his wooing of a beautiful older widow to rescue him from ruin and, worst of all, his guilt in a crime that makes all his other sins seem innocent. What she doesn't know is how she has lost her heart to him.   (180496—$3.99)